Greg Weston lives in the sleepy little town of Felixstowe, on the East Anglian coast. He lives with his wife Julie and with Emily, Jack, and Katie. He works as an accountant (which means he counts other people's money for them) rather than a children's author, but he does hope this won't be an isolated adventure into the world of writing… it has been fun.

This is Greg's third children's book. The first, Ocean View Terrace, was published in 2005 and was written about his daughter, Emily and based in his home town of Felixstowe. This tale continues the story!

Other books by Greg Weston:

Ocean View Terrace

The Man Upstairs

Log onto
www.lulu.com/gregweston
to see details of other
children's books by Greg
Weston.

Greg Weston

Ocean View Terrace and The Blue Pirate Eater

The story goes on…

First published in 2008 by

Lulu

www.lulu.com

ISBN: 978-1-4092-0278-3

For more information: lulu.com/gregweston

For Emily and Jack, without whom this strange story
would never have been born

And for all the other heroes of this tale: Fay, Joseph,
Jennifer, Isobelle, Ellie, Alice, Ollie, and Amy

Do you love chocolate?

I do.

When I was young I used to dream of chocolate... dream of living in a
place where even the very waves of the ocean are made of rich dark
gundgy chocolate. Could such a place exist, do you think,
somewhere?...

Em's Secret Diary
28 October...

'Dear Diary...

I just cant take it any more. Its been over a month since Whiskers blocked up the pasigways and not a word from him. Its just so anoying. Whats the stupid mouse playing at? ? ? ? And trevor called me a cow pat at school today and all the others laughed. I hate school. I hate everything. I need my secret door back. I want to catch the passitrain again and go and visit McG in Scotaland... go back to the castel and play with Princes Anabel and see the knights Sir Galavan and McDavish... just sit in the party room again. I just want... AAAAHHHHHGGGG... something to hapen... anything!!! Im desparate! I stood in front of my fireplace for a hole hour today when I shuld have been doing my homwork. I pushed everything on there which could have been a button. I kicked the stupid thing... nothing!

I want my passageway back. (and I havnt done any of my homework this week yet. Do hope mis R doesn't notice)'

It had all started over a year ago when Emily and Fay had discovered the secret passageways which ran below their street. And then the whirlwind adventure had started. Every night at midnight Emily would click her fireplace, it would swing open and she would disappear down the metal spiral staircase into a new and wonderful world. A world where she met up with her other friends too... mad Izzie and Ellie, her school friends and Joseph, Jennifer and Fay who lived down her road. A world where mice like wise Whiskers and the ever-excited Theo ran the passageways. And talked! Mice that talked, she could hardly believe it looking back. A world where tunnels ran all over town and where little wooden doors hid amazing adventures. A world where she could travel on the Passitrain all over the country, to see McG up in Scotland, Harriet her friend in London, or Mr Jinglepot at the Jinglepot circus. A world where she could travel back in time to visit Princess Annabel in Orford Castle.

And then it had all been ruined by Gravisham, the owner of Gravisham and Co Property Agents, when he'd discovered the passageways and Whiskers had been forced to close them down and fill them in.

Gone! They were gone. And with it, all the excitement of her life had just evaporated into thin air.

Chapter 1
The Picture...

Miss Robinson shut the front door of her little house behind her and dashed quickly down the front path towards her car. She had long dark hair and a very young looking face for a teacher, and she wore a very smart suit. Her high heels went click, click, click down the path as she ran. She glanced at her watch. She was slightly late. Miss Robinson was very organised and very confident. She was a teacher at a little school in the next town, near the sea front. She had been teaching now for a number of years. There was no classroom she couldn't manage, no child she couldn't bring into line and no situation she couldn't handle. She smiled to herself... after all she was the perfect teacher. I don't want you to get the impression she was a horrible teacher... in fact she was very kind. But she was single minded and determined. Her pupils would be the best. They would learn all she could teach them... they would excel in all areas. She took out her car keys and beeped the doors of her little yellow sports car. The lights flashed once to indicate the car was now unlocked. She looked up at the sky. Another nice day, she thought, perfect. She pulled back the soft-top of the car so the roof was open, put on her wrap around sunglasses and climbed in. She turned the music up to full volume, revved the engine and drove speedily out of the driveway.

Miss Robinson didn't realise that today was going to be different. Today was the beginning. The beginning of what, you're wondering? Well who would think that the perfect teacher's life could be turned upside down by one little girl, and a rather shy little girl at that. It all started with the picture...

Ten miles away, in their Victorian house in Ocean View Terrace, that little girl sat on her dad's bed. It was a very special day today. It was Dad's birthday, and they were going through the normal birthday ceremony. Mum snapped away with the camera, Emily's little brother Jack bounced up and down on the bed, and Tiger their big shaggy blonde dog ran round the bed barking and wagging his tail. Piles of ripped up wrapping paper lay across the bed and Dad held up his very last present to open. It was very flat, but very wide and it was very heavy.

"Go on, go on, Dad," shouted Jack excitedly. "It's a picture for you!"

"Jack!" everyone shouted at once.

"I don't think you're supposed to tell me that, Jack," Dad replied with a laugh. He ripped off the paper and stared at the picture. It was a painting. The scene showed rolling hills and, in the distance, the sea. The sun was breaking through the clouds and deep yellow rays of light were cast over the hills. The whole scene was encased in a thick wooden frame, with a spotless sheet of glass at the front.

"Wow, that is lovely." Dad looked all around the painting. There was so much detail. It was one of those pictures where you could spot something new in it every time you looked.

Breakfast was a hurried affair as Dad rushed out the door to work, shouting, "bye, I'm terribly late," and then he was gone. There was just enough time for Emily to run up to her bedroom before she left for school. She ran through her bedroom door, past the sign she had pinned up on the outside, which read in rather scruffy marker pen: '*No boys allowed beyond this point! (ESPECIALLY DAD!)*'

"Come on Emily!" Mum shouted from the front door. Emily stood in front of her fireplace, just as she had done every morning and evening for the last two months, and time stopped for a few moments. There was a buzz of excitement in the air. Just for a few seconds all the memories of their passageway adventures, which had ended so suddenly all those months ago, returned and as she had done every morning, she just wondered whether... just maybe... She reached down and let her fingers run over the cold metal of the fireplace until they found the hidden button. She paused. The button which had opened up her very own secret passage, her entrance to a world of adventures. Would it work today? A tingle of excitement ran down her spine. She shut her eyes, prayed and pushed the button…

Nothing. The dream ended and she rushed down stairs and off to school.

"Good morning Miss Robinson," everyone said in unison.

Miss Robinson smiled sweetly at the class, and then explained to them their first task of the day. She spoke with a soft Scottish accent. Emily's mind began to wander, as it had done every day since the beginning of term. Life was tough, she thought. How much stress was a little girl her age supposed to take? It just wasn't fair. All the fun they had had in the passageways, and then it's all cut off, just like that… the end. It was so unfair. And this was just so… so… so… so boring! Emily sat quietly gazing out the window, but inside she wanted to scream.

It had been over a year ago when she had first discovered the secret door behind her fireplace and she had entered the secret passageways for the very first time. The passageways ran directly underneath their road, Ocean View Terrace, and then branched out in all directions, all across the town. Her mind raced through all the adventures they had had as she and her friends had crept down there each night at midnight. The pictures were etched in her memory… they shot through her mind, just like when you press the fast forward button on a video. You may have read about these stories before in another book, maybe a long time ago, in another place and time. That's what it seemed like to Emily, a very long time ago… another age. She remembered the party room where they all met up, hundreds of children. They ate strange food, drank lemonade and listened to the mice band... because of course the passageways were run by the mice. Then she remembered the many little wooden doors with no handles, each of which led to a new adventure... she remembered the castle they had fought for and protected. That was when she had met Princess Annabel, who had knighted her friend Joseph, Sir Joseph the Brave. She remembered the passitrain, which could take them to different passageways all around the country... that was where they had met McG the Scottish lad and his six brothers in Edinburgh. She almost giggled as she remembered Albert, the totally incompetent mouse aeroplane pilot who had almost killed her... and Harriet her friend from London who they called Harrychoc since she loved chocolate and sweets so much. She couldn't walk and sat in a wheelchair but had been made better by the magic in the passageways... was it magic? She didn't know, but there was definitely something magical down there! And of course the magic room! How could she have forgotten that? Where she had travelled back in time to see her road when it was first being built. And she remembered the sad day when they had said goodbye to Fred, for there were two golden rules in the passageways, which were never broken and they were these: no adult was allowed to know about the passageways and secondly, at age ten you had to leave and forget all about them. Emily could never imagine forgetting the passageways. They were a part of her. Her memory was flitting around all over the place now. She missed all the mice terribly... they worked so hard to build and maintain the passageways. But most of all she missed Whiskers... she missed her friend, Whiskers, the mouse in charge of it all, and Theo the bouncy little mouse who helped him and was always hard at work marking things off on his clipboard. Oh, and there was so much more... it seemed like another life, somewhere in her distant memory. In her pocket she still had the little piece of paper. It was all crumpled and tatty now. It had been in her pocket for a long time. She took it out and unfolded it. It was Whiskers last note to her. It had all ended up going horribly wrong. The passageways had almost been discovered by a grownup (that was the worst thing that could possibly happen!) and so Whiskers had closed them down and filled them in. It tugged at her heart and almost made her want to cry when she thought of all that she loved down there, now gone for ever. She looked down at the crumpled piece of paper, Whiskers last note to her, and desperately holding back a tear, she read:

Dear Emily,

I just wanted to drop you a line. What a frightful mess we got ourselves into, didn't we. Theo has done an excellent job of finding homes for all the mice in other passageways around the country. Boris was a bit of a problem, but he decided to try his luck in Hollywood and left this morning on a boat set for America. I do hope you don't mind, but we couldn't find a home for Tiger and so I have left him with you. I know you will look after him.

Please don't be sad. Always remember all the fun we have had and all the things you have learnt. You are a very special girl.

Well, I am off now. I'm going to make my way up to Edinburgh. McSmallenby said he has some work, which needs doing up there. But I will be back in touch, so look out for me. Remember, always look out for the unexpected, especially the pink snowman.

Love, Whiskers'

Tiger the doggie was now part of their family and Emily giggled as she thought of Boris the monster. But look for a pink snowman? What was that supposed to mean? It was stupid…

"Emily, did you hear me? Emily… Emily Grace!" Emily was suddenly pulled back to the present by the soft Scottish accent. Miss Robinson never shouted. She had a way of being cross without shouting, and she only ever used Emily's middle name when she was cross. "Emily Grace, I would be pleased if you could listen along with the rest of the class rather than staring out of the window."

Miss Robinson stared at Emily for a couple more seconds to make sure she got the message. She didn't understand this little girl. Her report from last year had been very good, and yet this year, in the last few months her work had gone badly down hill. She didn't concentrate in class, didn't participate, and just seemed very unhappy. Miss Robinson always liked to know everything that was going on. She made a mental note that she would have to watch this little girl's progress carefully and she would have to work out what made this girl tick. Her eyes narrowed slightly as they lingered on the wiry thin girl, and then she pulled her mind back onto the day's lesson.

It was after lunch that the first sign came. It was only a very small thing, just enough to make Emily think. Just a fleeting moment... but definitely the beginning of something. It happened during Maths. There they were, sitting round watching Miss Robinson chalk on the blackboard, when something very small whizzed across the carpet. A number of the children's eyes followed as it darted across the room. The room went silent.

"That was a mouse!" whispered one of the boys. Suddenly there were screams and shouts, children running all over the room and out the doors.

Miss Robinson had also seen it. She was prepared for anything that could happen in her classroom... except a mouse, that is. The Headmistress was eventually summoned by the sound of shrill screaming from the classroom, and not just of the children but also from Miss Robinson, who by now was hopping on one leg on top of her desk, hurling books at it.

"Don't do that," shouted Emily, "You'll hurt him!" and to everyone's astonishment Emily ran over and picked up the little mouse. And not only that but she also seemed to be talking to it! When she glanced back at the classroom she could see that Miss Robinson was giving her that same suspicious stare her dad used to. Their eyes met, just for a second, and in that second Miss Robinson knew this little girl was up to something.

"Emily Grace, get that THING out of my classroom at once!" boomed Miss Robinson... who never normally raised her voice in class. Emily made a hasty escape.

To Emily it seemed like her world had come alive again. She had seen one of the passageway mice. What did that mean? OK, she had  crossed Miss Robinson, but then teachers were harmless, weren't they. She would just have to watch herself from now on. As soon as she got home from school she raced upstairs into her bedroom, slammed the door and wedged her chair in front of it so no-one could get in. She then paused in front of her fireplace. Surely it must be beginning again. She would press the button and the fireplace would click open as it had done before. She bent down, felt the metal, paused... shut her eyes... the tingle of excitement ran up and down her spine once again... and pushed the hidden button... nothing. She pushed it again... nothing. No! It must work. She pushed it again and again and then kicked it with all her might. Ouch! It just wasn't fair! She threw herself on her bed in frustration.

It was later that evening when everyone was asleep that she woke up. The nights were still warm, and the sky not too dark. She wandered out into the hallway and found Jack there. He was only a little kid, with short fair hair which stuck up at all sorts of funny angles, and piercing blue eyes which almost shone in the dark. He was standing on his stall with his head cocked to one side, which meant he was concentrating hard, and he was staring up at Dad's new picture which now hung on the wall.

"Look E, there's a house on it now."

Emily took a close look. Jack was right. Over on the left was a little wooden house (more like a shed). She had never noticed it on the picture before. It sat in the middle of the big meadow, surrounded by grass, with the start of the forest behind it. In front of it sheep grazed in the pastures. It was a very peaceful sort of picture. The kind that made you wish you could live there. Emily leaned in a bit closer. What was that, outside the little house? She stared hard... it couldn't be... she couldn't believe her eyes. There in front of the wooden house, looking totally out of place, with sheep grazing all around it, was a pink snowman. That was stupid! Who would put that there in a painting? It stirred something in the back of her mind... what was it now?... Whiskers' letter!!... *Look out for the unexpected, especially the pink snowman.*

That was just so stupid. How come she had never noticed it before? She put her hand up and pressed her finger up onto the glass of the picture, where the snowman was. But to her astonishment, rather than feeling any glass, her hand went straight through into the picture. It was the strangest feeling she had ever had. She could feel something pulling her hand. Her arm passed into the picture as well.

"Jack, quick! Grab hold." Jack just caught hold of Emily's other arm as the two of them were sucked right through the frame and into the picture.

Chapter 2
A Hole Called Rover...

They tumbled headfirst onto the grass. "Ouch!"

A nearby sheep bleated in protest at their intrusion. As they got up, with the sun shining around them, the little wooden house from the picture was now a real, life-size house, in front of them.

Suddenly the door of the house was flung open and out ran Fay and Amy, followed closely by Jennifer and Isobelle, known to her friends as Izzie. Em was very pleased to see them. They were all members of the Underground Gang. They had been a closely nit team of adventurers when they had explored the passageways together, all those months before. Fay and Jennifer also lived down Ocean View Terrace, with Em. Jennifer was the organised one and Fay the adventurer. Amy was Fay's little sister, and she could tell better stories than anyone, because she never stopped talking. Izzie was in Emily's class at school, and she had been introduced to the passageways when they had accidentally stumbled across a passage which ran below her house. Izzie was as mad as a hatter, and had long dark, wildly curly hair

"Wow! This is so pips!" Izzie squealed excitedly. Then a frown came over her face. "But what are we doing here?"

"There must be some reason we're here," Jennifer replied, in her normal efficient and organised manner. The thought hadn't struck Em until Jennifer had mentioned it, but she was right, there must be some reason.

The children looked around the valley and hunted around the house. There seemed to be nothing there of any interest. The house was an old log cabin, made up of two rooms. Just a basic kitchen with a big wooden table and a bedroom with a very small bed in it. "Not even a TV," gaped Izzie.

"Maybe we have to find some treasure or find our way back home." Amy paused for a minute, thinking. "Where are we anyway?"

"Good point," said Jennifer. "Your dad's picture, Em. Where was it a picture of?"

Em thought for a moment. "The picture was Levington Marina." Levington Marina was only a few miles away from where they lived, in Felixstowe. Yes, thought Em, this must be from the picture.

"We'll have to search the house again," said Jennifer. "Look for anything unusual, or tunnel entrances. Maybe we have to find our way in."

Though none of them realised it, the children were beginning to remember. They had only survived in the tunnels before by being a close team who worked together. Jennifer kept an eye on the clock. She was always the timekeeper, since they always had to make sure they were back in bed before morning. And it was as if the children had suddenly grown up from their carefree existence to the team of adventurers who explored the other world of the passageways, where they lived throughout the night. Of course, they were not all there. They were missing Joseph and Ollie, Alice and Ellie. But that was often the way. Rarely were they all together at the same time when an adventure began.

It took only a couple of minutes for Fay to find the note left behind the pot on the kitchen mantle piece.

The other children gathered round. Fay took the folded notepaper out of the envelope and read it out.

> *'Sorry to scribble such a rough note, but I have to be quick. They're here. We've been invaded, and we must keep them out. I had to use the picture to call you here because your passageways are closed. I need your help. You are my most experienced passagonairs. The mice have been captured you see. You have to rescue them. Find the secret door. You must rescue the mice before the Pirates get to them. Do hurry.*

And be careful.

Yours as ever,

Whiskers.

P.S. I left you the hole. He should be very useful. His name is Rover.'

Izzie frowned. "He left us a hole?" Fay turned the envelope upside down and what looked like a folded piece of black plastic fell out onto the floor.

Amy picked it up and unfolded it. It was a plain black plastic circle. It felt a bit rubbery and it stretched easily to change shape, a bit like an elastic band. Amy crinkled her nose up in mock disgust. "What's the point in that?"

However, something else was bothering little Jack. "Pirates!" he whispered, and a look of alarm came onto his face. He ran over to the window. He squinted his eyes and stared. To his left, across the marina he could see the docks, with their cranes working day and night. Beyond that was the wide open ocean. And there it was, sure enough. Out in the sea, in the distance he could just make it out. It wasn't a cargo ship sitting beyond the docks. It had a tall mast and billowing sails. At the very top of the mast was the skull and cross bones flag.

"Come on." Jennifer was getting restless. "We have to find the passageway entrance."

They raced out of the room in search of the secret door, which must lie somewhere in the house.

Jack continued to stare out of the window. Em lingered behind him. It was strange wasn't it? She had longed for the adventures to return, but had forgotten the worry and problems they might bring.

"Pirates," Jack said quietly. They had all heard the rumours before of pirates in the passageways. "If they catch a mouse they cut off its paws and tail. If they catch one of us, our hands and feet."

It was well known that the pirates used the sea tunnels to get in. If they brought the ships too close to land people would notice. But there were special secret tunnels that ran from the coastal passageways, right out to sea. The pirates had built them, and the gossip was that sometimes they use them to get in. But she had never seen one... had never really known if this was true or just imaginary.

"Maybe with the passageways closed, they thought they could take them over?" she wondered.

Meanwhile Amy was still holding the black rubbery plastic circle. She was trying to figure out what it was. She tried stretching it, pulling it, and rolling it up. But it didn't seem to have any real use.

"What am I supposed to do with you?" she tossed it from hand to hand. "You even have a name... Rover, wasn't it?" Amy always talked. It didn't matter if anyone was there to listen or not. She tried screwing the black plastic up onto a ball. It seemed to be turning more flexible and gooey in her hand. She threw it down on the floor. Splat! It hit the floor and spread out as it flattened against the wooden floorboards. Then to Amy's surprise it moved. It had landed about ten feet away from Amy, and it now seemed to be returning to her, as if it were on elastic. It stopped by her feet and she could hear it purring like a cat. Amy bent down to pick it up and to her astonishment her hand went straight through it. It wasn't a black spot, it was a hole. How strange, she thought. Amy reached out again but the hole moved away, just out of reach.

"Come on, boy," she coaxed. The hole moved closer again and purred loudly. Amy's fingertips felt for the edges of the hole. She could feel the slight ridge around the rim. She got her fingernails underneath, prised it up and up came the hole... a black, rubbery circle again. She looked down. The hole was gone from the wooden floorboards.

By now Jack and Em had noticed this, from the other side of the room.

"Amy, do that again," said Em, not quite believing her eyes.

Amy threw the black substance onto the floor and again it came to life, purring and moving about. Em took a step towards it, bending down to feel it but suddenly it changed. The soft purring changed into a growl and the circular shape changed immediately into the zigzag shape of sharp teeth, which barked at her. All three children jumped backwards in fright. The hole shot across the floor to Amy's feet and started to purr again.

"Em, I think you frightened him," said Amy defensively, before reaching down to stroke Rover.

"Unbelievable," said Em, "she has a pet hole?! This adventure is getting weirder by the minute!"

It was just then that Izzie returned through the door. "We can't find—" She never got to finish her sentence. Unfortunately for her the hole had positioned itself just too close to the door. She fell straight through the hole. The children heard a long scream, then a thud. And then to everyone's horror the hole gave a loud burp.

"What on earth..." started Fay as she entered the room. Her voice trailed off.

"You give Izzie back right now!" shouted Em as she made a lunge for the hole but it was too fast for her as it raced across the room. Panic then broke loose as the children started to chase the hole from corner to corner, but it was far too fast for them all.

"Right now, I said!" Em screamed.

"Please, Rover," Amy's little voice squeaked. The hole shot up to her feet, purred whilst it circled her feet a few times and then it shot up the wall and onto the ceiling. There was another sudden scream, which started off faint as if far off, but grew louder and louder and then Izzie fell out of the hole and landed with a thump on the floor. It was a very hard landing, the room shook, dust sprung up from the floorboards, which probably hadn't been cleaned in a few years and two books fell off the bookshelf near the door.

"Ouch!" Izzie slowly climbed to her feet and rubbed her legs. "What I was trying to say was, we couldn't find the entrance. What is that rotten thing?"

"Who needs an entrance," exclaimed Jennifer, "we can do better than that. We've got a hole. Amy, can you get that thing to stay still and let us jump through it?"

Amy ordered the hole to the middle of the floor and the six children climbed into it, falling about ten feet and landing on the hard damp concrete floor of what looked like an old abandoned and very uncared for underground passageway. Amy looked up and whistled, and as if by magic the hole dropped off the arched ceiling of the passageway, hitting the floor with a splat. Amy whispered some kind words to it and then rolled it up and put it in her pocket.

Em rolled her eyes. She had seen some silly things in her time, but talking to a hole had to be by far the silliest ever.

This was very different from going down the passages they knew and loved back home. For one thing, they had no idea where they were or for that matter what was around the corner. Everyone hoped it would not be pirates. For another thing, there was very little light down here. There were no candles in the walls and no-one, not even the organised Jennifer, had brought a torch. The tunnel was circular, like standing in a long tube of toothpaste, and the walls were damp, moss-covered brick. There were strange noises they could hear, water dripping, and strange clanging sounds, which echoed through the maze of tunnels. Fay led the way. They went along passages and down steps, through doorways and down more steps. The smell of sea and damp was very strong. Izzie was tasked to memorise the way back.

"How do we know we're going the right way?" Jennifer asked after ten minutes.

"No idea. This is going down hill though, and if they are holding the mice prisoners then they would be in the dungeons, wouldn't they?" Fay didn't sound very convincing, but then no-one else had any better ideas. "Also," Fay added, as she stopped, "if we were going the wrong way, we probably wouldn't be meeting them."

Everyone squinted in the darkness and could just make out the shape and features of people ahead. There were no voices, but the ringing sound of metal swords being drawn from their sheaths was unmistakable.

"If anyone has any good ideas, now would be a good time to share them," Em ventured.

Splat! Amy threw the hole onto the floor. "Go get 'em, Rover."

The black hole raced up the passage. "Ahgggg," shouted the first pirate as the stone floor disappeared under him and he shot down the hole. Then the next and the next. As the final pirate disappeared Rover gave a large burp and raced back to Amy's side.

"Unbelievable!!" exclaimed Em.

"Pips! That's pretty cool," said Izzie, looking rather impressed.

The children continued forward, but Jack lingered behind. He had heard the sound of the last cutlass falling to the ground, and rolling over to one side. He walked over and felt around in the dim light. There it was. He picked it up and swished it through the air a few times. Yes, it felt good in his hand. The confidence was returning.

Jack looked up. There was sudden confusion as a stream of mice appeared out of nowhere in the semi-darkness and everyone seemed to be moving in different directions. "Quick! This way," came the high pitch squeak of a mouse.

The long stream of mice ran by him. "Come on Jack," Em hissed urgently. "We've gotta get out of here NOW!" Behind them was the distinct sound of heavy running feet. They were being chased.

As he ran back, Jack noticed something on his right. It was a circular door. It was wooden, surrounded by a thick metal frame. He knew what it was. He had seen one of these before. It was a sea door. It was one of the doors that led out to sea… to the pirate ships. He had an idea forming in his mind.

"Jack, come on!" Em shouted. Behind them he could hear the distant sound of pirate voices. The escape had been discovered, the alarm raised.

"You go, E. I got an idea."

"No Jack. Are you mad? I'm not leaving you here. Come on!" The others had paused to hear the skirmish between the two of them.

"Go, Go," Jack motioned them on. "Amy, come with me. We can stop the ships."

"I don't think so," said Jennifer coldly. "Anyway, we need to hole to get out of here, remember?"

"We have to go now," Fay said nervously. The angry voices were getting louder behind them.

Jack wasn't budging an inch. He had always been an stubborn little toad, Em thought. A familiar little mouse voice piped up. "I know the way to the passage that leads out of here."

"Rufus!" Em cried, recognising the little mouse for the first time. Rufus was one of her best mouse friends... a mining mouse with a wicked sense of humour. She grabbed him up in her arms. He seemed lighter and more raggedy than she had ever seen him before. She guessed that life as a prisoner wasn't fun. She turned back to the others. "I'm not leaving Jack here."

"NOW!" shouted Fay.

"I'll go with Jack." It was Bart, another of the mining mice, who spent their days building new tunnels. Over the year Em had spent down in the passageways before, they had had lots of adventures together, and learnt to trust each other. "If there's a chance we can stop the ships…"

"There's no time for this," Jennifer said angrily. She grabbed Em's hand and before Em could protest she was being dragged down the tunnel. Jack grabbed Amy and, together with Bart, they turned to the sea door.

"How do we get through there," motioned a nervous Bart as the angry voices of pirates were getting very close, behind them.

"Hole!" Jack shouted. Splat went the familiar sound, as Amy threw the lump of black rubber at the sea door and they climbed through.

It was a long run down the passage to the ship. They climbed aboard through another sea door and found themselves in the cargo hold. It was dimly lit with lots of crates and boxes stacked around them. Up above they could hear the distant shouting and jeering of pirates up on deck.

"So what now?" asked Bart. "What's the great idea?"

"Easy," said Jack. "Amy. The hole?" Amy reached into her pocket and handed it over. Jack squashed it in between his fingers. "We sink her." And with that he flung it onto the side of the ship's hull. The black hole hit with a splat and spread into a wide black circle. They all watched for a moment. There was the distant sound of rushing water.

Bart suddenly looked worried. "But what about us, how do we get out?" squeaked the little mouse.

Jack screwed up his face, and swished his cutlass as he thought about it. Bart gave him a nervous sideways glance. Amy began to back away.

"I hadn't thought about that," Jack replied, as the sound of gurgling water grew very loud and the first torrent burst through the hole.

Chapter 3
The Sheep...

Thump, thud. "Ouch." The children shot through the picture and landed back on the hallway carpet. They had made it. Emily sighed with relief. They had ran out of the house in the green valley of Levington Marina, past the sheep and the fence and dived straight back through the picture. They hadn't even had a chance to chat to the mice. But as Emily looked around the hallway it took her only a few moments to realise the full extent of the problem they now faced. They had all returned through the picture, to Emily's hallway. All except the mice that is. How would Izzie, Jennifer and Fay get back home? And, Emily frowned, they were still missing Jack and Amy. Not only that, but there was a distinct bleating sound coming from beside her. Emily looked down. There was a sheep in her hallway.

There were lots of groans and bustling noise as all the children got up and brushed themselves down.

Emily glanced nervously at her mum and dad's bedroom door. "Ssh! Quick, everyone into my bedroom."

"Em, look!" Izzie was staring intently at Dad's picture which was still hanging on the wall. "We're on here."

"What!" said Emily in astonishment. They all crowded around the picture. Izzie was right. On the left hand side, next to the little wooden house, there now stood a group of six children. Emily bit her lip. Dad would kill her when he saw this. Would he notice, she wondered?

"Where did the sheep go?" Jennifer asked suddenly.

"Err, in there," Fay replied nervously pointing at Emily's mum and dad's bedroom.

"What!!" hissed Emily. She darted quietly through the doorway. The sight which met here eyes filled her with horror. Her mum and dad were fast asleep on each side of the bed and there snuggling down between them was the sheep. Emily was so stunned she couldn't speak. Fay and Jennifer put their heads round the door to see what was going on.

"What are you going to do, Em?"

"Out of here, you lot. You'll wake them up."

Emily watched the bed. The room was dark and quiet. The only sound was the clock ticking by the bed. Her mum shuffled a bit... "give me some room," she murmured sleepily. Emily held her breath, praying she wouldn't wake up. The sheep was laying facing Emily.

"Psst... psst. Come here," Emily said sternly under her breath, trying to coax the animal off the bed. Then she could have sworn the animal winked at her as he snuggled down further in the sheets. Dad snored loudly and to Emily's horror the sheep raised a hoof and kicked him in the back.

"Sorry dear," he whispered in his sleep.

"Here now, you dumb animal!" Emily hissed, but it did nothing. Emily was getting angry. She grabbed it and tried to wrestle it off the bed but it bleated loudly. Emily let go, fuming.

Jennifer came in behind Emily. "Try this." She handed Emily a cabbage.

Emily was now getting very cross. "What am I supposed to do with this?" she snapped.

"It's green... you know like grass. He might be hungry," Jennifer gestured. "Coax him off the bed with it."

"I'll take a carving knife to him soon, if he doesn't move," Emily muttered. There was more noise from outside the room. Emily stuck her head out. "Will you shut up!"

"It's Izzie. She's worried how she's gonna get home."

"Let me sort out the sheep first, OK?"

Emily and Jennifer tiptoed back into the room. Emily could feel sweat pouring down her face now. This whole thing was getting out of hand. She had been in many tight fixes, but she just wasn't sure she could get out of this one. And in the back of her mind she wondered where Jack might be now. She tore a leaf off the cabbage and gently placed it right in front of the sheep. He gave it a tentative nibble and then ate it up. "Glad you like it. We think it's disgusting stuff." She turned to Jennifer, "What now? He's not moving."

"Place the next bit a little further away. Make him move for it."

She placed another piece at the edge of the bed. The sheep strained his neck and then crawled forward for his piece of green stuff. Jennifer pointed and Emily placed another bit further towards the edge. The sheep shuffled forward a bit more. Emily placed two large leaves on the floor and the sheep finally crawled off. Jennifer grabbed him and pulled him quickly from the room, despite heavy bleating protests.

"OK, first problem solved," Emily sighed. She tiptoed out of the room, pulling the door to behind her. Then she hit the next problem.

"How do we get him down the stairs?" asked Fay. She gave the sheep a nudge, but the sheep bleated and backed away. "I guess sheep aren't used to stairs."

"Well this one will be," Emily said angrily. "Stupid animal!" and with that she gave it one almighty kick. Thump... thump... thump... thud... bleat!! The sheep lay at the bottom of the stairs.

"See," Emily smiled with satisfaction.

"Wow!" said Fay. The others just stared.

"What do we do with it now?" asked Fay as she raced down the stairs after it.

"I don't care," said Emily. "Just get it out of my house!"

Izzie was now getting quite upset. "I want to go home!"

"Maybe we have to go back through the picture?" said Emily.

"Nope," Jennifer replied reaching up and tapping the glass frame of the painting. It was solid. "No way back here."

"What about the fireplace?" Emily asked.

"Tried it. Nothing."

"Wait a minute. If the picture is solid, how will Jack and Amy get back?"

As if right on cue, a large black circle appeared in the hallway wall. There was the distinct sound of rushing water and suddenly, as if hit by a tornado, water started gushing out. A very wet and bedraggled Jack and Amy fell out with it.

"Quick, grab the hole," screamed Jack, sounding and looking like a drowned rat. Amy peeled it off the wall and the water stopped.

"Stupid boy!" shouted Amy and stormed off down the hallway.

Fay just stuck her head up the stairs to see what was happening when it was met by a wave of water flooding over the upstairs banisters.

Emily placed her left foot down on the carpet... squelch. She stared at the mess. "Oh, that's just great, isn't it! As if ruining Dad's picture and finding a sheep in the house isn't enough!"

"Sorry E," Jack shrugged.

"Come on. Let's get down stairs before we wake Mum and Dad up."

Down in the kitchen the six children sat around the table. Emily poured some fizzy drinks and Jack got a large tub of ice cream out of the freezer. If they couldn't think of any answers to Izzie's problem of how to get home, they could at least eat whilst they towelled down. Amy sat in the corner, wrapped up tight in a towel, shivering and still sulking. She scowled at Jack occasionally.

"So where's the sheep?" asked Emily.

"You don't wanna know," Fay replied. Emily wasn't going to enquire any further.

"Whiskers, you have a lot to answer for!" she muttered under her breath, to no-one in particular.

The sun was beginning to rise over the back fence of the garden. A few rays of bright light began to filter through the window and spread across the table. The children attacked the large tub of raspberry ripple.

All except Izzie that is. "How am I getting home?" she demanded, "I have no key to get in the house, we have an alarm… and it's dark out there!" She stamped her foot on the floor to get some attention.

Fay looked up and smiled. "Don't worry Izzie. We'll think of something."

"Any chocolate ice cream?" asked Jennifer.

"Err, yep," Jack replied sticking his head back in the freezer. "Choc chip?"

"Don't you lot care!" Izzie hissed.

"It's easy," said Emily. They all looked up. "We use the hole."

Emily was woken up by the sunshine coming in through her curtains. It was quite surprising that anything woke her after the night she had just had. The feeling of snuggled up bliss lasted about seven seconds before she heard her dad yawning and fumbling out of bed. Then the first squelch as he stepped out into the hallway. Then she suddenly remembered all that had gone on the night before. She hoped Izzie had got home alright. She quickly turned over and pretended to be asleep.

Squelch. Out on the landing, Dad lifted one soggy slipper off the carpet. "Oh no, we've had a leak." It was then that he started to stare at the picture on the wall. He frowned. There was definitely something wrong. He couldn't put his finger on it.

Mum came out of the bedroom. "Oh dear! You'll have to find the leak before you go off to work."

"This picture… it looks different," Dad mused.

"Don't be silly dear, what did they do, paint some more trees on it in the night?!"

By this time Mum was down in the kitchen. The sound of cutlery, plates and bowls being set out for breakfast drifted up the stairs. "Oh my gosh… have you ever seen… You'd better come and have a look at this, will you."

"What is it?" Dad replied, still staring intently at his picture.

"Well… err."

"Well what? Spit it out," called Dad.

"There seems to be a sheep in our garden," Mum said at last.

"A what!!" shouted Dad. He rushed to the back window. "Look what it's doing to my roses!"

Chapter 4
The Underground Gang…

"What's your name?… Amelia-Jane,

Where do you live?… down the drain,

What's your number?... cucumber,

What's the time?...ten to nine,

Where d'you hang it?... on the line,

Where d'you put it after that?... in the biscuit tin,

Then what d'you win?...another tin,

And what d'you lose?… a set a cruise,

Then what's the news?... a set a cruise gone to Caruze,

What happened to the line?... it got a fine,

At what time?… ten to nine,

And the policeman said…

What's your name?… Amelia-Jane,

Where do you live?… down the drain,

Singing... ey, ey, yippy, yippy, yi!... cucumber,

Singing... ey, ey, yippy, yippy, yi!... cucumber,

Singing… ey, ey, yippy… carrot got a hippy.

Singing... ey, ey, yippy, yippy, yi!"

Emily slipped on the wet grass and went flying. Victoria and Emily smiled at each other and laughed.

"You coming?" asked Emily as Victoria pulled her up.

"Gotta run. Hocky club, sorry!"

Vicky ran off.

Emily sauntered across the playground to where Izzie sat on the wall. Things were definitely not going well. She had blown any chance she had of getting on with her new teacher. The day after the mouse affair she had volunteered for staff coffee duty, hoping to earn her way back into Miss Robinson's good books again. She had carefully walked down the staff corridor carrying the tray of mugs, and been distracted by the mouse flying past her feet. Only for a fleeting second had her eyes left the tray and followed the mouse, but it had been enough. Miss Robinson had appeared from nowhere and Emily had clattered straight into her. Emily cringed as the memory drifted into her mind, like a black cloud on a sunny day. Why did it have to be Miss Robinson? Life had a funny way of kicking you in the teeth. The tray had seemed to spin in mid-air for an eternity, and then it had come down, with a very loud clatter, right on top of Miss Robinson. China mugs had shattered on the concrete floor, sending fragments spinning in all directions, and it seemed to Emily like every drop of tea and coffee had managed to spill down Miss Robinson's smart clothes. She had been furious… once they had picked her up off the floor that was. And she had walked with a limp for a week. Emily wasn't trying to make amends anymore; she just kept out of the way. But now, days had turned to weeks… and weeks to months, and there had been no further word from the mice. Not a thing! There were lots of children at the school who were part of the passageways and there was a definite sense that everyone was getting despondent and restless.

As if to add insult to injury, Christmas would soon be here and she had asked Dad for a mobile phone. "Not a hope, kid!" he had replied from behind the Saturday paper. "I mean (!), totally unfair!" Emily thought dismally. She had changed the sign pinned to her bedroom door. It now read: 'Dad, you're not allowed in my room till I get my mobile phone!'

It had been Izzie's idea, many months ago, to start the Underground Gang. Once a week they would all meet up in an empty classroom and exchange stories, remembering all the adventures they had had in the passageways back in the old days. Emily had been surprised to hear about even more places that some children had visited which she had never even known about. They had been great times, as they relived the memories. Izzie had often brought in some concoction she had made to drink, from her old passageway recipes. Friendships had deepened and it had made school a very exciting place. But now, Emily frowned, many of the children were even losing interest in this, since there seemed no prospect of getting back in the passageways any time soon. If something didn't happen soon it was all going to fall apart.

"Hi, Izzie. You done your diary homework yet for next lesson?"

"Oh yeah," Izzie enthused, jumping down from the wall. She bent down and routed around in her bag, coming back up with a green exercise book. "On Monday..." she started reading, running through a long explanation of tennis club and ballet. "On Tuesday..." and so it rattled on.

"OK, OK," Emily waved her to stop, a slightly annoyed look on her face.

"You done yours, Em?"

"Er, sort of."

"Well?"

Emily looked uncomfortable. "You don't really want to hear mine?"

"Yeahhh!" Izzie replied enthusiastically.

"Oh," Emily replied despondently. She sighed and opened up her book. "Monday Literacy... boring. Science... boring, break... cool, ICT... wicked, Lunch... yum, Philosophy... boring. Tuesday. Literacy... boring, PE... horrible in winter." Emily frowned. "Do you think that's what the old bat wanted? I thought that's what a diary was?"

Izzie smiled in a sort of sympathetic way you do to someone who has just had really bad news. That confirmed to Emily that she was dead meat. "I think she might have been looking for a bit more than that. Anyway," Izzie suddenly looked bright again, the frizzy curls positively bouncing. "You're it!" shouted Izzie slapping Emily on the arm and running. "No returns! Schools home plus three hours!"

"Ohhhh," Emily groaned. Typical!! This had been the longest running game of 'It' she had ever played, and the rules seemed to get more complicated by the day. Fay was still arguing that when they said 'school was home' that also included walking too and from school but no-one else agreed with her.

Emily glanced at her watch. "Telephone call. You coming Izzie?"

"You bet!" smiled Izzie. "No returns!" she added, just to remind Emily. Emily was pleased. Izzie was still a firm member of the Underground Gang. The two girls wandered across the playground. On the way they passed Jennifer. She was kneeling in front of the staff sports cupboard.

"Telephone call, Jen. You coming?" It had also been Izzie's idea to call it a 'telephone call' when they talked about the Underground Gang in the open, so that no-one would hear what they were talking about. It was top secret after all, and anyone who blabbed got their head flushed in the school toilets. That was the rule.

"No... I'm just... trying... it won't..." Jennifer was concentrating hard on her door. She had two knitting needles now and some hair clips. In their previous passageway adventures, before the passageways had been closed down, there had been many short wooden doors. These doors were there to stop the young children, 'Newbies' as they were called, from wandering into dangerous parts of the passageways. And behind each door was an adventure. The wooden doors had no handles, but would mysteriously creak open all by themselves, only to those children old enough and wise enough to enter that adventure. But Jennifer had cultivated the very useful skill of being able to pick the locks. She was the only one who could ever break through the wooden doors, with the use of her trusty knitting needles of course. Now she was trying to expand her skills to all sorts of doors and locks. But she didn't want to come to the Underground Gang, Emily sighed. "Come on Izzie."

Mr Baraclough, the school caretaker, passed them having a heated debate with the headmistress. They only caught a snippet of the conversation as they passed by. "I don't believe it!" He was ranting. "It's happening again! Another great big blomin' hole has appeared in the boiler room. All me tools have dropped down it. How can holes keep appearing everywhere?!" Emily and Izzie cringed at each other.

"Amy must have lost Rover again." Her pet hole was getting

totally out of control. The week before last it had been right in the middle of the floor in the assembly hall.

"We're having our last swim of the season tonight, Em. Do you wanna come?" Izzie asked. "It'll be really good fun." Izzie had a swimming pool in her garden, which was kind'a wicked.

That made Emily smile. "Oh yeah! I wouldn't miss it." The two girls ran quickly across the bit of playground which was open air (since it was pouring with rain) and dodged into classroom 5a.

There were about ten others in there already. In one corner Jack and Ollie were seeing who could make the loudest farting noise. Everyone else was ignoring them. They were all deep in discussion already. Scott was a small lad with clothes that were too big for him. He had a gaunt looking face with big eyes, and when he told stories he looked almost ghostly and everyone listened intently. "... and we found them in the smugglers cove."

"What smugglers cove?" Joseph asked, perplexed. "We never found a smugglers cove!"

"Down by the Ferry," Scott continued. The Ferry was the name given to one end of the little town of Felixstowe, out on a limb between the golf course and the sea. It was a ghostly little place that looked as if it hadn't changed for a thousand years. Going there was like stepping back in time. "We found their boat and you have never seen so much treasure."

Joseph was frowning uncomfortably. "I don't believe you!" he shouted. "Smugglers cove! There was no smugglers cove!"

"You calling me a liar?" Scott stood up defiantly. Joseph who was a short but stout and very brave boy, stood up too, and squared up to Scott.

"Hey," Emily put in uncertainly, hoping to break things up. "We've been down the passageways again recently."

There were sudden mutterings of "what?"... "never!"... gasps and looks of surprise.

"But the passageways were filled in," said a young girl with bunches and thick pebble glasses.

"But they're opening again!" Emily went on. A sudden sense of excitement buzzed around the classroom. The small group huddled in close, eager to know more.

"How did you get in?"… "What happened?"… "Who went?" The questions came thick and fast. Emily and Izzie began to unfold the tale of the picture and the pirates and the hole. For a few minutes it was like old times with wide eyes and excitement as they recounted tales, which would often became legends amongst the children. The girls relaxed into that comfortable dreamy sensation, when you could almost imagine you were still there. Fay and Amy were in the little gathering and they pitched in with details which Emily and Izzie had forgotten.

"So you went through a picture?" said the little girl with bunches, sceptically.

"…with a hole that moved around?" continued Scott. "Come on, even I can make up stuff more realistic than that!"

"But we did!" Emily protested indignantly.

Now Joseph had always been part of the team, but he had not been in the last adventure. He just wasn't sure. On one hand he loved the idea of the passageways opening up again. But the other half of him was very angry. Em and Izzie had been his friends, they had had so many adventures together and now, if it wasn't true, then they were making things up, lying to him and making him look foolish.

"It's like that story you made up last year," Scott spat. "You know, about a magic room taking you to a hidden castle. Ha! Rubbish. If you're gonna make up fairy tales at least make them convincing." And with that Scott upped and left. Everyone's eyes turned to Emily, as if for some proof that this whole thing and all the tales of the past year hadn't just been made up.

"But we did!" Emily protested again, but even she knew it sounded weak. All her friends were looking away. "Joseph…" she said weakly. "You tell them… You remember the castle…" Her voice trailed off. The whole gathering had lost steam now.

Joseph was in two minds. He did remember the castle. Of course he did. It had been his finest hour. He had been knighted Sir Joseph the Brave of Orford, by the princess. But now he was very angry with Emily for playing these games with him. "No I don't!" he said defiantly. "You know it was all a good joke Em!" His voice was quiet now. As the words came out he felt awful saying them. He was betraying his friend… but he couldn't go back now. There was a long silence. Emily stared at him, her eyes narrow and wet. Joseph stared back, defiant.

"Well, I'm off," said the girl with the bunches. "I think we should stop the Underground Gang. I mean what's the point?" And with that she left. There were murmurs of agreement all around, and with that it all seemed to finish.

"Hey Em, Maizy's having a makeup and sleep over party," Fay enthused. "You wanna come?"

"But…" Emily wanted to scream at everyone. They all seemed to be whittering on about things which didn't matter. "Ellie's coming too," Fay went on. Emily didn't answer. She cast one more daggers look at Joseph.

"Rat!" she hissed at him. Fay caught her arm and tried to drag her away.

"Come on," she pleaded. "It's not worth it."

"That the best you can do, butt face?" Joseph shot back. Everyone in the room had frozen. They were all looking very uncomfortable. Em hesitated, wondering whether to walk away, but she couldn't let him have the final word.

"No, I can do much better than that, Josephine!" she retorted sarcastically.

Joseph's eyes narrowed. "Cow!"

"Gutter vermin!"

"Snot for brains!" Joseph spat back.

Then Joseph's little brother, Ollie, joined in. "Pooh head!… Bogie brain… Ugly… Cow pat face!" Fay rolled her eyes and again tried to break it up.

"Ahhh!" Em hissed it frustration. "You… Ahhh!" Em couldn't think of any more insults so she just hurled a book at Joseph. It was only a maths book so it wasn't an important one. It hit him squarely on the chin, knocking him off the tabletop. "YES!" squealed Emily in delight… but she immediately regretted it… what was she doing?

Joseph was her friend.

"Emily Grace!" It was the ominous soft Scottish voice of Miss Robinson. "Go straight to my classroom at once!" Emily groaned. Why did it have to be Miss Robinson again? The hole she was digging herself with Miss Robinson seemed to be getting bigger by the day.

As Emily sat in Maths after lunch she felt worse than she had ever felt before. Everything was a disaster. Her whole world seemed to be collapsing around her and no-one cared. She wanted to scream and shout at someone. She stared at the list of sums in front of her. Her eyes glazed over. She couldn't do this. Her brain was all muddled. Suddenly she heard the pitter patter of raindrops in the classroom. She looked up. "Oh dear, oh my!" cried Miss Robinson. A hole had appeared in the classroom roof, just above her head. "Oh, that won't do at all. Now," she went on in her fine Scottish accent, "I'll call Mr Baraclough once class is finished. Please continue with your sums. Isobelle, please go and fetch a bucket from the staff rooms. Thank you." Miss Robinson rose from her desk and went to sit at one of the small tables near the front of the class. As Emily watched Izzie leave the room, she could see Amy standing at the doorway. She seemed to be waving an angry finger at the hole in the roof and shouting silently at it, whilst beckoning it to come to her. Rover was obviously having none of it. The children had all settled down to their work. There was a sudden repeat of "Oh dear, oh my!" from Miss Robinson. Emily looked up. The hole had split itself into two, and a second one was now sitting precisely over the new spot where Miss Robinson sat. The teacher had a very worried look on her face. Again Miss Robinson moved and the class settled down. Emily could still see Amy bouncing around franticly at the door. Emily watched the roof with horror as the hole split again and she saw the new hole whiz over to the point precisely over Miss Robinson. The hole then seemed to expand to let in as much rain as possible. Miss Robinson looked up again, jumping out of her seat. She looked distinctly unsettled now. "Well I've never seen such a thing!" she muttered. But now there were three large holes and the large triangular piece to roof between the three holes seemed to creak and strain. There were only small bits of metal holding it together now. There was a loud creak and then a cracking sound and with that the large triangular piece of roof crashed down onto the floor at the front of the classroom. It was well in front of the children and didn't hurt anyone, but it did demolish the blackboard, which had all the sums on it. Emily smiled.

At that point Mr Baraclough burst through the door and Miss Robinson announced that they would move to a different classroom. Out of the corner of her eye, Emily noticed the black spot race down the wall to the doorway where Amy peeled it off, rolled it up and put it in her pocket. She then wandered down the corridor giving Rover a good telling off.

On the way home from school they passed the little sweet shop on the corner. Outside Mr Bedgrow was standing on a stepladder fixing a large sign up to the window. It said, in large red letter, "CLOSING DOWN - FOR SALE."

"What are you doing to the shop Mr Bedgrow?" Emily asked.

"Hello there, Emily," he said chirpily, stepping down slowly from the ladder, but the smile then faded and Emily saw all the lines on his old face crinkle up into a frown. He scratched his head. "Well, we're 'aving to close the shop down, me dear. Not enough business to keep us goin' you see."

"Oh, I'm sorry to hear that, Arthur," Emily's mum said as she walked up behind them.

"Yes well…" there was an awkward silence. "Young Fred's very upset 'bout it, of course. Poor lad…" But Emily didn't hear the rest of the conversation. Her mind was drifting back. This was the little sweet shop they had broken into so often at night time. A secret passageway led right up underneath the floorboards to the hidden trap door. But what she recalled was her first ever trip there, when Fred had shown them around the passageways. What was it Fred had said?… He had stood there so proud of their night time expedition to his sweet shop. He had said, "Whiskers has it all sorted. He's been keeping this shop alive for years. He puts sweets on the shelves and money in the till. I reckon we have a better trade from the kids in the passageways than when we're open during the day!"… but now the passageways were closed weren't they, and Whiskers was gone. And Fred and Mr Bedgrow were having to close down the shop. It was so unfair!

Emily sauntered lazily down the road, as her mum continued to talk. She passed a rather fat man in a smart suit, clean white shirt and bright red tie. He was rushing up to a tall grey block of flats, leading a group of smart business men to show them around.

"Shoo, shoo, out of my way, little girl!" he dismissed Emily as he pushed passed her.

Emily scowled at him. His name was Oscar Gravisham. No-one liked him. He was a property developer, which meant that he spent his time replacing nice old houses with horrid new grey concrete blocks. He'd once, even tried to pull down Ocean View Terrace. And it was Gravisham who had discovered the passageways, and that was why Whiskers had closed them down.

Emily bent down and picked up a big clod of dirt. She reached back her arm and threw it at Gravisham's back, which was turned to her. The clod of dirt hit the back of his nice smart suit and stuck there, she was pleased to note. She smiled to herself. Gravisham looked around briefly, and Emily turned away. One day, she thought, I'll get my revenge on you for closing down my passageways.

"What a day!" Emily muttered as she collapsed on her bed when she got home. She didn't think she had ever had a worse day at school. And she was scared stiff of what Amy and her hole would get up to tomorrow. She had passed Dad in the garden on the way in. He had been feeding Norman. They still had the sheep in the garden. No-one would take him away. Dad had phoned the local farmers but it didn't belong to them. And he had phoned the local council but they said that sheep weren't on the list of things they were allowed to collect as rubbish. So the sheep remained, and Dad had called him Norman.

Just as she thought that the day could get no worse Mum walked in to break some bad news to her.

"Your Aunt and Uncle and Alice and her brothers are moving."

"Where?" asked Emily in alarm.

"A long way up North," Mum explained. Emily groaned. She and her cousin Alice were very close and Alice was one of the few left who seemed to still be devoted to the passageways. They all seemed to be dropping like flies. The whole thing seemed to be falling apart around her ears. She had never thought it would end like this. At least Izzie was still with her. IZZIE! She remembered. YES... she had invited Emily round to her swimming pool before they packed it up for the winter.

Izzie's house had an absolutely huge garden. It just seemed to roll on and on forever. It had various bits to it including the pond, and the vegetable patch, and half way up on the left was a large wooden building. It was the indoor swimming pool. Izzie and Ellie were already in there when Emily arrived. She got changed quickly and jumped in with a "Yippy!"

Izzie's dad was fiddling with all the knobs and dials around the edge which controlled the pool. "This is our last swim before we pack it up for winter, I think girls," he said as he was working.

There were lots of inflatables in the pool and a couple of minutes later Izzie's sisters arrived and jumped in too, together with a ball and a water gun. For the first time that day Emily was having a good time. At least nothing could go wrong here, she thought... but she thought wrong. Before the thought had even finished going through her mind, Izzie's dad twisted a dial by the pool and there was a very loud gurgling noise, almost like a loud burp.

"Err, what did I do?" Izzie's dad jumped back in astonishment. And with that the water level started to drop. It was as if someone had taken the plug out, but none of them could see where the water was going. Izzie's dad started frantically turning knobs and dials, trying to stop it but it was no use. All the girls screamed and grabbed for the side of the pool, not wanting to get washed away.

"Not again!" said Izzie despondently. "What have you done this time, dad? It keeps doing that!" she added for Emily's benefit. The final water drained away and they all looked down at the empty pool in astonishment. The girls stomped out of the pool, all giving stern frowns to Izzie's dad as they left… after all he deserved it. Emily frowned. Even her swim had been spoilt today. Life really wasn't fair!

Then Emily had a sudden thought. Her three hours were up. "Ellie?" she called as she pulled her bag over her shoulder to leave. Ellie looked around, and she wasn't quite quick enough. "You're it!" Emily tagged her and ran. "No returns! See you tomorrow!"

Chapter 5

The Lake...

More weeks passed. Christmas had come and gone (with NO mobile phone), and Emily had not spoken a word to Joseph. She refused to. She was so annoyed by what he had done. And that suited him too as he was sure Emily was still lying to him about the latest passageway adventure they had had. Easter also came and went and Emily had given up all hope of finding her way back to the passageways again. Maizy and the girls were now having regular makeup parties and sleepovers. They invited Emily but she just couldn't find the inspiration to go along and look interested. And the Underground Gang was all but forgotten. Emily's dad was still feeding Norman each day in the garden, and he still kept standing in the hallway and staring suspiciously at his birthday picture which hung on the wall.

"Em, was this ship here before?" he asked one day. Emily looked closely at the broad seascape picture. Over on the left, anchored in the bay, was a little ship. It hadn't been there before, Emily was sure. And what worried her more was that, if you looked carefully, it had a skull and crossbones flag on it. She didn't understand this picture, but she knew that it did seem to change to show things that were happening in the passageways. And a skull and crossbones flag could only mean one thing... pirates.

"Yeah, course it was there before Dad. You need glasses, you know," Em replied confidently.

Dad leaned in closer, squinting, which made his eyebrows do this strange up and down thing. "Oh, do you think so?"

He glanced back at Emily but she had disappeared into her

bedroom. As the door shut Dad could see the notice hanging there which now just read, 'MOBILE PHONE!!! Dad, get to it!'

Em had that strange feeling again when she woke up in her bed. She glanced at her pink pig clock with the broken ear... Midnight exactly. She never woke up in the middle of the night by accident. Her eyes narrowed. Something was going on. She climbed slowly out of bed and dressed. She tried the fireplace, but somehow she sensed that wasn't going to work. The whole world was silent around her as she stood still as a statue in the centre of her room. She was waiting.

"What you doing E?" came Jack's voice from the doorway. Em raised a finger to her lips. They waited. The moments passed.

"Beep, beep... Beep, beep." It was like the sound of an alarm clock, very faint. It was coming from Em's bed. She lifted the pillow. There was what looked like a watch there. She picked it up and turned it over in her hands. It was digital with a grey quarts face and a pink strap. She pressed one of the three buttons, trying to get the thing to stop beeping. The beeping stopped and the grey face flashed and suddenly turned into a multi-coloured display. The colours whirled around and formed into shapes... A face... a grey floppy eared mouse face which she recognised.

"Theo!" she exclaimed. "Where are you?... What is this?... What..." Jack was now peering over her shoulder too. It was a bit like having a video mobile phone but smaller and the picture was better quality and less jerky. "Wow! Roll over mobile phone... this is the bizz!"

"Hello Em. You like the passicom? Cool isn't it! It's one of Techno's inventions—"

"What's a?... And who's?..." There were so many questions, Em couldn't get them all out at once.

"Anyway," Theo went on, "Whiskers would have called you himself but he's just too busy dealing with the French mice you see. And he wants you down here quick because he wants to talk to you about the guardian... A great honour you know... And what with Techno here, there's so much happening..." Theo was babbling and

Em didn't have a clue what he was talking about. His little head was moving left and right on the screen as he whittered on, occasionally looking down to make a note on his purple clipboard. "Anyway, gotta dash. You get through your new secret door and get down here as soon as you can, OK?" and with that the watch thing bleeped off.

"What door, Theo?...THEO!" Em looked down at the confused look on Jack's face. She shrugged. "Don't ask. I haven't got a clue what he was talking about either. Looks like we have a new secret door to find." She strapped the watch thing to her wrist and then her eyes scanned round the room. Wardrobe... no, bed... no, sideboard... empty, floorboards... nothing. "This is hopeless!" Em fiddled with the watch thing to see if she could get Theo back... nothing. Em's ears picked up movement next door. Both her and Jack's heads snapped round at the same time. They had disturbed Mum and Dad. Em dived for the bed. Jack climbed into the right hand side cupboard of the antique mahogany sideboard. It had been Em's great grandma's and now it sat in Em's bedroom. Dad wandered sleepily to the toilet and then returned, stubbing his foot on the banisters and howling in pain as he did.

As she waited for Dad to settle again, Em realised she could hear a low buzzing sound coming from the antique sideboard. "Strange," she muttered to herself. She rolled out of bed and opened the sideboard cupboard door where Jack was. It was empty. Impossible! "Jack... Jack!" she hissed quietly. Nothing. The little cupboard was about two-foot square, very solid and had no other way in or out. Em climbed in to sit where Jack would have sat. Then she noticed it. A large square red button sat on the inside of the frame of the cupboard. She shut the door and pressed the button. The darkness around her vibrated and buzzed. She was in a lift! Unbelievable! she thought. She opened the door and climbed out into the familiar, and yet it seemed distant, world of the passageways. It was what she had been hoping and praying for, for so long, yet now she was here she was uncertain what to do. She felt rusty at all this stuff. And there was something unfamiliar here. There seemed to be cables and wires laying everywhere, which was very unlike Theo, she thought. He was in charge of the passageway planning committee and he was very organised, always making sure cables and wires were hidden away. In the old passageways, the walls had been covered with strange pictures and carvings, but here there were none. In fact, thinking about it, were these even the same passageways? After all they had been filled in before.

"Jack!" she hissed again. He had obviously charged ahead. Typical! She wandered slowly down the passage. It was like walking through a dream. On either side teams of mice worked; hundreds of them. She walked around one corner and her dream was broken as a tiny axe flew past her right ear. She had walked into an argument. On one side of the tunnel she recognised her old friends, Rufus, Dufus and Bart, the mining mice, in amongst a large host of angry looking mice. They were facing another set of mice across the tunnel, who Em didn't recognise. They were dressed in berets and blue and white stripy shirts and holding up spades, shovels, drills and axes as if they were more weapons than tools.

"Why you *un-ger-lish* rat fink!" the largest blue and white stripy shouted in a strong French accent. "You *call-a* this a tunnel? Pooh!" He waved his axe dangerously. Em began to back away.

"You laughing at our passages, frogy?" Dufus growled.

"*Wee, un-ger-lish* rat fink! *De dead-a* snail I 'ad for lunch could tunnel better *dan* this!"

"GET OUT! This is our site. We're building here, frogy."

"Na, na, na, we... how you say... 'ave to mend *your-a* mistakes, *un-ger-lish* rat f—"

"Why you!" Em saw a brief glimpse of Whiskers as he haired round the corner, obviously intending to stop the fight. Shovels and spades flew like missiles across the passage and the two groups of mice descended on one another. The passage suddenly exploded into a large cloud of dust. Em could hear the chink of equipment being dropped as more mice dived into the fray. Em turned and ran, afraid of being drawn into it.

Stepping over cables and toolboxes, she rounded the corner, and stopped dead in her tracks. The noise seemed distant now and something had caught her eye. It was a wooden door. There was nothing particularly special about it. It was small (about her height) and it was locked tight with no handle on her side. It was one of the many wooden doors the mice used to stop children entering dangerous areas of the passageways. But for her it brought back so many memories. She ran her fingertips over the rough wood. Memories of doors like this one, which had led to the magic room, the passitrains, the zoo, the cinema, and the list went on. The sweet shop... and with that thought she remembered that the shop was closing down... how many places would now be gone? Maybe it would never be the same down here now. She pulled herself away from the wooden door and away from her thoughts. She dropped down a series of stone steps and found the passage opening out into what you would immediately assume to be a party room. But it was definitely not the party room she was used to. It was a very large circular room. Right in the centre was a large circular counter where twenty or thirty mice were busy mixing ice cream and lemonade cocktails and concoctions of all sorts of bright colours. Others were taking food orders. It seemed like hundreds of mice and children were milling around, and clambering to get served. The rest of the floor was littered with lots of different types of seating. There were armchairs, sofas, wooden tables and chairs, and little booths tucked away. The stone walls were draped with large sheets or tapestries, between the many tunnel entrances. They had wonderfully colourful pictures and designs on them. Some had pictures of mice on, whilst others just had colourful patterns. The ceiling was miles up in the air, and seemed to have a large hole in the centre which went dark inside so Em couldn't see what was up there. Light radiated from hundreds of different coloured spotlights high up in the ceiling.

"E... E!" called Jack. Em spotted him sitting in a little booth with Fay, Amy and Ellie. Em's eyes lit up and she ran across. They had so much to talk about and there were so many questions, Em didn't know quiet where to start. Em slid into the booth, next to Ellie. They all had large glasses in front of them. Ellie and Fay had red fizzy drinks with cocktail umbrellas in them. Em looked closely at Ellie's glass. Maybe her eyes were deceiving her but it looked more like sparks than bubbles coming out of her drink. Jack and Amy's glasses had mountains of ice cream in, Jack's covered with chocolate sauce and Amy's covered with strawberry.

"Em, you have to try one of these," Ellie raved. "It's called a Mexican sparkler. Izzie!" she shouted. She raised her hand in the air, three fingers raised. "Three more!" she shouted. Em glanced over at the bar, where Izzie gave a thumbs up. And Em recognised the small square shape of cook, one of the mice, busily running up and down the wooden top of the counter. "Izzie's enjoying herself," added Ellie. "You should see some of the concoctions her and cook have been brewing."

"This is fantastic," was all Em could say.

"Isn't it just!" Fay replied.

"Wicked!" added Jack, spraying ice cream over the table.

"So how long have you been here?" Em asked.

"Only an hour or so. It was quiet when we arrived," Fay continued, "but it's been filling up quick." Em could sense the excitement building up around the room.

"Any sign of Whiskers?"

Fay took up the story whilst Ellie drained the last of her Mexican sparkler. "Theo said he wanted to make a welcome speech but he's just overrun with problems with the French."

"Yeah, I noticed them," Em replied. "Who are they?"

"Apparently this is the biggest passageway build in Europe at the moment and Whiskers has all the best building teams from all over the place here to help."

"But he didn't figure on all the problems they would cause!" Ellie added.

Em picked up the menu, which stood in the corner of the table and glanced down it. It was an Ice cream and lemonade menu. She scanned down the list... '*Birmingham blitz*'... '*Arabian split with banana and Worcester sauce*', yuck she thought. '*Warbaswick whistler*'... '*Mexican sparkler*', that was it. She read the ingredient:

'*5 Strawberries,*

Add 1 spoon of clotted cream,

1 chopped and grated red pepper,

Then add the lemonade (be careful... It'll fizz over the glass),

A dash of chilli sauce to give it some bite,

Plus 2 diced glow worms and some star dust to give it the sparkle.'

"Ahhg! I'm not drinking that!" she said as the drinks turned up.

"It's OK. Tastes gorgeous." Em examined it closely. The surface was definitely on fire with bright yellow sparks. "They cook the glow worms first and you don't taste them," Ellie went on.

"They're not real sparks," Fay continued. "They won't hurt you." Em looked doubtful.

But before she had a chance to try it out the little mouse, Theo, arrived. He scanned round the table, grabbed the pencil from behind his ear and started ticking names off on his purple clipboard. Em smiled. It reminded her of the first time she had met the excitable and likable little mouse. "Hello everyone!" Theo positively exploded, as if now his official work was done he could talk. "What do you think?" he gestured the whole room expansively with both paws. He didn't seem interested in an answer. Before anyone could utter a word he was whittering again. "My design, you know! Especially the circular ice cream counter." Of course, Em remembered, Theo was in charge of the planning committee.

"Must be a busy time for you with all the planning for the rebuilding." To her surprise the smile faded from his face.

"To be honest it's all a bit of a strain. And it's far too much for me. Whiskers has brought in the best, you know. From France and Italy, and McSmallenby has sent all his best teams from Scotland. But," the little round mouse sighed, "we can't agree on any of the plans. I leave them to it now." He sounded so depressed. Suddenly his voice took on a more buoyant tone. "But I've been helping Cook with the ice cream and lemonade menus. What do you think? We've added some real corkers!"

"Er... they're ... different," Em replied. "Yes, definitely never had this before."

"Hey, someone you just have to meet," Theo raved on, seemingly unconcerned what answer Em gave. "He's the best, he is. TECHNO!" he called over the noise of the crowd. "McSmallenby sent him down," Theo continued, turning back to them. "He's a whiz with electronics and anything technical. Built your lift, Em." Em suddenly perked up, a bit more interested. Theo rushed off for a second and returned pulling another mouse by the paw. The other mouse was older and wore spectacles. And he had a pack on his back with a strange curly metal aerial sticking up in the air. He didn't seem to care about being dragged around by Theo. He seemed to be looking aimlessly round the room.

"This is Wellington, but we call him Techno," Theo announced. The children all nodded. "Say hello, Techno." Techno raised his hand absently. He still seemed to be staring round the room.

"Need to adjust the light density," he muttered to Theo.

"Yeah, yeah. Tell them about the passicoms. Go on Techno."

"The what?" Ellie asked.

Theo pointed at his wrist. "Passicoms. Brilliant idea." He patted Techno on the shoulders. "I really don't know how he does it! McSmallenby swears by them. They're all fitted with them up there."

"Still need to lay all the transmitters though," Techno butted in. "Only sectors five through ten done so far. Need more cable."

"What do they do?" Em stared down at the watch thing on her wrist, which she had seen Theo's face on earlier.

"What does it do!" Theo exclaimed in mock surprise. "Did you hear that Techno?" but Techno had got bored and was now examining the old fashioned jukebox, playing music by the wall. "It only allows you to locate and contact anyone in the passageways," Theo went on. "Just say a name." He demonstrated, saying very distinctly, "EM". He pressed one button and it showed a tiny map with Em located in the party room. He pressed another button and Em's wrist beeped again.

"Wow!" all the children said in unison. They were just beginning to realise how useful and important this might be.

"So does it work outside the passageways?" asked Fay.

"With limited range." And with that the excitable mouse changed tacks completely. "Oh, oh... I must show you! Come and see this. Get Izzie to. She'll love this." He grabbed Em's ankle with his paw.

He led them out of the party room and they walked down a long tunnel. Theo was bouncing and sprinting excitably, his long tail curling with anticipation. They seemed to be going down deeper and deeper underground. They were all beginning to realise they were going to have to rediscover the passageways. Everything was new and different.

Finally they entered a huge expanse of a cave. "This is our swimming pool. We call it The Lake."

Em could see why. When you looked at the edge of the pool in front of you it looked just like a public swimming pool, with a ladder and tiled steps leading down into the warter. But it didn't stop. It was huge. No that was an understatement. Em couldn't see the end. It was like an ocean.

"Some pool!" said Fay.

"Wow, E!" Jack said excitedly, jumping up and down.

The ceiling was very high… it must have been a mile high. The whole cave was massive. She couldn't tell where the light was coming from, but the lake seemed well lit. There was lots of space around the lake, all of it the normal cold flat rock. "Could do with a beach, Theo," Em commented.

"Yes. They're working on that."

Over to the right was a large brick building. You could only see the front of it since it appeared to be built into the rock face. In front of it was a tall stepladder with a seat at the top, and there was a motorboat moored at the edge of the lake. Suddenly the door of the building burst open and a mouse ran out. He was wearing a black wetsuit and wrap around sunglasses, which Em thought was probably a bit unnecessary in an underground cave.

"Oh yes!" exuded Theo. "It's Buster. Let me introduce you. Bus—"

"Good evening ladies," Buster interrupted smoothly. He looked rather muscular for a mouse. "Now no need to be concerned. I'm the lifeguard here. Here for your safety. We have wetsuits and life jackets, for you youngans, in the cabin." He rubbed his hands in anticipation.

"Only showing them round, Buster," said Theo, and with that the lifeguard mouse's expression seemed to drop.

"No way," said Jack. "I wanna swim."

"Me too!" came shouts from the others.

A broad smile leaped back onto Buster's face again. "We have diving boards to the left, the shark pool a bit of a walk up the towpath and the log flume ride to the right behind the cabin."

The children scattered excitedly in all directions.

"Er, Theo, are they safe with him?" asked Em.

"Oh perfectly. Buster, he's great. Brought up in Hawaii you know. You should hear his pirate stories. They had to fight off pirates in Hawaii when he was just a lad."

"So where does all the water come from?" Em asked, dipping her hand in at the edge. It looked clear and fresh. It can't have been from the sea. It felt warm.

"Oh, you see that hole," Theo pointed up at the ceiling. Em and Izzie looked up. They could just make it out a large hole in the ceiling. "Well," Theo looked very pleased with himself. "This is really clever, what we've done here. We positioned The Lake right below a swimming pool, so we can drain off some of the water from up there and bring it down here."

There was silence for a couple of seconds while this fact sank in, and Theo's tail quivered with pride.

"So..." began Izzie slowly.

"Designed it myself, you know."

"...what pool does this come from then?"

"Had to take the water tunnel round the gas main and... Er, what pool? Oh, I dunno, just a pool in someone or other's back garden."

"WHAT! But that's my pool!" exclaimed Izzie,

Chapter 6
The Blue Pirate Eater...

"We need a few more things to play with in here, don't we Em?" said Theo, gazing out over the Lake. It was a few hours on. Jack and Amy had grown tired and returned to bed. The rest had explored more of the newly built passageways and eventually found themselves back at the Lake again. Theo pondered for a few moments. "Yes! That's it." And with that he rushed off. "Come on Em," he called behind as he went. He led Em back to the lift and they buzzed back up to Em's bedroom. Theo dived enthusiastically out of the lift, his tail quivering with excitement. Em followed him into her bathroom. The bathroom had tiles half way up the wall and then there was a ledge with lots of pretty ornaments on it, all of which had something to do with the sea. There were shells, rocks, boats, little beach huts, and starfish amongst other things.

"Perfect!" announced Theo. "Right. Collect them all up. Come on, quick, Em. I know just what to do with them."

Em gave the excited little mouse a quizzical glance. "But Theo... what use is this lot? You can't exactly put these in the lake, can you? I mean, they're too small, aren't they?"

"No problem," Theo announced. "We can upscale them." He said it without any explanation, as if Em should have known exactly what he was talking about, and as if the matter was all settled.

"Upscale them?" Em asked.

"Yep. You'll see. How do you think mice move everything about? Most stuff is too big for us. So we move it while it's small and then make it bigger... Upscale it. I'll show you. Now grab those bits." Theo pointed to the bathroom ledge.

Em picked up all the bits obediently. She was curious to see this.

"How do you think we got all that water for the Lake?" Theo whispered as they tiptoed back to the lift in Em's bedrooms, trying not to wake anyone in the otherwise sleeping household. Em hadn't thought about it, but she realised he was right. It couldn't all have come from Izzie's pool. The Lake was far too big. "We drained Izzie's pool and then upscaled the water. Worked a treat it did!"

"But how—"

"You'll see," Theo cut her off. He examined each article before he put it in the lift... the boats, beach hut, rubber duck and starfish all went in. There was a plastic man on a windsurfer. Theo pulled the man off and threw him aside, and placed the windsurfer in the sideboard cupboard.

Theo reached inside the cupboard, pressed the red button and then shut the cupboard door. They stayed in the bedroom and watched as the lift moved down, with a low buzz. "Excellent!" said Theo with a broad smile, and rubbing his little paws together in anticipation.

"What about this one, Theo?" Em asked, picking up a little blue sailing boat, which had obviously been dropped on the way back from the bathroom. Theo examined it. It was about four inches long, with a tall majestic mast. It was a tiny replica of a very impressive boat.

"Never mind. We'll send it down in a minute." Theo whistled and tapped his paw on the side of the blue boat as they waited for the lift to return. Em was lost in her thoughts... it was just so good to be back in the passageways. She felt a buzz of excitement. Ideas were springing into her mind... back down to the party room each night... competitions on the Lake... mounds of ice-cream... she would visit McG in Scotland, Princess Annabel in Orford Castle, and Harriet in London... so many friends she had down there who she hadn't seen for ages. And she wouldn't let anything go wrong this time...

There was a little high pitched yelp at her side and Theo jumped back in shock, dropping the little blue boat onto the floor. Em looked around but couldn't see anything wrong. It took a few moments for her eyes to lock in on the problem. It was the boat. Very slowly, almost indiscernibly, it was growing bigger. Theo frowned for a moment, and then a look of panic slowly came over his face. Em couldn't take her eyes off the sailing boat. It was incredible! It was now a foot and a half long and still growing. As it grew bigger, more details appeared on the boat, which hadn't been there before. The sail, which had just been a piece of material stuck onto the mast, now had rigging, pulleys and ropes attached. A rudder had also appeared. It was now four foot long.

"What?... How?..." Em blurted.

"It's been upscaled," said Theo

"So how big is it gonna grow, Theo?"

Theo had turned quite pale. "Er, full sized," he replied in almost a whisper.

"What?" she said with a nervous laugh. It was slowing down a bit now. It was very pretty, she thought. Full size?... No, couldn't be. Theo was kidding her. Why wasn't it stopping?

"Theo, why doesn't it stop growing?" There was no answer. Full size?... FULL SIZE!!!

"Oh nuts!" Em exclaimed. Her mind reeled for a moment as it tried to work out what to do. Then she quickly grabbed the boat and rushed it to the door, but she was too late. The hull was already too wide for the doorframe. "Double nuts! What are we gonna do?" No-one answered her. The two of them just stood and watched in wonder as the ship grew bigger and bigger. This was going to be a mega disaster any way you looked at it, thought Em.

She was carefully watching the tall mast of the ship as it grew closer and closer to her pink ceiling. Now it was touching. Em bit her lip as, with a loud crack, it punched a hole in the ceiling plaster and continued to grow. The wooden hull grew longer, wider and stronger. It pushed her toy box aside and crushed it against the wall. Then the front (which is called the bow) of the boat made contact with the doorframe. It creaked and strained, and Em hoped it wouldn't be able to grow anymore. But with the sound of splintering wood it burst through the doorframe, leaving a rather large boat shaped hole. Then to Em's horror it continued to grow, snapping through the banisters at the top of the stairs and even pushing through the wall opposite into the bathroom. And that's where it finally came to a halt, with about two feet of the very tip of the front of the boat sticking through the bathroom wall and resting precariously on the glass shower door. There was the sound of tinkling glass, and Em looked at the back of the boat (which is called the stern). The stern had pushed right through her nice bay windows, shattering the glass, and was now sticking out into the street. The boat was now about twenty foot long, with a tall mast, and a slim sleek look about it. It almost looked like a racing boat, Em thought. On the side was a nameplate, which bore the inscription, 'The Blue Pirate Eater.' Neither Em nor Theo quite knew what to say.

"Well, it's a nice boat," Theo said hopefully, as he pinged a nearby rope, unfurling a large sail from the boom, which shot up the mast, knocking down the light fitting and making an even bigger hole in the ceiling.

More plaster and dust fell around them.

"Oh that's just great, Theo. Thanks a bunch! What am I s'posed to do now?" asked Em, furiously. "And don't touch anything else!" she added crossly. Then Em remembered her mum and dad and rushed out to see if, by some miracle, they had slept through all the noise. She had to climb over the side of the boat and duck under the top of the doorframe (what was left of it) to get out of her room. Yes, still asleep... a miracle.

Jack wandered out of his room, rubbing the sleepy bits out of his eyes. He saw the boat and rubbed his eyes again, as if he obviously wasn't seeing properly yet. "Er... E, there's a—"

"I know, Jack," Em cut him off. "Now shut up, I'm thinking."

When Em climbed back into her bedroom the sight, which met her eyes, was even stranger than before (if that were possible!) "I thought we might need some help," Theo ventured. Em could hear the lift buzzing over by the window. There were already about thirty mice clambering over the hull of the boat. Techno was hanging upside down from the mast. "Very well designed bearings on this boat, you know."

Em sighed. Oh, this was all she needed! There were also three boys from around the corner standing on her bed, trying to position the rudder, under the direction of a very official looking mouse.

"Hey!" Em protested, "who let you in? And get off my bed!" But before she could complain further the lift door opened and Fay and Izzie climbed out.

Fay's hand shot up to her mouth in surprise. "Oh Em!" was all she could say. A heap of French mice were unpacking saws and drills from a large toolbox. They rushed out into the hallway and Em could hear the sound of sawing.

"Oh no!" she moaned and ran after them.

"Be careful of the boat," called Techno, cheerily. "She's a beauty. Don't want to damage her."

"Aggghhhh!" Em screamed and waved her fist as she ran past. Annoying… horrible… detestable little rat, she thought.

Out in the hall the French mice, in their berets and stripy shirts, had already sawn a large chunk out of the banister rails.

"Hey!" Em shouted. "Get off that! It doesn't belong to you!" One of them motioned to his mouth and shrugged lazily. He was French. He couldn't understand what she was saying. Then she noticed a little, nervous looking mouse in a red baseball cap, standing down the hall. This was Benji, she remembered. He was in charge of emergencies. Well, I guess this is an emergency, she thought.

"Benji!" she called. He was wearing a worried expression, sweat pouring off his brow. He seemed to be sealing up her mum and dad's bedroom door with thick brown tape. "What are you doing?" she asked.

"Oh, er, Em, yes." He was a very nervous little mouse. "First things first," he replied. "We have to soundproof the doors so they won't be disturbed." He dabbed his brow with a red hanky and looked around nervously. It didn't fill Em with confidence.

A couple of young lads passed Em in the hallway. One had his camera out taking pictures of the boat. "Who are you?" she asked.

"This beats the games room for entertainment, doesn't it!" the camera boy said cheerfully as he passed Em. "Hey," he added, raising a glass. "They're dishing out lemonade and ice cream cocktails in that bedroom over there if you want one. Don't know what this is but it's delicious! Ferocious on the throat though."

Em was incensed. "Who does he think he is?!" she muttered under her breath. She stuck her head round Jack's bedroom door and sure enough there was a queue of mice and children, half of whom she had never set eyes on before in her life. They were queuing in front of a make-shift counter where Blotch and Cook were dishing out drinks. A sign above the counter announced, 'Please queue on the right for ice cream delights, and left for hamburgers and hot dogs.' And all this was happening in her house in the middle of the night.

"Le Disgusting!" commented a fat stripy mouse, in a French accent, as he took a sip from his drink, screwed up his face and tossed the cup out of the window. "They *donn-a* serve this drivel where I *come-a* from!"

"What are you calling drivel?!" Cook retorted angrily.

This was ridiculous, thought Em. They would be selling tickets soon!

Down the hall she could hear a loud motor sound. She stuck her head back out to take a look. A large mouse with a wide-eyed mad expression on his face had just started up a chain saw, which he was waving around dangerously.

Right, she thought! This had gone too far. She marched out into the middle of the hall, brushing past crowds of happy onlookers and bellowed, "Everyone just stop what you're doing right now!" She no longer caring if she woke her mum and dad. "And SHUT UP!!"

There was a sudden silence. The sound of the chain saw motor revved slowly down to a stop. Every eye turned in her direction and waited. She gulped. "OK... Thank you. Now... er... Excuse me... put down the saw. Yes you," she pointed to the mad-eyed chain saw mouse, "before you kill someone. Then everyone please, kindly... GET OUT!!" she screamed. No-one moved. "Stop staring at me,"

Em continued in a very frustrated voice. "Leave... Scram... GO AWAY!" Everyone continue staring for a couple more seconds and then simply resumed their activities. The mad chain saw mouse started up the motor again, and Blotch continued selling his cocktails to the ever increasing crowd.

"Who does she think she is?" a small boy behind her sneered to his friend. "Thinks she owns the place!"

"Fine!" said Em quietly to herself. "Absolutely fine! What do I care! It's only MY HOUSE!!" she bellowed in a rather panicky shrill voice, at a little girl with red hair who almost jumped out of her skin. "I'm losing it," Em muttered to herself.

She backed away from cook, who was now angrily wielding a carving knife at the fat French mouse, and shut Jack's bedroom door quickly, to keep the noise down.

The mice now had all the banisters down, the carpet was rolled up and there was a large hole in the floor where they were lowering one half of the boat, which they had dismantled, down on a sophisticated pulley system. Em put her head in her hands. Fay and Izzie came up to try to comfort her.

"Oh look, drinks!" raved Izzie, "I adore ice cream soda! I might just... would you like one, Em... perhaps... er..." Her voice trailed off as she saw the look of annoyance on Em's face. "Maybe not," she smiled weakly.

It was half an hour later that Em watched the boat being levered out of the French windows onto the back lawn. By now there was a huge crowd of children enjoying the spectacle under the moonlight. There was a loud crunching noise as the boat landed with a crash onto the patio. Norman bleated, and the crowd cheered. Em groaned as she saw next door's upstairs window open. Mr Bradshaw stuck his head out.

"What is going on?!" he called in an exasperated voice. "Unbelievable!" he continued. "They're not content with a sheep! They've got a boat out there now. And they're having a party! HEY!" he called, pointing to his watch. "It's quarter past one in the morning, you know!"

"Wanna drink mister?" shouted someone from the crowd.

"Sorry Mr Bradshaw," Em called weakly. Norman gave another bleat. Em gave the sheep a kick to shut him up. Mr Bradshaw shook his fist one more time before disappearing inside and slamming the window closed behind him.

The last of the mice disappeared into the lift having abandoned the boat in the garden next to Norman's make-shift pen. "Great party!" said the kid with the camera as he left.

"Yeah, great entertainment," said his mate. "That was a classic!"

"Eat snot, pin brain!" Em replied crossly. "Now get lost."

Em was left alone with Fay and Izzie, who was still sipping on her ice cream soda, which seemed to be mixed with some steaming blue liquid and had a cocktail umbrella stuck in the top. Benji had made a surprisingly good job of the boat removal. The bathroom wall and the hole in the floor had both been repaired. He had said that the paint on the bathroom wall should be dry by morning. The doorframe had been patched with thirty-seven tubes of wood filler. In fact, the thing that was most noticeable was all the stains on the carpet where people had spilt their drinks and ice cream. And with all the abandoned cups and bottles (and tools and building materials), the place looked like Em had been having a party while her parents were away.

"I'll start doing some clearing up," announced Izzie. Em smiled.

"Thanks, Izzie."

"They forgot that," said Fay pointing up at the pink ceiling. She was quite right. In the centre of Em's ceiling was a hole about six inches across, where the mast from the Blue Pirate Eater had pierced through the plaster.

"Oh nuts!" replied Em, biting her lip. She was utterly exhausted now and all she wanted to do was flop out on the bed.

"Don't worry. I got it," said Fay. And with that she climbed onto a chair, placed precariously on top of the remains of the toy box, took the chewing gum out of her mouth and used it to fill the gap. It was pink and blended perfectly. Em grinned. Seventeen pieces of gum later and it was done... Not perfect but after a night like this it would do.

Em flopped on the bed. It was then that Izzie came running in. "What do you want me to do with the cement mixer in the kitchen?" But Em was already snoring.

Em was still fast asleep when her dad woke up and went for a shower the next morning. He yawned and stretched. It had been a restless night for some reason. He had dreamt about the house being overrun by mice. Yuck, he shivered. He groped around at the bathroom sink for his toothbrush, still half asleep.

"YOUCHHH!!" He put his hand in the cup by the sink and a sharp pain dug into his fingers and shot up his arm. He pulled his hand back instinctively. There was a mouse trap attached to the end of his fingers. He removed it and flexed his fingers. Yes, still in one piece but, ouch, that hurt. Then he noticed the note which read:

'Dad,

Ha, ha. Gotcha!

Love Emily. XXXX'

Dad's mouth gave a twitch of annoyance.

"Right! This is war," he muttered to himself. "You just wait, little lady."

After his shower he popped into the garden to feed Norman, and was immediately confronted with the imposing sight of The Blue Pirate Eater and a rather rusty cement mixer. He would have been surprised except he was getting used to strange things turning up in his garden now. He was hoping that maybe a new sports car might turn up there one day. Whilst he was having a nose around the boat a head popped up at the fence. It was Mr Bradshaw.

"Morning Hector," called Dad.

"Now, I don't like to be a spoil sport but—"

"Like my new boat?" Dad cut him off, not really listening to a word he was saying.

"Er, yes... but I draw the line at raves in the early hours of the morning. I mean—"

"Oh yes, I quite agree Hector. Terrible."

"You do? But—"

"Mmm..." Dad pondered, dreamily. "I've always fancied taking up sailing you know. I could take her for a spin. It's not quiet a sports car though. Maybe next time, ay Hector?"

"Er, yes... What?... I say. I wanted to complain about..." but Dad had wandered off thinking about his sports car.

Dad picked up a remaining cocktail glass of blue steaming liquid, left over from the night before, and drunk it while he ate his cornflakes. He had given up wondering how all these things happened. Mmmm, nice taste, he thought.

Mum ran into the kitchen. "We've got a boat in our garden!" she yelled accusingly.

"Yes," said Dad calmly over the top of the morning paper. "Nice shade of blue, isn't it."

"WHAT?"

"Thought I might take it down the beach for a sail."

"But you've got work today!" Mum fumed.

"Who needs work when stuff just drops into your garden?"

"Well I want it OUT of my garden!" Mum yelled

"Yes dear," Dad smiled sweetly.

"AHHH," Mum screamed. "Am I the only sensible person in this house? And what are you drinking?!"

"Dunno. Nice taste though. You want some?" Dad replied. Mum stormed off. Dad relaxed. "This might be a fun day," he thought to himself, wondering where he would sail his new boat to. "Wonder if Em wants to come out in it too?"

Chapter 6 ½

The Gobble Button...

They were all in the party room when Theo arrived. Techno was close behind him, his gaze working its way aimlessly round the room as it often did.

"They're packing up, the last of the Scottish contingent and heading back. Techno's off too," Theo bounced excitedly, "but he's left you a present. Go on tell 'em Techno, tell 'em!" Techno looked round at Theo and scratched his head. That was enough of a cue for Theo, who proceeded to babble on. "He had some spare time this afternoon, since they had finished all their work and stuff, so he got out of the tunnels for a stretch and had a play with your dad's car."

"What?... my dad's car?" said Em with a look of concern.

"Yep. He's installed..." Theo went on very slowly, as if talking to a two year old, "a - gobble - button."

"A what?" asked Em, her look of concern turning to a look of horror.

"Oh Yeah! A gobble button!" shouted Jack excitedly. He seemed to like the idea, though he didn't have clue what a gobble button actually was.

"Yeah, tell 'em Techno," Theo bounced.

"Yes, well, you see. It's a spring fitment attached to the coil behind the dashboard which when pressed enacts the springs underneath the left—"

"Yeah, thanks Techno," Theo interupted. "They get the idea. What he means is, when you press the button it gobbles up whoever is sitting in the front seat, next to the driver."

"WOW!" raved Jack. "OH YEAH! A gobble button!"

"Well what's the point in that?" asked Em, the look of horror turning to a look of annoyance.

"Point? There's no point," answered Theo

cheerily. "It's just a gobble button!"

"Er... but... isn't it a bit dangerous?" Em persisted. "Which button is it anyway?"

Theo pondered this for a moment. "No idea. Techno, which butt..." but Techno had lost interest and wandered off. Theo rushed after him, muttering to himself, but they never returned with an answer.

The next day was Saturday and Dad announced they were going out to Walberswick beach for the day. "Whose car shall we take?" he shouted up the stairs.

"Mum's! Take Mum's," Emily shouted back nervously.

"No, take Dad's!" Jack replied with an evil grin on his face.

"Mine it is then," Dad announced. "Tell you what Em, you can go in the front if you like. I'm sure Mum won't mind."

"Er... no thanks. No, NO! Definitely not... It's OK," Emily replied, totally failing in her attempt to put on her best innocent, I no nothing sort of voice.

"OK, Em, no need to overdo it," Dad replied. "I only asked."

They loaded up the car and climbed in. Emily watched very carefully as Dad started up the car. His hands moved quickly over the dashboard pressing buttons and pulling levers. The sunroof opened and the radio came on. With every button pushed Emily winced, waiting to see if that button would be the gobble button. Mum shifted around in the front passenger seat, getting comfortable and relaxed for the journey.

They drove along happily for twenty minutes before Jack announced, "Press the gobble button, Dad." Dad looked at him in the mirror with a quizzical look. Emily gave Jack a kick and got scolded for it. But Dad soon caught onto the idea. He would let his finger hover over a button on the dashboard for a few seconds whilst Jack shouted at him. Then he would push it, shouting, "Gobble you up!" Emily screwed her eyes tight shut every time he pushed a button. This was torture.

It was the third time, and his finger hovered over the button.

"Go on, Dad!" Jack shouted.

"Stop it, Dad! This is a stupid game." Emily retaliated. "I'm not playing!" But she watched carefully as Dad's finger very slowly moved towards the button... now it was touching it... her heart skipped a beat... it seemed like an eternity passed... and slowly the button pressed in until there was a click. To Emily's horror there was a large mechanical noise and suddenly something whizzed and flipped up in front of here. "Aaaaaaahggg!" she screamed, almost flying out of her seat in fright, but it was just a cup holder unfolding mechanically from the dashboard. Everyone laughed. Emily was furious and sulked for the rest of the journey.

They arrived at Walberswick safely. Dad pulled into the gravel car park and climbed out to pay the parking attendant. They could smell the sea air through the window and see all the kids standing with their crab lines on the bridge, which ran over the little stream. They were suddenly eager to get going. Their crabbing equipment was all stored safely in the car boot. Mum stretched and yawned in the front seat. Emily undid her seatbelt and leaned across to Jack, to help him. She pressed the seatbelt release button, CLICK, and her head snapped quickly left as she heard a loud SNAP... WHIZZ... FLIP sound. There was brief flaying of arms from the front seat, a blur of movement as the base of the front seat appeared to flip over and Mum was gone.

Emily just stared in shocked disbelief. "Cool E!" Jack announced in a deeply impressed voice, "you pressed the gobble button!" Emily recoiled quickly from the button. It wasn't possible... she couldn't have.

Dad then stuck his head back into the car. "Where's Mum gone, Em?"

"Er... "

"The gobble button got her!" Jack shouted.

Dad smiled at him. "Seriously Em, where did she go?"

"Er..." Emily was at a total loss for words. Dad continued to stare at her, waiting for an answer. "Well..." she started, and then stopped. There was an uncomfortable silence.

Suddenly a hand reached out from underneath the car and grabbed Dad's left ankle. He gave out a little yelp of surprise and jumped. Mum crawled out from underneath the car and slowly stood up. Her hair was matted with dust and her T-shirt was covered in dirt. She tried to dust herself down without success.

Dad had a very confused look on his face. "What are you doing down there?" he asked.

But Mum had a similar confused look on her face. "Ermm... I dunno." When they had finished crabbing, eaten the picnic and gone for a swim, Mum squeezed into the back beside Emily for the trip home. Funnily enough, no-one wanted to sit in the front passenger seat.

That evening Emily had serious words with Theo and Techno, demanding that they remove the gobble button immediately. The two mice trudged off begrudgingly. Half an hour later Techno returned and announced to the waiting world that he had removed the offending gobble button... and replaced it with a rather natty ejector seat. "Latest model, you know," he added.

Chapter 7

The Pirates...

Jack lay in bed fidgeting. Emily kept telling him he had to wait till Mum and Dad were asleep, but he couldn't be bothered with all that. He was listening carefully. They were still moving around. He lasted a full seven seconds, before diving out of bed and climbing into the bottom draw of his chest of drawers, where his secret door was hid.

Emily also lay in her bed, listening carefully. She wouldn't move till they were asleep. She glanced over at her TV, which now sat on top of the sideboard. If she did it quietly, maybe she could watch TV? No, Mum would notice. She used this time to think instead. There were still a number of things which bothered her. Amy's hole was still causing havoc at school. Mr Baraclough, the caretaker, was now finding holes all over the place. Yesterday he had found a hole in the wall of the girls' toilets and all the girls had refused to use them until he fixed it. And it was getting closer and closer to end of term. That would mean summer holidays again, but also school reports, and she was still convinced that Miss Robinson hated her, which in turn could mean a bad school report. Emily had tried her best to make things up but Miss Robinson just seemed very cold towards her. She really didn't understand why. And then there was Joseph, she sighed. She was desperate to make friends with him again, but she was determined not to make the first move. After all he was wrong, wasn't he. He was avoiding her in the passageways, she thought, since she hadn't seen him down there at all. But at least the passageways were back, she smiled. But lying there in her bed, the smile turned into a frown. Theo had mentioned pirates again yesterday, and she recalled the ship which had now appeared on Dad's picture... suddenly she noticed the shadow cast across her bedroom floor. The curtains were not quiet shut and the moon shone through. But the shadow had a distinct person shape about it. She pulled the duvet up around her neck.

"CHING," came the distinctive sound of a sword being drawn from a sheath. She could see the shadow raising the sword above his head...

Emily shook her head. The shadow had gone. She had been dozing. She scolded herself for having dozed off. She glanced over to the corner of the room. Nothing, no pirates. Pirates... the picture, she remembered. She glanced at the pink pig. Eleven thirty. She listened... no sound. She climbed out of bed and tiptoed into the hall to examine the picture. The pirate ship was still there, which was not good. Her eyes scanned across the hills and valleys, the aeroplane up amongst the clouds, the bays and vast ocean... hang on... aeroplane? What aeroplane? That hadn't been there before. It was a little plane with a single propeller at its nose and an open cockpit; kind of old fashioned looking. Curious, she thought. Another thought suddenly struck her. She had never thought of that before. Every room she had entered, down in the passageways, had mice standing guard on the doors. Why would they have guards on the doors? Perhaps they were scared of a pirate invasion. She would have to ask Fay and Jennifer. They were the best adventurers, good at plotting and scheming and things. They would have noticed.

Then she remembered the passicom. She dived back into her room and found her passicom under her pillow. It just looked like an innocent digital watch. Her one was pink. She pressed the top and bottom buttons at the same time. Theo had said that was an anti-parent device. Parents weren't intelligent enough to figure out pressing both buttons together. Emily whispered into the passicom, "Fay." It buzzed, clicked and the face of the watch went fuzzy. Fay's face came into view. It was all wet, with her hair clinging to her face.

"Em! Get down here. We're in The Lake. It's brill!"

Emily immediately forgot all her questions and worries, grabbed her swimming costume from the bathroom and dived for her sideboard cupboard. She pressed the big red button and the lift buzzed into life, descending into the depths of the passageways.

Everyone seemed to be in the lake. It was fantastic. There must have been hundreds of children there. There was a buzz, ding, and then a voice came over the speaker system. "The next boat trip to the shark pool will leave the pier in five minutes." Em spotted Ellie over to the left. She was dressed in a smart wet suit and standing on a wind surfer. She seemed to be taking directions from an older boy. There was a look of distinct concentration on her face, as if this was something she was determined to master.

About a hundred meters out a speedboat raced past, sending a large spray of surf towards the shore. The people in the boat seemed to be waving in her direction. She could make out the shape of Fay in the boat.

Buzz, ding. "The wave machine will be starting in two minutes," ding. Em spotted Amy to her right, building sand castles and digging holes on the beach. She was talking to herself, or was she talking to the sandcastle? Em wasn't sure. Both were equally worrying. And there was Buster, with the same wrap around sunglasses on and holding a megaphone. He seemed to be having two discussions at once, alternating between giving some directions to a group of swimmers through the megaphone and having a heated debate with her little brother, Jack. Well that should be interesting, she thought. I don't think Buster will win that one.

Buster held out the life jacket. "All the youngans have gotta where them if they go in the pool. That's the rule. And," he poked Jack in the left knee cap (which is as high as he could reach), "you, kido, are no exception!"

"No! Don't want it. It's pooh!" Jack shouted back.

"I don't care," Buster replied. "No jacket, no pool! Got it?"

Jack gave the little mouse one of his mean looks. Then he picked him up by the tail.

"PUT ME DOWN, YOU HORRID LITTLE TOAD!" Buster shouted, swinging his paws at Jack, but it was no use.

Em watched, quite amused. If it were any other mouse she would have gone to help, but there was something about Buster she found quite annoying... his smoothyness. Jack grabbed the megaphone, placed it so that Busters head was dangling inside the end of it and then shouted through it, "I AM NOT WEARING YOUR STUPID LIFE JACKET! UNDERSTAND?" Then he dropped Buster onto the floor where the poor mouse sat, his head still vibrating from the noise. Jack proceeded to stomp down the beach to the waters edge, where he seemed to turn back into a little kid again and started jumping the waves.

There was a sudden CLANG... CLANG... CLANG. Em looked round to see the square shape of Cook standing at the entrance to The Lake. She was banging a spoon on the bottom of a saucepan. "Lemonade and Ice cream bar's open!" she shouted, and a cheer went out from some of those huddled on the edge of The Lake. They began to make their way across to the tunnel. Cook had a frustrated look on her face. CLANG... CLANG... CLANG, she bashed again. "Today we have specials on chocolate ice-cream sundaes, and coke floats. Can you beat the three litre choco-ice challenge?" she shouted. A few more interested looks and she smiled and disappeared.

Em wandered up to the party room keen to see the three-litre choco-ice challenge. The room was filling up now. Izzie was serving at the circular counter in the centre. Em wandered up to say hello.

"Em, I've got just the thing for you!" Izzie squealed excitedly. She grabbed a couple of bottles, emptying the contents into a large glass. She flipped one bottle neatly over her head. It flew through the air in an arc and landed with a clank it the bin. Em was impressed. Izzie was enjoying herself. "I just adore cocktails! This one's gorgeous, you'll love it. It's pips." One hand deftly threw a lemon into the slicer and she finished by placing the lemon and umbrella into the large glass of... ahhh, what was that. It looked gross.

"Er, thanks Izzie. What is it?"

"It's a bug juice special. It tastes absolutely mega pips."

Em looked at the bright blue liquid. It was giving off a hissing sound and it was bubbling, but not like a normal fizzy drink. Large bubbles were slowly coming to the surface, rising up and drifting off over the crowd. "Any chance of a plain lemonade?"

"Try it. You'll love it," grinned Izzie as she disappeared to poison another customer, her curly hair bouncing around as she went.

Jennifer popped up next to Em. "Wouldn't drink that," she said. "I tried one the other day. Not good." Em abandoned it on an empty table and the two girls wandered over to the crowd, which had formed around one table.

Em and Jennifer pushed their way to the front. Sitting at the table was Jemima. She was a large, tall girl with long ringlets, with bows in. She also had a large personality. She was loud and always the first for an impossible challenge. And so there she was, spoon in hand, licking her lips, sitting in front of the largest ice-cream you have ever seen. It was a choco-ice challenge. It was in a glass, which looked like an oversized wine glass, so large that Jack could probably have sat in it. It was stuffed full of ice-cream, chocolate sauce, biscuit, fudge, brownies and topped with whipped cream. It was so full that cream and chocolate was running down the side as it melted. If anyone could eat it then Jemima could. There were shouts of, "come on Jem!"... "you can do it!" But before she could start a second choco-ice challenge was placed on the table opposite her. Everyone stared, astonished, as little Jack sat down. Jemima stared across the table.

"That's bigger than you are, kid."

"Yeah, I know!" Jack replied with a wide-eyed look of wonder in his eyes. Everyone gathered round were shaking their heads... no chance of him making it. Both launched into the gigantic ice-creams. Jemima took dainty mouthfuls and made steady progress, whilst Jack had his head bent down close to the glass, seeing how much he could fit in his mouth in one go. Both reached the halfway mark, and by this stage Jack's face and pyjama top were covered with ice-cream. By the three quarters mark Jemima was definitely slowing down. Jack still seemed to be going strong. They were getting near the end. Jemima had now turned a distinct shade of green. Every mouthful looked like an effort, and she was taking long breaks between each one. Every now and then a groan escaped her lips. Everyone knew she was suffering. Jack, on the other hand, was now slowing down but apart from that didn't seem to be showing any other signs of a problem. Jemima watched as Jack took his final mouthful and placed his spoon down on the table. Everyone held their breath, waiting to see his reaction. He rubbed his tummy.

"That was yum! Can I have another one?"

"What!" exclaimed Cook. "That's impossible!"

Jemima groaned. Then she bolted from the table. "Get out of my way! I'm gonna be sick!"

Buster was now standing at the doorway shouting through his megaphone. "Dolphin ride and water skiing now open. Bring your drinks through."

No sooner had everyone wandered back to The Lake, than Cook reappeared, with Izzie at her side, banging her saucepan and announcing that tonight's entertainment was now commencing, which was a very special visiting mouse circus from Russia. Everyone started traipsing back to the party room yet again. Buster looked furious. It was evident that there was a bit of a battle going on here between Cook and Buster, who were obviously not the best of friends. Buster then appeared in the party room (plus megaphone) to announce the beach party karaoke, followed closely by Cook announcing the official launch of the new party room. When Buster then appeared and called everyone back to The Lake again, everybody was getting very confused and irritated. Buster could then be seen barricading the door so that Cook couldn't get in.

As Cook and Buster were squaring up to one another in heated debate, Theo appeared at the girl's side. "Hello Em. Have you got a minute? Whiskers wanted to have an important—" but Theo never got to finish.

"What's that?" shouted a small boy on the edge of the pool, pointing out over The Lake. Everyone turned to look. There was definitely something large on the horizon, and coming closer. It was difficult, in the artificial light of The Lake, to see it clearly. Buster broke off from his argument and collected his binoculars from the cabin.

"It's a bloomin' great ship alright, but it certainly ain't one of ours." He hit a button on the side of the cabin. Red flags unfurled from the lifeguard tower. Ding, "The red flags have been raised. Will all swimmers please leave the water." Ding.

Theo dropped his clipboard. "The pirates! They've breached the passageways. It's a disaster!"

"Pirates?" Em questioned but Theo gave no response. As all the children swam to shore and were rushed out of the cave, it dawned on Em for the first time that most of them were younger than she was. She remembered 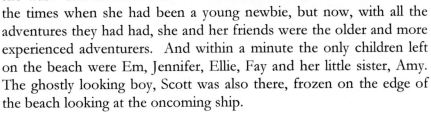 the times when she had been a young newbie, but now, with all the adventures they had had, she and her friends were the older and more experienced adventurers. And within a minute the only children left on the beach were Em, Jennifer, Ellie, Fay and her little sister, Amy. The ghostly looking boy, Scott was also there, frozen on the edge of the beach looking at the oncoming ship.

They all watched until they could distinctly make out the skull and crossbones flag.

"So what's the plan, Theo?" asked Jennifer.

"Buster's in charge of guarding The Lake," Theo replied. "Buster!" he called.

Guards?... Em's thoughts from earlier came back to her. "So it's true... you've placed guards on all the passageways. Why?"

"No time to explain. I need to get Whiskers. Buster will take care of the pirate ship." And with that the little panic stricken mouse collected his clipboard and went scampering down the entrance passage.

Buster, the muscular lifeguard, burst out of the cabin clutching thee large sports bags.

"OK, what's the plan?" Jennifer repeated her question.

"Plan?" Buster asked.

"Yeah. Like you taking care of the ship out there. Theo said—"

"Look lady, it's like this," Buster interrupted. "They're pirates... you know, chop your tail off sort of pirates. And I'm a mouse... I'm a lifeguard, there's nothing in my job description about pirates!" Buster shouted the last bit as he ran down the passage.

"So what are we supposed to do?" called Em angrily.

"RUN!" came the shout from deep in the tunnel.

"Oh great!" said Jennifer, "we're dead meat," she continued, putting words to what everyone was thinking. The children looked around. They were all alone. The ship was getting bigger and was heading straight for them. As it got closer, they could make out more details. They could see the dirty brown sails, and the rigging with lots of pirates crawling all over it.

"So it's true then?" said the faint voice of the ghostly Scott. He was looking even more white and pale now, as if he was going to faint. "You know, about the pirates... the picture and the hole and all that?"

"Hole! That's it. Amy, where's the hole?"

"Er," Amy looked a bit sheepish. "I lost him. Well I haven't exactly lost him, I just can't find him. At the moment, that is. I think he ran away. Actually! Well maybe he..." Jennifer left Amy rambling on to herself as if she was at a teddy bears picnic.

Fay was standing at the very edge of the pool, ankle deep in water. She could smell an adventure in the air. Em's eyes were wide, looking at the pirate ship, which now seemed to dwarf the view. "Jen!" she whispered, feeling the panic welling up inside her. "We need to do something. Quickly!"

"Hang on. I'm thinking."

"We need to get out of here," came the sensible voice of Ellie. "We can't fight pirates."

"We can't fight them, you're right Ellie," Jennifer replied. "But we can't let them get into the passageways either."

"Why not?" said Scott. "I like the idea of getting out of here."

"Look, there is only one entrance to the lake. We block it up," said Jennifer.

"NO WAY!" shouted the voice of Izzie as the curly haired girl ran into the cave. "You rotton lot! Have you forgotten? That hole in the roof leads up to MY garden... MY pool, remember? You can't leave them here! They'll invade my house!" They all looked at each other. Izzie jumped into the nearest boat. "Come on!" she shouted. They watched as she readied herself for the battle, floated out six feet and then capsized, flipping the boat over with great shouts and splashes. Fay rolled her eyes.

This is a total disaster, Jennifer thought. Here they were... they couldn't fight, and now they couldn't run. They were all glued to the spot, helpless.

Jennifer's thoughts were interrupted by Scott's shout. "It's stopped!" He was right. The pirate ship had stopped. They watched as, to their horror, five or six small boats were lowered over the side of the large ship. Seven of eight pirates dropped into each one. Swords and ropes were then dropped down to those in the boats.

Em gulped. "Well, at least it can't get much worse." There was a sudden ear-bursting explosion, which shook the ground. Whizzzz...

"Cannon!" shouted Scott. The cannon shot landed in the water about thirty feet out, with an even louder explosion, which sent all the children diving to the ground. Fay climbed to her feet first. She could see the smoking cannon on the bow of the big ship. The pirates were loading up another round and adjusting the angle so that it would reach the beach next time, then it would be curtains for anyone left on the beach. "Need to hurry," Fay whispered to herself. Then she turned and shouted, "Hurry! They're reloading!"

"We've gotta move, now!" shouted Ellie. "Let's get out of here."

"NO!" Izzie shouted back. The two girls glared at each other. Still no-one moved, and the pirates finished adjusting the cannon. The five or six small rowing boats were getting closer, and they could now make out the angry faces of the pirates. They had dark sunburnt skin and black hair and beards. The lighting glinted off the broad curved blades, which lay in the boats, ready for use.

"We're toast," said Jennifer, in a very depressed tone.

Suddenly there was a soft buzzing sound. Em could see a little spot in the distance, like a wasp buzzing around in the lofty heights of the vast cave. The pirates had also seen it and were looking.

"It's a plane!" said Scott in surprise.

"It's Alfred!" shouted Whiskers with glee as he popped up beside Em.

"Whiskers!" exclaimed Izzie. "Pips! We're saved. Look... Pirates and..." but no-one was listening. They were all staring at the little plane, now clearly visible. It was a bright yellow single propeller plane with an open cockpit, just like Em had seen in her dad's picture. On the side was a picture of a large mouse, donning a top hat worn crookedly atop his head. It was definitely Alfred in his circus aeroplane, Em groaned. She remembered that she had once had a terrifying ride with him. He was a lunatic! "Alfred..." she moaned. "Did things just get better or worse?"

Whiskers frowned. "Better I hope. Otherwise we're up the creak without a tail, as they say."

"You have a plan?" Jennifer asked, looking worried. "Someone around here must have a plan."

"Er... No," Whiskers replied calmly, "but it's not quite time to panic yet."

"NOT TIME TO PANIC YET!" shouted Ellie, now totally losing her cool. "You're totally IRRESPONSIBLE!" she yelled. Whiskers carried on looking calm and humming a little tune as if she had just invited him to afternoon tea.

"He's got help," Whiskers went on, pointing. "Look. Joseph and Ollie are with him."

"What!" they all looked up in surprise.

Up in the aeroplane Alfred, Joseph and Biggles swooped lower to see what was going on. The wind blew through their hair and left them almost breathless, in the little open top, single prop plane.

Joseph thought it was the most exhilarating feeling he had ever had, as he gave a loud "whoop" of excitement, which no-one heard over the sound of the engine. They all wore flying goggles, and Biggles had his lucky scarf trailing behind.

It had been the strangest of adventures which had brought Joseph and Ollie into contact with the mad little mouse, Alfred. They had found him hanging upside down by his ankles in a butcher's freezer... it was a long story, Joseph smiled to himself. And over the last weeks and months since the passageways reopened, they had spent almost every night with Alfred, learning to fly. And they'd spent almost every day desperately trying to stay awake during school. As it turned out, whilst Joseph loved his flying, he had to admit (somewhat reluctantly) that it was his little brother, Ollie who had a real talent for it. Ever since they started learning Ollie insisted on wearing his lucky scarf and being called 'Biggles' every time he donned his goggles, after his, now favourite, flying hero from the really old comics and books his dad had. And, Joseph's thoughts drifted a bit further, Ollie was a whole different person behind the stick of the aeroplane. He would stick his tongue out slightly as the eyes narrowed in concentration, and he would fly wickedly close to things and through incredibly tight spaces. He bordered on being a real maniac when you put him in an aeroplane. But he wasn't as bad as Alfred, who was, let's face it, utterly loopy, as well as deaf.

Joseph's mind had drifted. He quickly pulled himself back to reality. It didn't look good down there. The ship was firing cannons and five little boats were rowing to shore. It was very strange flying in a cave, but the roof was high enough to give them lots of manoeuvring space.

"Geronemo!" screamed Ollie, gritting his teeth.

"What? Lower, you say?" Alfred tipped the stick forward and dive-bombed directly for The Lake.

"AHHHG!!... NOOO!" screamed the two boys.

Alfred overflew the first two rowing boats, about four feet above the surface of the water. One of the pirates made the mistake of standing up and was rewarded for his stupidity with a direct hit, centre forehead, by the left wing. He flew twenty foot threw the air and landed in the other boat with such force that he sank it.

Alfred immediately pulled the plane up into a steep climb, flipping the plane over spectacularly as it went, which is where their problems began. Half way up the engine gave a fatal stutter and then died.

"Oh crumbs!" said Joseph.

"What was that?" shouted the mouse, distracted by Joseph's comment. "Want some rum, you say. Oh my favourite. Be right back." And with that his head disappeared into the cockpit. Joseph and Ollie just stared as the plane slowed its accent and came to a complete halt in mid-air (still no Alfred to be seen). Time seemed to stand still for a moment and then the nose of the plane sank down and it started to drop. Alfred's head popped back up. "Here we are!" he held his hip flask up high for everyone to see. "It's an excellent brand of... Oh..." he looked around and suddenly noticed they were in trouble. Then the plane started to spiral wildly as it fell and Alfred fell out.

On the shore, everyone had been getting hopeful as they saw the spectacular low dive over the boats. Now they watched as the little mouse fell into the water with a loud splash. Em rolled her eyes. She knew Alfred was a walking disaster (or rather, a flying disaster.)

"Do you think they'll be alright?" Fay asked. No-one answered as they all watched the stalled plane spiralling towards The Lake.

"Biggles! Grab the stick!" Joseph shouted, as he kicked, punched and cursed the engine. He gave it one last hefty kick and the engine lurched back into life. Ollie pulled back on the stick and they cleared the water by inches. Joseph looked up to see a blanket of white in front of him, as the little plane ripped through the main sail of the pirate ship.

"Nice one, Biggles!"

Ollie grinned. There was a loud explosion behind them and a cannon shot past them, which Ollie neatly avoided by rolling the plane.

"OK! Time to sort them out I think, Biggles." Ollie pulled sharp left and the ship came back into view. "I have an idea!"

The children watched from the shore as the little plane careered straight for the large ship.

"He's not gonna...?" Fay started, "Is he?"

"I think he is," Jennifer replied. "He's mad!"

The plane dived in low, scattering pirates in all directions. The right wing struck the base of the mast. It ripped most of the wing from the plane and the plane went spinning off, somehow managing to stay airborne. The mast rocked, then creaked, then tipped, splintered and fell over the bow of the ship. The heavy mast smashed through the upper decks creating a large gash in the front of the ship. A fire now blazed, as the rigging and sails caught alight. The fire must have reached the gunpowder for the cannons as, with a loud explosion, the left side of the ship was blown out. And with that the ship keeled over and began to sink.

The pirates, who had been sitting, very confused, in the rowing boats decided they had had enough and turned to rescue their fellow crewmen, before fleeing from the cave. The little plane, now spiralling wildly out of control, did a full loop and dived low over the water. This time it didn't manage to clear the water but hit the surface head on, with a splash so big that it sent water up to the roof of the cave and looked more like an upside down waterfall.

The cave was suddenly silent.

"Joseph! Ollie!" shouted Em and Fay together, and they started splashing through the water towards the wreckage of the little plane.

"Well, that went rather well, I thought!" said Whiskers cheerfully

"Well?" replied Jennifer in horror. "What a disaster."

Chapter 8
Project Stormbuster
How it all Began...

After they had dredged the remains of the aeroplane from The Lake, Whiskers settled them in the Committee Room. They all felt wet and tired. After all the excitement of the night, it all seemed rather flat now... and rather confusing. They still had no idea why all these things were happening. They snuggled, wrapped in blankets and sipping coco, listening to the commotion next door and taking in the smart surroundings of the Committee Room. Em remembered this was the place where the Passageway Committee met and made all the important decisions. Wow, she thought. The room was dim, lit by only three candles placed atop the deep brown mahogany ring doughnut shaped Committee table. It was a low table, which they sat around on cushions and beanbags. Em starred at the row of paintings on the wall; all portraits of mice who had led the Crinkle Point passageways since they had been built in, when was it, 1896. The last picture on the wall was of Whiskers.

Everyone seemed content to sit in silence. They listened to the heated argument going on in the room next door between Whiskers and Spondic, who was a rather old and rather irritable mouse.

"...Absolute balderdash, young Whiskers," Spondic was hissing angrily. "You left the passages with minimal defences and were totally unprepared. I mean really! Placing a mouse like Buster in charge of a key doorway?!!"

"He'll learn. He has to—"

"You're an irresponsible and rash young mouse," Spondic interrupted. "Just like your father! Full of fancy ideas. A load of claptrap, it is! No control of what's going on at all! Don't know how you've lasted this long!" Spondic was a very old mouse, bent over with age and wrinkled with the experiences of life. In fact he was the oldest mouse in the passageways. All the passageway children avoided him because he was always so miserable, and he would often wave his walking stick and shout at a boy or girl, accusing them of committing some supposed crime or other. Em didn't know why Whiskers put up with him.

"My dear Spondic," Whiskers gushed, as if he had just been told how wonderful he was. "That is as it maybe... and you may be right, yes you may. But we owe these children an explanation. They need to understand what is happening. They need to understand what they are up against."

"Absolutely not! This is our responsibility." They could hear Spondic cracking his walking stick down hard on the stone floor. "You cannot put this sort of pressure on them. They are children, for goodness sake!" The children listened, wondering what pressures and responsibilities the mice were arguing about.

"This is our responsibility, you are right. But they are part of us now." There was a silence and all they could hear was Spondic huffing and puffing. "I have made my decision Spondic. Will you join me with them, please?" Whiskers asked softly.

"NO I WILL NOT!" came the rattled reply from Spondic. "You're a fool!" Spondic retorted, "just like your father."

It was only the older children sitting around the Committee room: Fay, Em, Joseph, Jennifer, Izzie and Ellie. The youngsters had been packed off to bed. The ornate grandfather clock struck two am. It was late. Joseph was sitting opposite Em. He was bruised and his arm was in a sling, though it was not broken or seriously damaged. They could just see each other across the top of the doughnut table, and all of a sudden their eyes met. Neither of them twitched a muscle, not wanting to give way an inch and scared they might inadvertently smile at the other.

"Rat," said Em.

"Scus bucket," replied Joseph half-heartedly.

"Gutter vermin," Em said with half a grin on her face.

"Snot for brains."

Em smiled. "Nice flying."

"Thanks." There was a pause, as they both seemed to find something incredibly interesting to examine on the grey stone floor. "Sorry about—" Joseph started.

"That's OK," Em cut him off. It was strange. She had been waiting months for an apology and now she didn't want him to say it. She just wanted everything to be how it used to be. They held each other's gaze for a few more seconds, not really knowing what else to say, and then it was suddenly broken by the noisy entrance of Whiskers.

Whiskers jumped up onto the doughnut table with a glass of lemonade in hand and surveyed the children.

"Right, well, sorry about that." He seemed to be collecting his thoughts for a few moments. "I think I owe you all an explanation."

"Those weren't real pirates, were they?" interrupted Ellie, unable to hold back the questions going through her mind any longer. Her very sensible mind had been busy thinking through all the possibilities and just couldn't make sense of it. "I mean pirates don't exist do they? So this was just a passageway magic thing... er... like the magic room?"

Whiskers smiled. "Of course, a very important question. Everything you experience down here, even in the magic room is real. Every adventure, every danger, every person or animal or monster. This is no dream. And, yes, pirates do really exist—"

"Will they be coming back?" Jennifer asked.

Whiskers took a sip of his lemonade, thinking how to phrase his answer. "Yes, they will. There is no reason to think tonight's events, however well you did (and you did do well!) will stop them."

Murmurs started up around the room.

"We will have to be better prepared next time," Jennifer concluded.

"Yes, precisely! Which is why I need all of you on the Committee." A silence spread across the room.

"Us?" said Jennifer sceptically.

"Yes, you. If you hadn't realised, firstly you are fast becoming the oldest children down here. Secondly, you are the most experienced adventurers I have. And thirdly all the previous Committee led by our Guardian, Fred, have left." They had all liked Fred, the son of Arthur Bedgrow, the shopkeeper. He had reached ten years old last summer and had to leave the passageways. "And most importantly," Whiskers paused, "you care." Em looked around the important looking stately room, where all the important decisions were made. And to think... it would be them in here making them. "But I must ask you... are you willing to take on this responsibility? It is not something to be taken on lightly." The children all glanced round at each other. They all nodded.

"What's a guardian?" Fay asked. "You called Fred the guardian."

"So I did," replied Whiskers. "There are a number of important roles and things which you have to do. But ultimately there must be one mouse and one child chosen to lead the Crinkle Point passageways. That is the rule, and it is the same for every set of passageways. That child is called the Guardian of the passageways. Without a Guardian we are not allowed to open." The children all looked around at one another wondering who the Guardian would be. Em thought it should be Jennifer or Joseph, since they were the best at leading their little group. "But before we choose someone, there are some other important things we need to do." Whiskers went on. "Everyone on the Passageway Committee has a special job to do. Jennifer and Joseph, I would like you to concentrate your skills on the defence of the passageways. As you have already said, Jennifer, we must be better prepared." Joseph and Jennifer both looked at each other, reached an unspoken agreement and nodded their consent. "Very good. Now, Ellie and Izzie I would like you to take responsibility for domestic arrangements: catering, party room, and entertainment.

Izzie with your gift for it and all the work you have already been doing with Cook."

"Why me?" Ellie asked, a little confused.

"I need you, Ellie, with your firm hand, to start sorting out some of the problems, starting with Buster and Cook." Whiskers' tail gave a quiver of annoyance. "Fay, I would like you to work with Theo on the enormous task of... Wooden doors. Planning out the passageway adventures. It is so exciting at the moment, building a whole new set of adventures for a whole new set of passageways, don't you think?" Fay, who was always fidgeting for the next adventure was licking her lips in anticipation. "And so that leaves you, my dear Emily. And I would ask you to do the humblest of jobs and be the Guardian of the Passageways." Whiskers smiled at her.

"Me? I could never—" Em started, but Whiskers upraised paw cut her off.

"Go on Em," said Fay. "You should do it."

Em glanced around the room and there were nods of agreement.

"Excellent!" enthused Whiskers, clapping his hands. "In that case I declare the twenty sixth Passageway Committee formed and now in session. So this is our first meeting. Of course there will be a few more members from the mouse contingent: Theo for planning, Rufus on building and maintenance and, of course, Benji for our all important emergency response. I asked them not to attend tonight so I can spend a little time with you alone." Whiskers sighed and the lines of age and worry appeared on his brow. "And Spondic. Of all the mice, he is by far the most important." Whiskers saw the look of disbelief on the children's faces. "Oh yes, don't be fooled. Spondic, and I know you see little value in what he does and you call him, what is it..."

"The old git," Joseph said helpfully, with feeling.

"Ah yes, a pleasant term of endearment!" Whiskers joked. "Spondic is my most valued friend and advisor." Again looks of disbelief came from around the room.

"But he calls you stupid and wants you kicked out!" Joseph said, being helpful again.

Whiskers smiled. "What you will come to learn is that Spondic and I disagree quite considerably when it comes to how we should teach you."

"Teach us?" The children had never thought of it as teaching.

"Oh most definitely. And Fay, you need to understand this more than anyone if you are to plan the adventures, which exist here. The purpose of the passageways is not fun or adventure or enjoyment, although we hope all this is part of it, no the purpose is to teach. To teach you more about life... it's dangers, the importance of your friends, and just how much you are capable of, for you can do much more than you could imagine... in fact you already have! To teach you more than you will ever learn in a classroom. Anyway, Spondic. We disagree quite considerably when it comes to how the passageways should be run. You have to understand that Spondic comes from the old school, which says we should control all that happens and keep you children far away from any danger or challenge. You see Spondic cares about you more than anyone does. But I always think we learn from the adventures and dangers we face, and I always find it fascinating to see how life works things out for us. Look at tonight for instance!"

Ellie frowned at him.

"Ahh, but Spondic is so right," Whiskers went on, "I do cause myself problems far too often."

There was a long silence. "Goodness me, I'm rambling. I came here to offer you an explanation for the strange things, which have happened of late. It is a long story and I had better start from the very beginning. Sit back and make yourself comfortable. I would not share this burden with you, except that you need to understand the extent of the problem we now face, and this will also give you a glimpse of the whole reason we are here. Right, where to begin..." There was a sudden buzz of excitement in the room. They were finally going to get answers to some of their many questions. Whiskers had a far away look in his eyes. The room had a heavy rich atmosphere as each word hung in the air. The smoke slowly rose from the candles as the wax ran onto the mahogany table. The grandfather clock struck three am.

"Well, I suppose it all started with the Prime Minister." The children were suddenly looking around wide-eyed at each other. "You know, the man in charge of the whole country. A nice chap he is."

"Yes, we know who he is, but what has he got to do with our passageways?" asked Ellie impatiently.

"Have you met him then?" Joseph blurted.

"Only the once," Whiskers replied. "Very nice chap." The children again exchanged astonished glances and then settled down to hear this most amazing of tales.

"Yes, it all started with the Prime Minister. He knows all sorts of things that you would never get to hear about and things you just wouldn't believe, because he's in charge you see. It must be over sixty years ago when they first discovered that us mice weren't just dumb animals. It was about the time of the war. Bombs falling all around us, every day more casualties. They wanted us to fight, you know. Ridiculous really, when you look back. They had invented something they called the dog mine. They would attach explosives to the back of a dog and then train them to run under the enemy tanks and heavy artillery. Then they would detonate the mines and destroy the enemy position. Didn't work of course. They had trained the dogs using British tanks so when they set them loose with the mines the dogs, not being too bright, ran under the wrong tanks and blew up the British ones. Anyway, when they discovered mice were intelligent, they tried to get us to do it. Spondic's father was in the first mouse mine programme. They all abandoned the mines and made a run for it. Well they didn't want their tails blown off did they! After this it was Spondic's grandfather, Jeffers Spondic, a very honourable and distinguished mouse who sought a meeting with the then Prime Minister. He wanted to argue for mouse rights and also to offer their services to the Prime Minister, if they could be of use.

Now, it just happened that, about this time, the Prime Minister, or PM as he is known, had a number of difficult problems on his plate. One was the children and the other was the pirates. This was back in the days when children as young as seven or eight would be sent to work down the coal mines and in the workhouses. They were, for want of a better word, slaves."

"Never!" Ellie interrupted, wide-eyed. "That's criminal!"

Whiskers adjusted his position and took a sip of lemonade. "That's the problem, you see. It wasn't criminal."

"But why didn't he stop them? This PM man."

"People were making lots of money out of it, you see. Even someone as powerful as the PM was, has to do what the people want. He was trying to persuade them of course, but it was taking a long time and he was concerned for the children. The second problem was the pirates. They were attacking the shores, raiding villages and ships as they left harbours and—"

"But why didn't he just send the navy fleet out to destroy them?" asked Joseph.

"Well of course the navy could have whipped their tails, but the PM couldn't do that."

"How come?"

"The pirates were very clever. They never came into shore in their ships, they kept away from the shipping lanes and they kept themselves very secret. They only ever picked off one ship at a time in an area before moving on. They relied upon the fact that no-one believed they existed." Whiskers paused to let this sink in, and to refill his lemonade glass from a smart drinks cabinet in the corner.

"Oh I get it," said Joseph. "So if the PM announced he was launching an attack against the pirates no-one would believe him!"

"Exactly!" Whiskers looked pleased with his pupil. "He would be a laughing stock. They would think he was mad."

"So where do they come from, the pirates?" Fay asked.

"Good question. We aren't totally sure, but we believe they live off the coast of a country called Bermuda. There is a large stretch of ocean called the Bermuda Triangle where many ships mysteriously disappear. Nowadays sailors are afraid to go there. We think that perhaps the pirates live on islands there."

"And do they really cut off hands, feet, and tails?" asked Izzie in a ghostly whisper.

"I'm afraid they do, if they don't kill you first." A hush fell over the room. Izzie's eyes were so wide Em thought they might fall out. Suddenly the clock struck the half hour.

"Ahhg!" Izzie jumped.

"Goodness, the time!" Whiskers continued. "Jeffers Spondic, that's Spondic's grandfather, offered their services. The mice could spread the word through the vast mouse network in the sewers (that's where the mice lived then.) They could watch and, where necessary, contact the children. And they could start a secret war against the pirates. And in return they would be allowed to exist in peace. The deal was struck. It was nicknamed Project Stormbuster, after the name of the first pirate ship, which had attacked British shores. Over time the mice organised themselves into squadrons in each town and city and built their own network of passageways. They fought the pirates, and they gave a secret life to thousands of sad children, feeding them, encouraging them, giving them a reason to live and a chance to be someone... just like the secret life you live. Of course conditions for children are much better now than in the past, but there are still many many who need our help, and the passageways give lessons in life which no school could. Spondic was but a small lad then, but he was one of the first Committee members here, as was my own grandfather. And for a while it all went well. They did other jobs too, you know. The PM and all the other government ministers used to keep their secret papers in red boxes. The mice used to deliver all the red boxes through the secret tunnels. It was the safest way to transport things, you see. But then things began to crumble." Whiskers sighed. There was total silence in the room now. All eyes were on Whiskers and the only sounds which could be heard were the ticking of the grandfather clock and the dripping of wax off the candles.

"There was a new Prime Minister elected, and the whole deal with the mice, Project Stormbuster, was scrapped, paperwork burnt, and that was the end of that. This left Jeffers with a difficult decision, but he decided to continue the work being done. Then we realised too late that the pirates had been cleverer than we thought and were actually using our network of mouse tunnels to get in shore and raid the coastal towns. They were building secret sea tunnels out into the sea, so they could latch straight onto our network from their ships.

"That's what we saw in the Levington passageways!" exclaimed Fay.

"That's right. But the worst disaster," Whiskers continued, "was the rebels. And the worst of them was Gravisham."

There were gasps and sharp intakes of breath around the room, at the sound of that name. Oscar Gravisham was a well know name to the children. Only a year back Gravisham, who was a property developer in the town, had tried to destroy their Terrace and uncover the passageways, and they had stopped him. But they thought they had seen the last of him.

"That's right," Whiskers went on, "when I told you he was dangerous I didn't just mean he could catch you. He is dangerous because he knows about the passageways. He knows everything!"

"But you let us go right up close—"

"No," Whiskers cut Ellie off, "I told you that under no circumstances were you to go near him, if I remember rightly, but you didn't listen."

The dreamy look came back into Whiskers eyes and he continued. "By this time the first generation of passageway children were growing up. Most of them turned out well. We helped so many children, you know. But a few didn't turn out well. Why? I've often wondered. I think they felt left out when they had to leave."

"Gravisham." Whiskers spat the name out. "Of course the first Gravisham was not the one you know. No, it was his grandfather, but since then it has all passed down to his son and grandson. He was once Guardian of the passageways, the first Gravisham."

It was now very late. Em yawned, her eyelids fluttered and her mind drifted lazily. As Whiskers continued to talk and his words wafted gently around the room like the slow curling smoke of a cigar, Em imagined the scene before her...

A young Gravisham senior sat in the front living room of his tall Victorian town house. The coal fire blazed. He prodded it with the poker. He was only a young man of sixteen but still the lines of worry creased his forehead. "It's the business, Charlie. Gravisham and Co Property Agents is just... well, it's not doing well at all. The bills were piling up." He threw a stack of envelopes up into the air. "I have to do something!"

Opposite him sat a close friend, Charles Attenbury. Charlie sipped his glass of port. Both men were dressed very formally in suits and ties, as was the custom in the olden days.

"I can help, of course?" said Attenbury raising his eyebrows questioningly. "If you're willing to take the risk."

"Anything, Charlie. Really, I'll do anything!"

"I have a small proposition which might interest you." Charlie narrowed his eyes, assessing his friend. "But I must warn you. These are serious people I'm dealing with."

Gravisham was curious. His friend, Charles was one of these people who seemed to know lots of people and drift easily through life. Gravisham nodded. "Go on."

"I know a man... he is a rather strange fellow... who is willing to put his money into your business while you get started. His name is Nathaniel Mitra Bruthersharken"

"Really!?" blurted Gravisham. "How come? What terms? How—"

"All he wants in return," Charlie continued, ignoring the barrage of questions, "is your help in a small matter. You deal in houses and properties along the coastal towns. He needs access to a network of secret passageways which run from many of the houses in those same coastal towns."

Gravisham frowned. "Secret passageways? Is this legal? Who is this fellow?"

Charlie paused before answering. "This is where it gets interesting. Do you believe in pirates?"

"And so the deal was struck," Whiskers concluded, "The Pirates paid Gravisham the money he needed and in return Gravisham helped the pirates get into the passageways. And the Gravisham family has been tied up with the pirates ever since, right up to this day. It was a betrayal of the worst kind which Gravisham made!" Whiskers spat in disgust. "But there's more. The mice had to act quickly, and this is where Spondic and my grandfather had their first major disagreement.

You see Spondic wanted it all done by the book. The passageways had been discovered and we should do a full closedown and fill in, and move out of all the coastal towns, including Crinkle Point here it Felixstowe. But my grandfather disagreed. He wanted to take the risk of staying open because of all the children who were being helped. It was an impossible decision. They fought bitterly over it, and eventually Jeffers himself stepped in and ruled in favour of my grandfather. But despite being overruled Spondic did not begrudge it, in fact he responded magnificently. He led the emergency response team in what was a very dangerous game. He kept the passageways guarded, he fought off every attempt by the pirates, single-handed sometimes. He saved us, you know, and received medals for his courage and bravery." There was a mixed look of awe and confusion in the eyes around the table as they all struggled with these new revelations about Spondic. "Spondic has never been given the job of running the passageways though he should have been, and he would dearly love to. No-one has ever voted him in because of his tough nature. They say he lacks the love for the children, but they don't know him as I do. There is no-one more committed to the work. And so the running of the Crinkle Point passageways passed to my father and eventually to me." Whiskers smiled. Two of the candles had burnt out and there was a darkness covering most of the room. The clock struck four. "Goodness me, the time. You need to go."

"Whiskers?" Fay enquired. The old wise mouse looked up. "Can we come here again and hear more about all that's happened in the past?"

Whiskers scratched his head. "Thought you'd find it all a bit boring really, but of course you can if you'd like." There were eager nods of approval for the idea, and so in a different sort of way the Underground Gang was reformed, as they would meet up as often as they could, in what eventually became known as the Story Room.

There was little talking as the children left the passages that night. They were all lost in their thoughts. A whole new world had been opened up to them.

Em hung back in the Committee room. There was still one thing concerning her, one question she was burning to ask. "Whiskers, er... Why did you choose me as the guardian... Is it just 'cause I couldn't do any of the other jobs... no use for anything else?"

"My dear Emily, is that what you think?" The mouse put a comforting paw around her ankle as they walked out of the room together. "No. I chose you because your heart is here in this place. You care more than anyone else. You will fight harder when the time comes. You proved that last year when you overcame all your fears to face Gravisham. But be careful. That heart of yours will lead you to very dangerous places." A silence fell between the two of them as Em thought about the words of the wise mouse. "Love's a very special thing you know," he continued. "When you give it out, it always returns to you. Not always in the way you expect, but it does return. Remember that My Dear, it's important." Whiskers smiled. "And of course, more than anything, you are my closest friend."

"Will Gravisham return?"

"Yes," Whiskers replied, "we will have to fight him again."

Em gave the wise old mouse a hug and returned home for a sleepless night. Her mind was far too busy to sleep. What would the next move be by the pirates, and where did Gravisham fit into the picture? Eventually she dozed and had the same dream she had had the previous night, about the pirate standing in the corner of her room, except this time it was a fat pirate with the face of Gravisham.

Chapter 9
School Reports...

It was as Fay and Emily walked to school that they saw it. It was that time of year when everyone is yearning for summer to come, and hoping that this year will be that blazing hot sort of summer you dream of, especially when you live by the sea and can look forward to all those days on the beach. Fay's school bag dragged along the pavement, giving a faint rapping sound as it hit the edge of each paving slab.

"So why did Whiskers say the pirates attacked Britain first of all?" asked Emily in a far away confused sort of voice. Everything which Whiskers had told them yesterday seemed hazy after a night's sleep and she was trying to piece it all together again in her mind.

"Dunno. Who cares," Fay replied.

They were both yawning and still thinking on the stories of the night before. It seemed to have changed everything, thought Fay. One minute she had been enjoying a boat ride and the next they had been attacked by pirates and suddenly found themselves in the middle of a chilling adventure. But she was pleased. There was a shiver of excitement running down her spine.

"How long do you think it'll be till they come again?" asked Em. "Do you think we'll be ready?"

But Fay didn't answer. Her jaw had dropped at what she had just seen. They were at the round-a-bout at the end of the high street which was just around the corner from their school. On their right was a rather large brick building, which no-one ever went in or out of. Mum said it was the telephone exchange. On their left was a smart hotel and coffee shop. Parked rather dangerously outside was a small yellow sports car. Fay nudged Emily and pointed to the coffee shop window. The two girls watched Miss Robinson, Emily's form teacher, through the window as she was talking rapidly and smiling. Sitting across the table from her, in the coffee shop, was the large bulk of Oscar Gravisham, sipping his coffee. Miss Robinson rose from her chair, pointed at her watch (she was obviously late for something... school, Fay realised), lent over and kissed Gravisham on the cheek before running out and beeping the little yellow sports car.

The two girls looked on in stunned amazement. It was suddenly making sense to Emily.

"She's plotting with Gravisham! That's why she doesn't like me!" Emily said, thinking aloud. "She knows!"

"She can't know," Fay replied more in hope than for any other reason. Everything Emily said made sense.

"If she knows everything and is working with Gravisham we've got big problems," Emily replied as the yellow car sped off, leaving skid marks on the pavement.

As they entered the school playground, the girls passed the large sign pinned to the music block door. It read, 'Music Block temporary out of use.' Then they could see that Mr Baraclough had scribbled after the notice, 'Due to more bloomin' holes!!' They could see an angry looking Mr Baraclough through the window. Emily shot Fay a concerned look.

"Oh well," Emily shrugged. "STAMPS!" With that announcement of one of Fay's least favourite games she stamped firmly on Fay's left shoe.

"Ouch!" Fay stamped back but was too slow. Just as Emily was feeling rather smug, however, with the speed of her footwork, Izzie's foot clamped down on hers with enough force to break a toe, and sent Emily hopping around in agony.

"Gotcha!" announced Izzie. "Oh and you're IT too!" she shouted, tagging Emily whilst she was still writhing around in pain. "No returns! Schools home plus three hours!"

"Nuts!" shouted Emily.

Emily walked dejectedly into her classroom and handed in the note her dad had given her for her teacher. Miss Robinson ripped open the envelope and silently read it, her eyes scanning quickly across the letter. A broad grin then began to spread across her face.

"Certainly I will," she said, handing the letter back to Emily. "Come and see me at break," she said with far too much pleasure in her voice. Emily quickly glanced down at Dad's letter. It read:

'Dear Miss Robinson,

Emily has been miserable all week, and quite frankly, a real pain in the bum. I would be grateful if you could arrange some extra homework for her.'

WHAT! That was outrageous!! Emily slapped the palm of her hand on her desk in frustration. How could she have been so stupid? This was one of her dad's little jokes. "Aggghhhhh!!" So annoying! Her dad was getting totally out of control. She couldn't believe she had been caught out by someone as dim as her dad!

"Today we have two new pupils joining our class," Fay's teacher announced, as the class settled down at their tables. Fay's classroom was just down the hall from Emily's, since they were not in the same form class. "They are going to spend the last few weeks of term with us so they can get to know you all, and then they will start in your new class next term, after the summer holidays."

Fay looked at the girl and boy standing at the front. The girl looked very smart, she smiled sweetly but nervously and her hands were fidgeting. She had shocking red hair, which was very curly, and tied back in bunches. "This is Miranda Ivy Attenbury." What a mouthful, Fay thought. The name sounded familiar, but Fay couldn't think why. She was sure she didn't know the girl. Miranda came to sit at the spare desk next to Fay. The boy was both tall and wide. He had a disinterested look on his face, and his mouth seemed to have a permanent scowl on it. But he was also a little nervous; Fay could tell, as his feet were tapping. Everyone recognised him straight away, and no-one wanted him sitting near them. Fay was relieved that Miranda had taken the spare desk next to her. "This is George Gravisham," the teacher announced cheerfully. He was known around town as GG. He was Oscar Gravisham's youngest son. You had to be careful. If you crossed him, it was well known that you would end up meeting his two older brothers after school. His father had withdrawn GG from his last school, since the school threatened to expel him. This was just great, Fay thought. What with Miss Robinson and now GG, the Gravishams were well and truly invading her school.

At break Fay was playing hopscotch with her new friend, Miranda.

"So how come you've changed schools?" asked Fay.

"Moved house. We used to live up North. Something to do with my dad's work," Miranda replied. She did speak with a very strange sounding voice. Must be a northern accent, Fay thought.

"You know anyone round here?"

"Not really," and Fay noticed the smile slip from Miranda's face. "Sort of tough having to move and leave all my friends behind." She wasn't a very coordinated girl, Fay noticed. She sort of splodged from square to square on the hopscotch, rather ungracefully, as if one leg didn't move in time with the other. Hop... jump... hop... jump... jump.

"No, you're supposed to hop that one," Fay pointed out.

"Really? I thought..."

"Don't worry," Fay dismissed it with a wave of her hand. Not the brightest kid on the block either, this one, she thought. But she liked Miranda. Fay didn't get a chance to finish the thought.

"Telephone call!" Jack shouted, running up to them. He placed his hand up to his face as if it was a telephone receiver.

"What?" said Fay, confused. They had stopped the Underground Gang ages ago.

"Telephone call. Urgent!" Jack repeated obstinately.

Fay glanced at Miranda and made a quick decision. "Come on Miranda, I've got something to show you. You won't believe this!"

At the edge of the playground stood a number of playhouses. One was painted as a castle and one like a shop. Another was like a cafe and another like a Wild West fort. They were large wooden playhouses like you might have in your garden at home. Jack led the girls over to the castle one. "She can't come!" he said loudly pointing at Miranda.

"Don't you tell me who I can and can't bring!" Fay shot back angrily. She pushed him out of the way and brushed past, pulling Miranda with her. Jemima was standing outside, guarding the castle playhouse.

"What's going on?" asked Fay.

"Quick. Get in." Jemima replied.

The two girls ducked into the castle. Inside there were pictures of knights and queens painted on the walls. In one corner there appeared to be a trap door which was flipped back open. They could see the top of a ladder at the opening. Miranda's eyes almost popped out of her head. She leaned over the trap door but all she could see was darkness.

"Gosh! What on earth..."

"Come on," Fay grinned.

"But—"

"Trust me. I'll explain later," Fay was already clambering down the ladder. Miranda stepped off the ladder behind her into the passageways. She looked around in surprise.

"Isn't this cool!" Joseph called as he ran past Fay. "We can even get down here at school! It beats double maths!" He ran off and disappeared around a corner.

Miranda's jaw dropped in astonishment. She couldn't believe her eyes. "Isn't this... I mean aren't we... Where are we?"

Fay was pleased. It would cheer up her new friend a bit.

"Come on," she called, grabbed Miranda's sleeve and with that she was off.

"What are you up to?" Mrs Salmon asked.

"Oh nothing," answered Miss Robinson from the staff room window. She glanced at her watch and lowered her binoculars. Strange... very strange, she thought. She had been watching the playhouses all through break. Eleven and a half minutes. Seventeen children had gone into the playhouse and none had yet come out for a full eleven and a half minutes. That wasn't possible!

The afternoon at school was developing into a bad one for Emily. There was an ominous looking pile of envelopes on Miss Robinson's desk, Emily thought.

"Right," said Miss Robinson in the quiet Scottish accent, "since we are fast approaching the end of term and summer holidays, I have your school reports for you to take home to your parents." For the first time ever Emily had a sinking, panic stricken feeling in her stomach as she walked home. She avoided the others, hiding in the toilets for ages, until they had all left, and then she walked home all on her own, clutching the school report. What would it say, she pondered? Could she open the sealed envelope, have a peek and then seal it up again so that her mum wouldn't notice? She didn't think she could. And even if she were able to, what would she do if it was a bad report? She couldn't exactly just bin it could she. With every step she took home, worse thoughts came into her mind about what might be written there. By the time she was in Ocean View Terrace she was dawdling along at snails pace, scuffing her shoes along the pavement and the envelope felt as heavy as a brick. At the last minute, as she reached her front gate, she made a decision and stuffed the report to the bottom of her school bag. She stroked Norman the sheep before she went in the house.

Heaven only lasted half an hour and then Mum went through her school bag.

"Emily, what's this?" Mum ripped open the envelope. Emily stopped and stared. The envelope being torn open sounded as scary as a lion roaring to her. Mum opened the folded bit of paper and scanned down the page. Emily put on a forced smile. Maybe she was over reacting… maybe it wasn't that bad at all. "Emily, that's…" then the telephone rang. Mum snatched it up and started talking. Emily stared round the room. She had that feeling you get when you're in a dentist's waiting room, waiting for your teeth to be pulled out. Mum made a yapping motion with her hand. It was going to be a long one. Emily tried to go back to the game she was playing but it was no use. She really couldn't enjoy it now. The phone receiver went down.

"Emily," Mum said sternly, "this report is terrible! You just wait till your father gets home!" Emily groaned.

Eventually she sat in front of Dad, braced and ready to receive her lecture.

"Now Emily," he began. He cleared his throat and shuffled uncomfortably in his seat. He really wasn't good at this stuff. Mum must have told him to do it, Emily thought with a smile. "This report really isn't... erm... good enough, you know." Emily just smiled innocently with her best half upset, soppy look. That tended to work best on men. He ran through all the C and D grades Emily had been given. The final comment at the bottom of the piece of paper stuck in Emily's stomach. Miss Robinson must have scribbled it on. It seemed a rather terse remark. Maybe she had written it after going through lots of reports and she was getting fed up with them. 'I am very disappointed with Emily's performance' it read. But then it went on... 'I just haven't got a clue what she has been doing all year, except for staring out the window. And I don't want her bringing any more rats into school!!'

Dad stared at her and shook his head. "Rats?" he said in a surprised voice.

Emily bit her lip and just shrugged.

"In my day, Em, we wouldn't have been allowed to get a report like this. It wouldn't have been tolerated. I would have been whipped to within an inch on my life, you know."

"What by Nanna?!" Nanna was Emily's grandma. She was as kind and soft as they came. She couldn't imagine her whipping Dad to within an inch of missing his snacks between meals, let alone his life.

"Yes. She might seem nice and fun to you, but she was very strict with us you know. Kept the cane under the doormat, she did. We had to work hard. And I expect no less from you. And as for trying to hide your report! Well, what can I say? You need to be a bit more honest, my girl. From now on you will start working hard. No more staying up late at night and being tired during your classes. No more day dreaming! And no more scuffing your shoes... look at the state of them!... what do you do to get shoes that muddy?... and no more coming home looking like you've been dragged through a hedge backwards. Understand? You know, I might even think about getting a cane to put under our door mat." Dad eyed her sternly in one of those, 'well that's shown her, give her a piece of my mind,' sort of looks. "So!" he continued confidently, looking down his long nose, "what have you got to say for yourself?"

Emily paused.

"You've got hairs sticking out of your nostrils, Dad. It's disgusting."

"What?... erm... have not!"

That night a very despondent Em made her way down to the party room. She was surprised to find a despondent Jennifer and Fay there too. "So you got a bad one too?" asked Fay looking at the frown on Em's face.

"Dad gave me a right telling off," she replied.

"So did my mum," said Jennifer. "I've made a decision," she announced. "I'm not coming down here anymore." Em and Fay stared at her. "Don't look at me like that! I've got to improve my grades. I can't do both."

"But you can't stop..." Fay started but the words faded. Without a further word Jennifer rose and walked out of the party room. It was just then that Whiskers arrived, looking very happy and pleased with himself. He jumped up onto the table top.

"It's so nice being rid of all the building parties. It almost feels like being back to normal. Thought I might take a holiday, you know." He looked around at the girls. "What's with all the glum faces?"

"School reports," murmured Em under her breath.

Whiskers took a long sip on his lemonade. "Ahh yes," he said, as if he knew all about it. "Reports! Horrible things. Yours are bad ones I take it. We often get this problem, but it's easily solved." Fay  and Em looked at each other. "Over rated they are, reports." Without a further word Whiskers placed something small and golden on the table, winked at them and wandered off. Em picked it up and turned it over in her fingers.

"What is it?" asked Fay, intrigued.

It was a small oblong piece of gold-foiled paper. It had some words printed on it and a hole punched in one side. "It's a bus ticket... a golden bus ticket." She read all the little writing on it and stared at the date. '6 August 1979.' The two girls stared at each other.

"Sounds like an adventure to me!" Fay grinned.

The two girls were wandering down yet another passageway. "This is hopeless!" said Em. "I thought you were supposed to be in charge of organising all the adventures now. Shouldn't you know where everything is?" Fay just shrugged. They had now been wandering aimlessly for the last half an hour. As they passed what must have been the hundredth little wooden door it creaked open a couple of inches. This must be it. They could hear a faint ding, ding... ding, ding, coming from behind the door. They looked at each other and Fay grabbed the door. As they ran through Em could feel the breeze blow hard on her face and see a mist around her. Then she knew they were in the magic room. Em held her breath, wondering where they were going to end up.

"Tickets please!"

"Er... what?" said Em as the mist began to clear. The floor jerked and she fell sideways, falling on top of someone. "Oh sorry."

"Hold onto the handle there please, missy. Ticket please. Come on now, I haven't got all day." Em looked around. They were on a bus. She grabbed the handle beside her before the bus took another corner.

"Em, the ticket!" coaxed Fay.

"Oh yeah, sorry." She fished around for her golden ticket, and held it out. This wasn't like a modern bus where you paid the driver as you climbed aboard. It had a bus conductor, who collected all the tickets. The conductor took the ticket and tore it in half. He was a short fat man with a blue cap and a jacket which wouldn't have buttoned up over his stomach if he'd tried.

"Tar, love." He said. "Which stop you goin' to, missy?"

"Er... dunno."

"Here'll do," said Fay, grabbing Em's hand and pulling her off the bus as it pulled into a stop.

"What d'you do that for?" Em retorted.

"Look," Fay pointed. "This is where all the other kids are getting off." Em looked around. It was now bright daylight. They were standing by a small triangular green, which had roads on each side, and all the roads seemed to be blocked with traffic. There were the sounds of car horns hooting and the smell of fumes. Beyond the roads were tall buildings and shops and town houses. Ahead of them a stream of school kids sauntered along slowly. The two girls giggled. They looked very strange. The boys all wore shorts and caps. And they had very boring grey uniforms. The girls all had straw hats and hideous green and yellow stripped blazers.

"I wouldn't be seen dead in that," laughed Em. It must have been about three thirty in the afternoon. They were all going home from school. "Where are we?" Em asked.

"What does it say on your ticket?"

Em looked down at the golden ticket, now torn in half. It said they were on the 281 bus route... Twickenham Green... London. "London," muttered Em... "That's where my Nanna and Grandad live."

"And where your dad lived as a kid, right?" Fay asked. "And we're in the year 1979. You worked it out yet, Em?"

Em hadn't worked it out at all. But then one of the boys caught her eye. He looked remarkably like a picture, which hung on the wall at home. It couldn't be, Em thought. Fay saw the shocked look on Em's face and followed her gaze. "What is it, Em?"

Em stared, stony-faced, and murmured hesitantly, "That's... my... dad." The two girls watched the boy, who was perhaps a couple of years older than they were. His collar was lopsided, his shirt untucked and he had a splodge of mud on his face. His shoulders seemed to sag and he dragged his school bag along the pavement.

"Doesn't look like your dad," said Fay, crinkling up her face in concentration. "Actually, come to think of it, he's got a big nose, like your dad. OK, let's see what he gets up to." The two girls followed at a distance just far enough to see and hear what was going on.

"Nah, that can't be my dad, Fay. No way. My dad was a right goody two shoes from what I've heard. There's no way that could be him." Fay gave her a doubtful look.

"All parents tell their kids that. Don't you know anything?" Fay gave the scruffy boy another look. "Well, if I had looked like that, I wouldn't have admitted to it either."

The boy was wandering along with a group of four or five others. They sauntered slowly down a side road, which led down to a park. He seemed to be walking disinterestedly three or four paces behind. On the corner was a little sweet shop. "Hey!" one of the others shouted, "you gonna get any sweets?"

"Nah, no cash," replied the boy.

"Well hang on." A number of the boys dashed across the road and into the corner sweet shop.

The scruffy boy sat on the wall and dumped his school bag down on the pavement. Another boy, taller and slimmer, with longish blonde hair, waited with him. The scruffy boy, who they suspected might have been Em's dad, suddenly pulled a small book out of his bag. He rifled through the pages and started scribbling in it.

"Oh, put that away you big girl!" the blond-haired boy called in an embarrassed voice.

"Shut up, Russ. I just want to get this down. We haven't seen that number before. It was one of the old style trains."

"He's a train spotter!" giggled Fay. She dug an elbow into Em's ribs. "Your dad's a train spotter!" Fay had to turn around to hide her giggling, so the boys wouldn't notice.

"That's not my dad!" Em hissed.

"It's not bad enough that you collect toilet roll holders," Russ continued, "why do you have to be a train fanatic as well. I mean seriously. Get a life!"

Em's face fell. Toilet roll holders? He collected toilet roll holders? Surely not. Why would anyone do that? There was absolutely no way this was her dad! That was final! She glanced down at Fay who was now lying on the pavement having convulsions of laughter and silently mouthing the words "toilet roll holders". Em gave her a hefty kick.

"You coming down tonight?" asked Russ. "You know... down down." He made a pointing motion down towards the pavement. Em couldn't believe her eyes and ears. What did that mean?... "down down." Could her dad have known about the passageways? Was that possible?

"Nah," the scruffy boy replied. "Need to label my toilet roll holders tonight." Em covered her face, in embarrassment. There was no way this guy was her dad. Her dad did some daft things but seriously... This guy was a total loser... He had to label toilet rolls?... get real.

"What you gonna do about your report?" asked Russ.

"Oh nuts!" said the scruffy boy, pulling a plain brown envelope from his bag.

Emily's face froze in alarm. What had he just said?... "NUTS!" That's what she always said when she was in trouble. This was terrible. This really was her dad, after all. She knew it was. He did kind of look like that picture on the wall back at home. She just didn't want to believe it. This was worse than terrible... this guy was soft in the brain... a total moron... he collected toilet rolls!

Her dad turned the envelope over in his hand.

"I bet that's his school report," said Fay, appearing back at Em's side, the giggles now firmly under control. Em looked on, suddenly very interested. The other boys ran out of the sweet shop, their hands loaded with sweets.

"Oh let's have one?" asked Em's dad.

"No way! So what you gonna do with that." The boy pointed at the brown envelope. "It's gonna be another bad one."

"Yeah, I know." And with that he ripped open the top of the envelope and pulled out the report. The other boys gathered around to read it with him.

"Wow! Look at that," one of them laughed. "Heck! You can't show that to your dad. He'll roast you."

A couple of girls stopped close to the boys. They were older than the boys. One of the girls marched over. "You're not supposed to read that. You're supposed to give it to Mum."

"Oh, get out of it, Deb!"

Em stared in amazement. "That must be my Aunty Debbie! She's older than Dad. Look at that blazer. It's gross!"

"Mum is gonna kill you!" Aunty Debbie went on.

"Not if she doesn't know," Em's dad replied. And with that he held the report out and very slowly ripped it in half, and in half again. Then he very dramatically dropped it into the litter bin at the side of the road.

"Come on... footie." The boys raced away onto the park and one of them produced a ball from his bag. Aunty Debbie looked on angrily for a few minutes and then walked away, shaking her head.

"Come on," said Fay. The two girls wandered up and sat down where Em's dad had been. Fay rummaged around in the bin, extracting the ripped up bits of report.

"I can't believe he did that!" Em fumed. "And after he lectured me for hiding my report in my school bag." They pieced the jigsaw together eagerly. Em scanned down.

"The lying little rat," she stormed, going red in the face. "Look at the grades he got. He told me he always worked hard and got good reports. Look at this. F... F... F....F. He's got the lowest grade in everything! What was it he told me... 'Wouldn't have allowed that sort of report in my day'," she mimicked her dad's voice.

"What does it say in the comments?"

Em scanned down to read. "Er... yep, here we are. Lazy, daydreams... a hopeless case."

"A teacher hasn't actually written that, have they?" They both looked at the crumpled, torn piece of paper. It said in big bold writing, underlined, and in red… 'A Hopeless case!' They stared up across the field. Em's dad was running for the ball. He missed his kick completely, and skidded across the ground, leaving grass stains all up his trousers and shirt.

"Em, he can't even kick a ball. He's useless!" Fay was right, thought Em, though she didn't like to admit it. And he collected toilet rolls!

The two girls watched until the boys got bored playing football and then they followed Em's dad until he said goodbye to his mates and walked up the street home. Em immediately recognised her Nanna and Grandad's house. Dad slipped in through the back door.

"I've gotta see this," said Em.

"How? What are you…" but Em had gone. Fay watched in horror as she ran up the driveway and slid into the back door where her dad had gone in before her.

Em hid in the utility room, which was attached to the side of the kitchen. She could hear all that was going on inside.

She spotted her dad's school bag abandoned by the door and had an idea. She withdrew the crumpled pieces of school report and scattered them by the side of the school bag. Then she hid herself beside the large washing machine.

"Good day, pet lamb?" she heard a rather younger than normal Nanna's voice. Pet lamb… who called their kids pet lamb? "What have you done to your clothes?" Nanna continued.

"Oh, dunno, Mum. Just happens, sort of."

"Did you get your report today?

"Er… nope. Didn't give them out. Get 'em next term I guess."

Em fumed with annoyance, thinking of the lecture she had received earlier today. What had her dad said… 'You need to be a bit more honest, my girl'. "Lying toad," she muttered. Her eyes twinkled as she saw Nanna come out and pick up the school bag. She could just see around the end of the washing machine, as Nanna bent down and read the crumpled pieces of paper.

"It doesn't matter though," her dad continued confidently from inside the kitchen. "You know I've been trying much harder this term. Yeah, teacher reckons I'm gonna be a rocket scientist. Thinks I can take my O levels three year early."

Em watched as Nanna straightened up, turned and walked back into the kitchen. There was a long silence. Em waited for the explosion. She tried, with a distinct note of pleasure, to imagine the look on her dad's face. Would Nanna go for the cane under the front door mat, she wondered?

"Never mind, Dear," she heard the voice from inside the kitchen. "But no third piece of chocolate cake today!"

"Oh, Mum!"

"Well, maybe only a little third piece then."

WHAT!! That was so unfair, Emily fumed. The rat got away with it.

Em had heard enough. She slipped out the back door. But one thing niggled in her mind as she walked back to the bus stop, still fuming… If her dad had visited the passageways, then he must have forgotten all about it. It worried her. Would she also forget when it came her time to leave?

It was the next day at breakfast that she asked the question. "Have you still got your old school reports, Dad?"

"Er… don't know that I have, Em," Dad replied nervously.

Mum coughed from where she was, preparing sandwiches at the worktop. "I'm sure you have, dear. Upstairs in the attic."

"Er… well, I guess maybe."

"I'd love to see them," pushed Emily.

"Yes, that would be good," said Mum with a grin on her face. "Show Emily a good example of how she needs to improve and do better."

"Actually, erm… gotta dash. I'm gonna be late for work." And with that Dad dashed out the door. Mum gave Emily a wink.

At that moment the phone rang. Mum went to pick it up, but Jack shot out of his seat and reached it first.

"Ask who it is!" hissed Mum.

But Jack just grabbed up the phone and blew a loud raspberry into it, before dropping it back into the cradle.

"JACK!" Mum and Emily shouted together.

"Honestly!" muttered Emily, picking up the phone and dialling 1472. "That might have been one of my friends! Brothers!" She listened. "It's Nanna." She pressed the redial button for Nanna.

"Hello Nanna!"

"Hello, pet lamb," came Nanna's voice. It sounded distant down the phone and just a touch older than it had done last night in her adventure.

"Nanna? Did you really have a cane under the door mat when my dad was a boy?"

"A cane?!" came the distant surprised reply.

"No, I thought not," Emily said slyly.

"But I'll tell you something," Nanna went on. "I thought about getting one. Your father! You wouldn't believe the things he got up to! You know, I remember when he brought his school report home once…"

Emily just smiled.

Chapter 10
Miss Robinson...

It was late at night, the following Monday evening, as Miss Robinson sped across town in her little yellow sports car. She moved up a gear and pushed her foot down heavily on the gas. She was dressed in black and a torch sat on the seat next to her. Miss Robinson was a very precise lady. Everything she did was planned and done properly. She lived on her own, didn't have a boyfriend and concentrated on her work and the children she taught at school. And she liked fast cars. But it was all turning rather strange. She was perplexed. She didn't like things which she couldn't understand and so tonight she had a task to do... a rather strange task, she considered. Was she being stupid, she wondered? No, she needed to work out what was going on. So many strange things had happened over the past months. The mice in her classroom (she shivered), the holes appearing all over the school, the strange comings and goings in the playhouse, and at the centre of it all... Emily Grace! Miss Robinson had been looking through Emily's school file. It had all been fairly ordinary until she had reached that particular page. It was a story Emily had written in class the previous year. A story which was so well written, with so much detail, it was almost as if it was true... no, couldn't be, Miss Robinson shook the thought out of her head and dismissed it. And yet... maybe... the story had been about secret passageways, which ran under her road. "I must be mad," she muttered to herself. This was so unlike the normal Miss Robinson. She didn't take risks, she always did things properly. And yet here she was, intending to break into Emily's house while her family were away on holiday.

The road behind Ocean View Terrace was dark and silent as a

graveyard, as the yellow sports car's engine purred slowly down the road, looking for the back fence of just the right house. Miss Robinson flicked off the car headlights. She had already visited the school. She had spent over an hour hunting round the little castle playhouse, inch by inch, meticulously, but had found nothing. Then Mr Baraclough, the school caretaker, had found her and wondered what she had been doing there at that time of night. "Oh, just forgot some books for marking," she had replied unconvincingly and made a hasty retreat. Miss Robinson fumbled with the steering wheel nervously. This was not a normal thing for her to be doing and her hands seemed to be shaking with nerves. That's probably why she put the gear stick into reverse instead of forward, and backed straight into the fence with a deep clunk, which reverberated down the silent road.

"Oh bother!" she hissed. She was getting flustered now. Her right foot hit the brake pedal hard, but it was the wrong pedal. The engine revved furiously, before smashing straight through the fence and skidding round in quite a neat handbrake turn on the garden.

"Bother, bother, bother!" Miss Robinson fired up the engine again. It revved a few times and then died. She tried again… it died. And again… nothing. Miss Robinson sat very still, breathed deeply and made herself calm down. "It's OK," she said to herself. "There's no-one home. So no-one will care about the back fence. You can fix it later." She grabbed the torch and slid out of the car door.

Something behind her started to nibble her fingertips. She screamed with fright, jumped back, tripping over a watering can and landing in a heap in the flowerbed. She looked up. "A sheep! What have they got a sheep for?" she mumbled. "Strange family!"

She brushed herself down and tried the back door. "Locked. To be expected, I guess." Kitchen window. Locked. The back of the house was a new building added onto the old Victorian house. It had a flat roof. Miss Robinson shinned up the drainpipe and climbed onto the flat roof. The bathroom window was not locked. She pulled it open and climbed into the house. She was in.

The hallway was dark, except for the shallow rays of light shining in from the doorways where the children's lights were switched on. Miss Robinson walked slowly and silently down the hall. Why was she being careful? There was no-one here, they were supposed to be on holiday. She stopped dead. Something wasn't right. What was it?

Then it hit her. The lights! Why would there be lights on in the children's bedrooms if they were away? She could now feel a rising panic in her chest. She tiptoed up to Emily's bedroom door and glanced in. She wasn't there, but her bed had definitely been slept in, her duvet hanging onto the floor. "I wonder if she's in her secret passage?" She glanced in Jack's room and was just in time to see Jack's little back legs disappear into the bottom draw of his chest of drawers. The drawer shut with a bang. "Strange!" She pulled the drawer open. It was empty. She pulled it right out of the chest and looked in the empty gap. Yes, there it was, a hole at the back of the drawers. "Could I crawl in there?" she wondered. Miss Robinson was a very slender lady. She lay down flat and pulled herself in, and through the hole. All of a sudden she realised, too late, that there was no longer any floor below her and she tumbled loudly down the metal spiral staircase.

"Ouch!" she said, straightening up and rubbing her hips. Then she smiled... she had found it!... It was true, Emily had a secret passageway. "Unbelievable! Well would you credit it?"

Now the passageways were not built for grownups. Indeed, grownups were not allowed to even know of their existence, so Miss Robinson found herself stooping as she walked along so that her head didn't hit the roof. She marvelled at the passageways as she wandered through them, seeing all the little wooden doors and dark tunnels leading off in all directions. Just as she was about to conclude that they were empty and deserted, she heard distant voices behind her. She ducked into the shadowy entrance of a smaller tunnel as the voices came closer. She recognised them.

"Come on," said Fay. "I want to try out the flumes tonight on The Lake."

"But we've got so many projects to do over the summer!" Em replied despondently.

"Who cares!" Fay replied. "We have all summer to do it. Really Em, you've got to get a life!" Em frowned. She was more a get it out of the way sort of girl, whilst Fay preferred to leave it to the last minute. "At least you won't have old battleaxe Robinson next year."

"Well thank goodness for that. Not sure I could take another year with that witch!"

Miss Robinson crouched silently in the shadows, desperately trying to stop herself from stepping out to surprise the two girls as they sauntered past.

"Do you reckon she's on to us yet?" Fay asked.

"What, the passageways? Nah, she's a real dumbo... totally brainless. She wouldn't catch on if you stuffed a mouse up her dress."

Miss Robinson clenched her fists... her face had turned red and if you looked carefully you could just make out the steam coming out of her ears. She followed the two girls down the passage, careful to stay far enough back so that she wouldn't be seen. There seemed to be more noise ahead now and as she looked around a corner her eyes went wide. The passage opened up into a large room and there seemed to be hundreds of children. What were they doing? There were balloons and the clinking of glasses, and the smell of food. It was almost as if they were having a party.

Em and Fay had settled down on some bouncy cushions next to Ellie and Izzie, and also conveniently near the food. Whiskers had jumped onto the little table with a glass of red smoking lemonade and had just launched into a rather funny story about Spondic having a go at water-skiing. Fay was just seeing if she could fit a fourth scotch egg in her mouth, when Miss Robinson stepped out of her hiding place into the room.

It took less than a second for the room to turn from noisy hubbub to total silence. Whiskers choked on his lemonade and Fay sprayed small pieces of Scotch egg over everyone in a five foot radius. All eyes were on Miss Robinson.

"Blinkin' heck, it's a grownup!" came a voice from the back of the room.

Miss Robinson's eyes surveyed the scene and then settled on Em, who by now was squirming in her cushion, desperately hoping for the world to end... very soon!

"So," said Miss Robinson, slowly. She was going to enjoy this. "What was it you said? Let me see if I can remember... she's a real dumbo... totally brainless. She wouldn't catch on if you stuffed a mouse up her dress. Was that it?"

NOW! thought Em, I want the world to end right now!

"Right. Who's in charge here?" asked Miss Robinson sternly.

All hands pointed instantly at Em. After all she was the guardian. "She is," Whiskers whispered in a high-pitched squeak. Miss Robinson's smile broadened into a grin.

"Oh nuts!" said Em.

There was a whirring sound of something flying through the air. A large chocolate gateau flew thirty feet across the room and smacked Miss Robinson clean on the chin. Chocolate mouse and sauce splattered down her face and the front of her jumper. There was a very long silence. You could have heard a pin drop.

"What a waste of cake!" said Izzie. Em shut her eyes in horror.

"Get her!" shouted the disruptive voice from the back of the room, and with that sausage rolls, sandwiches, and scotch eggs shot across the room like ammunition. Em raised her head and was struck on the right ear by a large scoop of yellow banana ice cream, which ran uncomfortably down her neck. A pizza then whizzed over her, like a Frisbee, and would have chopped Miss Robinson's head off if she hadn't ducked.  But Miss Robinson was standing very close to the food table, which she immediately tipped over and ducked behind to form a barricade and from there she launched her attack. So many missiles shot out from the table that you would have thought she had five arms. Her head popped up over the table and her eyes zeroed in on Em. Two seconds later Em was struck full in the face by a three litre choco-challenge, with so much force that she flew back into the jukebox, which immediately started playing 'Food glorious food'.

Emily's dad woke up the next morning feeling very refreshed. He went through his morning routine while everyone else in the house slept. He was always the first one up. He had to get up early to go to work, he thought, begrudgingly. He washed and shaved, cutting himself three times with the razor. That was about average. He then picked his toenails and cleaned the fluff out of his bellybutton with Mum's electric toothbrush… well he didn't want to use his did he… it tasted horrible. Then there was the big decision of the morning… would it be cereals or an extravagant two slices of toast with butter… or if he was feeling really adventurous he could put the whipped cream on his corn flakes. Wow, he did live a boring life didn't he? He grabbed hold of the kitchen blind and said his normal morning prayer… "Go on, let it be a sports car in my garden this morning. Just this once… please! A nice red one…" No, it was trendier to have yellow these days, wasn't it? Ferrari did yellow now, didn't they? He pulled up the blind and stared. He blinked. He pulled down the blind again. His eyes were playing tricks on him. He picked up the rolling pin from the kitchen dresser and hit himself on the head with it. "Ouch!" Yes, he was definitely awake. He pulled up the blind again. There it stood. A little yellow sports car… in his garden.

"Thank you God!"

Chapter 11

The Fire...

Em grinned with satisfaction as she stared at Miss Robinson. Well, wasn't it every kid's dream to do that to their school teacher? She couldn't remember the last time they had had so much fun. They had been lucky though. The fight had ended when Miss Robinson collapsed on the floor in a fit of giggles. Said she was having more fun than she had had in years. And so they now had their first ever grownup member of the passageways. How strange? Em thought. And a teacher of all people... and Miss Robinson! It was unbelievable!

"Well that should do it," said Miss R, as she was now becoming known. She had overalls on and her arms were covered in grease up to her elbows. They were on the beach by the Lake and, together with Joseph and Ollie, they were mending Ollie's plane.

"Wow, Miss R," Ollie exclaimed. "I'm impressed."

"It was my dad. A great car man he was. I spent hours... days in the garage with him." There was no doubt about it, thought Em, she was a cool teacher. And Em was extremely relieved finally to have Miss R on her side. But there was something else on Em's mind today.

"So how do you know Mr Gravisham?"

"Old Oscar?" Miss R replied in surprise, trying to wipe the grease off her hands with an old rag. "He's my Uncle. A sweetheart, he is... old Uncle Oscar."

"A SWEETHEART!?" Joseph retorted shrilly. "He's a maniac! He tried to kill us!"

Miss R rocked back laughing. "Oscar! He couldn't hurt a fly if he tried!"

"No, really, he did!" Joseph persisted.

Em nodded. "He did, Miss R."

"I'm sorry," she replied wiping a nice line of grease across her face as she tried to control her giggles. "You lot... I'm just amazed at all you do down here, but you must have got the wrong end of the stick with Uncle Oscar. He's a pussycat, honestly. Now more importantly, Em," Miss R continued with a stern note in her voice. "Do you remember what you are taking to the passageway committee?"

Em sighed. "Yes, I remember. Rules... We can't stay down more than two hours in an evening and no more than two evenings a week during school days."

"But that's no good!" said Joseph. "Two hours? You can't get anywhere in two hours!"

Em sighed again. Miss R was cool, but then again she was a grownup and this is what happened when you had grownups... RULES! But then again she could party with the best of them, and she was wicked on the karaoke. She seemed to manage it well... to be a teacher during the day and a little kid at night.

Miss Robinson was staring intently out of the staff room window with her binoculars again.

"You are a nosy so and so!" said Mrs Salmon sitting down next to her.

"They're very interesting, children" Miss Robinson replied. "Know a lot more than we realise."

"Ha! I don't know about that. Just interested in making rude noises and avoiding work if you ask me. You listen to me. I've been in this teaching game for many years." Mrs Salmon tapped her forefinger to her nose in a conspiratorial sort of way. "Kids are just skin deep. You can read 'em like a book. You can always tell what they're up to."

If only you knew, thought Miss Robinson as she watched the twenty fifth child disappear into the play house.

The afternoon lesson was approached by all the children with a sense of dread. Miss Robinson had said they were starting a new big project. As everyone entered the classroom they saw that it had a very different look about it. All the classroom lights were off, the blinds were down and the room was lit by candles. Emily, Ellie and Izzie sat down, rather puzzled.

"What's she up to?" whispered Emily.

"I tried to winkle it out of her last night in the passageways but she wouldn't tell," said Ellie. It was approaching summer now and so the sun was still blazing through the edges of the blinds.

"Now," announced the soft Scottish accent of Miss Robinson. "Who can tell me what this is?" She held up a rather old roundish metal object.

Trevor's hand shot up. "It's a helmet Miss, a Roman army helmet."

"Well done Trevor! I borrowed this from…"

"Oh no!" groaned Emily in a whisper across the desk. "I don't want to do a project about army helmets!"

"Boring!" agreed Izzie.

"Hey, I forgot to tell you." Emily hissed quietly. "It's my birthday in the holidays and I'm having a sleepover. You two are coming, aren't you?"

"Yeah!" Izzie and Ellie whispered excitedly together.

"Who else are you gonna invite?" asked Ellie.

"Well Mum said I could ask three friends along so I'm gonna get Fay along too."

"Wicked!" said Izzie.

"…Emily Grace! Can you stop whispering and listen with the rest of the class please." Emily shot up straight. Although Miss R still

called her Emily Grace, she was sure that her tone had changed. She
didn't seem quite as harsh these days. "Now, in the days of the Celts
and Romans," Miss Robinson continued, "they didn't have electricity
for lighting or heating. That is why today we have candles." There
was a murmur of understanding, which rippled around the classroom.
"So your task is to find out as much as you can about the Celts and
the Romans. The differences between their habits, how they lived, the
history of the time and the reasons for their war. I will be bringing in
lots of books from the library, and you can look up some good sites
on the internet which I have written up on the board for you. You
will be doing the project in pairs…"

"Who's gonna go with who?" hissed Izzie.

"I'll go with you!"

"No, me with…"

"And I," continued Miss Robinson, "have decided who will be
partnering who."

The three girls looked up in alarm. Emily was sure she noticed
the twinkle of a very slight grin on Miss Robinson's face. Miss
Robinson seemed to take ages to read down the list. "…and Emily
with Trevor."

WHAT!! Emily almost blurted. NO WAY! Nuts, this was so
unfair! Emily glanced across at Trevor. He was a small lopsided kid,
with hair that would never flatten down. He always called Emily, "a
pile of pooh," whenever they crossed paths… so Emily called him,
"Tinkerbell," or, "Tink," for short. He was one of those annoying
little kids that messed around but managed to look as good as gold
when the teacher turned their gaze in his direction. He glanced across
at Emily. He looked as annoyed as she did with the pairing for the
project. He stuck two fingers in his mouth and pretended to be sick.
He then picked up his spelling book, a small square grey book, which
he now and then used as a Frisbee and flicked with deadly accuracy at
the back of people's heads. He glanced quickly at Miss Robinson to
make sure she was distracted, pulled back his arm, and flicked his
wrist, catapulting it through the air. The little grey book spun across
the classroom, taking a slight ricochet off Ellie's left shoulder, and
missed Emily's head by inches as she ducked sharply. She looked up
and followed the spelling book as it slowed down and dived off the

left, slicing through a candle as it went. The book landed harmlessly on Paula Hempwhistle's desk, but the candle toppled to the left and fell onto the window blind. There was a collective gasp from around the room as the flames immediately shot up the blind and seemed to ripple across the ceiling. Miss Robinson's head snapped round. She immediately reached out and punched through a small red piece of plastic - the fire alarm, Emily thought. A shrill high-pitched bell started to ring.

"Please keep quiet, stand and follow me out of the classroom," Miss Robinson said in a still very calm, but very commanding voice. Some children stood, but others were panicking. At least two had dived under their desks and another couple were staring at the ceiling, mesmerised by the sky of orangey blue flame above them.

"Now!" said Miss Robinson sternly, heads spinning towards the raised voice.

"But we can't Miss," called Graham. "Look Miss, the door!" He was right. The door was a fireball of flames. In fact flames were now cascading down the blinds on all of the windows. A black film of smoke had hidden the fire above them and seemed to be descending towards them with amazing speed. Emily was finding it hard to breath and her head was spinning.

There were shouts coming from every direction, but louder than all of this was a shrill scream piercing Emily's left ear. She glanced around. Izzie looked as if she was having a fit, arms flaying all over the place. If she flapped them any harder she would take off. Emily glanced around the room. Since the door and all the window blinds were on fire, there was no escape. Miss R had obviously noticed too.

"I want everyone down underneath their desks please," she said, still in the strong calm Scottish accent. Emily and Ellie ducked down under the desk.

"Izzie! Get down here." Izzie was still flapping.

"Passicom!" shouted Ellie. The fire was making a very loud roaring noise now and they had to shout to be heard. The smoke was lowering, as if reaching down towards them with black curling fingers.

"What?" replied Em.

"Passicom! Have you got a passicom? The mice. They may have

more tunnels!" Brilliant thought Em. Ellie was just brilliant! She didn't have a passicom on her, but Izzie did.

"Izzie! IZZIE!" It was no use. Em grabbed both her ankles. This was gonna hurt. She yanked hard. Izzie slammed onto the floor, knocking the wind out of her. Em took the opportunity to grab her wrist and yanked the strap off. She didn't really care if the hand came with it. She pulled the passicom towards her and fumbled with the buttons. Her mind was suddenly blank. Which buttons did she have to press? Er? "COME ON!" she shouted, mostly to herself. There was an emergency signal wasn't there. How did she do it? She couldn't remember. To her left, Izzie shook her head and sat up, paused for half a second and then started screaming again. Em gave her a sharp slap round the face. SMACK.

"Ouch!" Izzie shook her head clear.

"The emergency signal! What is it?" Em screamed.

Ellie looked blank. Izzie reached her hand across, clamped it around the passicom and pressed the top button on the left and right, together. The face of the passicom started to flash red. The three of them collapsed flat on the floor and waited. They could feel the heat from above them, and they could see Miss R as she swept all the children down onto the floor and towards the centre of the classroom in her normal calm and efficient manner. Em was now beginning to panic. "Please!" she prayed. "Please, get us out of here!"

As if in answer to her prayer she suddenly felt the floor give way beneath her. The room was getting hotter and hotter around her and it was harder to see or to breathe. As she felt the ground below her give way, she immediately thought she was beginning to drift away. Then her chin whacked hard against something, sending an unbearable pain shooting down her neck, and a second later her whole body hit the stone floor. NUTS! That hurt! She looked up. She had fallen through a trap door and into the passageways. And she could still see the swirling mixture of fire and smoke through the passageway trap door above her. Then she saw the tirade of bodies jumping through after her. "Ouch… aggghhhh… nuts… ooooch… crumbs." There was a fresh lurch of pain as each body smacked down on top of her.

When Em finally fought her way from under

the pile of bodies the trap door above was closed, and the familiar smell of the passageways was around her. The feeling of panic had ebbed away and there was no fire in sight. Her heart was still beating fast but she felt safe and secure. She glanced around her at the strange sight. Mice were rushing around. Children were unfolding themselves from the knot of bodies. Half of them were rubbing their aches and pains, but other than that were relaxed. The other half, those who had never before entered the passageways, were looking around in stunned amazement. Em spotted Whiskers and Theo in animated discussion.

"What!" screamed Theo, holding his head as if trying to stop it falling off and rolling away. "New passageways... for ALL of them?!"

"They're here now, Theo," Whiskers replied as calmly as ever. "We have to have new entrances for all of them."

Theo wandered straight past Em, muttering, in a world of his own, and clearly in shock.

Whiskers cleared his throat, and the tunnel grew quiet. "Well, if you would all follow me, your new classroom awaits. Wouldn't want you to miss your lesson now, would we."

They all followed, and Em could hear comments all around her such as, "Was that really a mouse?"... "Don't be silly, this is some sort of joke they're playing or something!"... and, "I think I banged my head too hard, for a minute I thought that mouse spoke."

They all arrived in a wide, low ceiling cave. There were desks set out and on each desk sat a large glass, like you would get holding a large ice cream sundae. They were all filled with different things, all a vast array of different bright colours.

"Em, isn't this amazing!" said a voice in Em's ear. It was Julia. Her eyes were wider than Em had ever seen them. "Hey," she said suddenly, as if she had just woken up, "Izzie says you're having a sleepover party. Can I come?"

"What?" replied Em... "Er, yeah, kay."

That made Em think. Izzie, Ellie, where were they? She spotted them and ran across. They all settled down into their seats. Around them astonished children were still glancing around the cave, whilst others tried out their drinks and still others examined their drinks suspiciously. Trevor took a sip of his and his hair suddenly seemed to have a distinct green tinge to it.

Whiskers then jumped up on the table at the front and lessons began... But not like any lessons they had ever had before. They were treated to a mouse acrobat exhibition, had a lesson in cocktail ice cream mixing, followed by a lesson in one-legged water-skiing. By the time they had finished, they all sat mesmerised, and when Miss R started talking about returning to school Em realised she had totally forgotten there had been a fire at all.

The class reluctantly said their goodbyes to the mice and returned to school. "What are we gonna do now, Miss?" asked Izzie ten minutes later as she surveyed the charred remains of classroom 4A, and bit her lip. "Will we have all our lessons down in the passageways, Miss?"

"I don't think so," Miss Robinson replied. "It is a bit of a state, isn't it?" Their classroom had been in a block in one corner of the school, and that corner was now gone... vanished and replaced with what looked like a large lump of black gundge. It still smouldered with patches of red and ash blowing about in the rising smoke.

Emily looked up to see the fire engines pulling away, and behind her the rest of the school was running in to admire the scene, with shouts of, "Ooooh... Wow!... Wicked." Her class now appeared to have taken on a hero status.

Emily wasn't quite sure how she, Ellie and Izzie came to be sitting in Mrs Gorbison's office. The day had just been a whirlwind and to be honest Emily felt in a bit of a daze and just a tad flustered. But sitting in the comfy, rather deep armchair, drinking hot chocolate, she suddenly felt relaxed and tired. She could have just put her head to one side and closed her eyes.

"Well, well, well," said Mrs Gorbison. "Quite a shock for all of you." She gave a smile. She was the school's head mistress. She was a tall thin lady with very grey hair and yet a very young kind face. She made Emily feel comfortable. "Now how are you all feeling?" They all gave encouraging nods and were rewarded with a warm smile.

"So a trap door in the classroom? How very odd! I am very pleased it was there though. Things do have a habit of working themselves out." Another warm smile. The three girls just curled up in their armchairs, exhaustion overtaking them, listening as Mrs

Gorbison chatted away.

"A trap door in room 4A," she pondered. Emily watched as Mrs Gorbison eyes closed halfway in concentration. She looked as if she had grasped the very end of a thin thread of a thought, and couldn't quite find the rest of it in her memory. "You know, I'm sure I recall something strange about that classroom... No, I just can't put my finger on it. A trap door... Yes..."

Emily watched and wondered. Had Mrs Gorbison once been a child down in the passageways, like Emily's dad had? But none of them could remember. A horrible thought flitted through her mind. What would happen when she had to leave? Would she remember? She hoped so. She rested her head on her shoulder as a picture of a young Mrs Gorbison ran through her mind. She bet Mrs Gorbison had been a guardian. Emily's eyes slowly shut and her breathing deepened... phew... phew... phew. She was fast asleep.

Chapter 12
The Detectives...

Of all the strange things you come across in the world (and lets face it there are some strange things around) Sealand is one of the strangest. It lies in the ocean, six miles off the coast of Felixstowe, and on a clear day you can see it from the beach if you look very carefully. It is a platform about quarter of a mile wide, with two very thick and sturdy legs which run all the way down to the bottom of the ocean. Most platforms you find in the ocean are drilling platforms or oil rigs, but this one was built over sixty years ago as an army fortress. Since then it's been owned by a number of different people. It's been invaded three times, once by the French and twice by sea pirates, and right at this moment it's owned by Prince Bret Beltcher. I say 'Prince', because... well it is a funny thing... but Beltcher stood up one day and announced to the waiting world (none of whom were particularly interested) that he was declaring his platform to be a separate country. He named it Sealand and declared himself the Crown Prince of Sealand. He printed his own money, issued his own stamps and even started to sell people passports! (Most people thought he was as barmy as a cuckoo).

There wasn't much on the platform these days. There was a lookout building and an old World War One gun turret. Beltcher lived in one of the legs of the platform, which were wide and hollow, and were sheltered from the wind, rain and sea spray.

Today however he had a sense that something strange was afoot. He didn't know why, he just sensed it. He stood with his binoculars to his eyes, in his oiled waterproof, his grey hair and beard blowing in the wind. He was an old man, Beltcher, his skin wrinkled by the wind and sea, a limp in his right leg from the war wound, which hurt more and more as the years passed. His eyesight was also fading which was why he didn't notice those things going on around him.

Nathaniel Mitra Bruthersharken III was known to his fellow pirates as 'Shark'. He had brought the small rowing boat in under the platform by cover of night the previous evening and had then waited. He now climbed silently up the leg of the platform. He was a pirate, but not an old fashioned pirate with a pirate's hat and a wooden leg, like you would see in a film on television and perhaps laugh at. No, Shark moved fast and silently across the platform. His well oiled blade didn't make a sound as he drew it from his belt. His ship waited just out of sight, over the horizon. The pirates had decided that the platform would be the perfect place from which launch their attacks on the coast. After all, from here they had a direct link into the passageways.

Emily climbed sleepily out of bed, and planted her feet shakily on the floor.

"NUTS!" she screamed as a freezing cold pain shot up her legs. She whipped her feet back under the covers, and peered out to survey her room. Someone had left a large bowl of ice cold water there, the ice cubes still bobbing up and down on the surface. A note was sitting next to the bowl.

"Dear Emily,

Time to get up.

Ha, ha.

Love dad. xxxx"

Emily fell back on her bed. "Daaaaad!"

Emily sat eating breakfast, ten minutes later, eying her dad suspiciously as he read the newspaper. "It's terrible," Dad commented, waving a piece of toast at the paper. "You wouldn't believe it could happen in Felixstowe of all places, would you?"

"What's that, dear?" Mum asked from the chopping board.

"It's vandals again. They've been burning down beach huts and stealing boats from the Ferry boat yard. A number of the coastal houses have also been broken into, it says." There were a few minutes of silence as Jack played disinterestedly with his food and then piled it into Dad's bowl whilst no-one was looking. "Listen to this," Dad continued. "It says here... Sergeant Travis stated yesterday that they believed this was an organised gang of young people. The police are working on a number of leads. The gang is believed to be operating under the name of the Underground Gang." Dad tutted. "Young people today," he added. "Hope you don't grow up like that, Em!" He looked sternly down his nose at Emily.

Emily had stopped in mid-mouthful, her mind reeling. "The Underground Gang." Had her dad really said that? What was going on? "The police were working on a number of leads." What on earth did that mean? Did the police think she was doing this?... were they onto her?... following her and her friends? She was frozen with fear. What would her dad say if the police arrived to say she was involved in all this? He was tutting again from behind his newspaper.

"Telephone call!" was the word that could be heard all around the playground at the first break, as half the children in the school seemed to be disappearing into the castle playhouse. Miss Robinson noticed... but then she knew what was in there and smiled.

They sat on the floor in the tunnel just below the playhouse entrance, so they could meet quickly and then go back up to school. People would notice if they were gone too long. They all wore glum expressions. Scott had even cut the article out of the local paper for everyone to see.

"They're making it look like we did it!... Burning beach huts and breaking into houses!" Ellie said. Em hadn't thought about it like that. She had just assumed it must be a mistake, but now she thought about it, Ellie was right.

"Who's making it look like us?" Miranda whispered to Fay.

"The pirates," she whispered back.

"Of course!" said Joseph. "Whiskers said that the pirates kept themselves very secret. What better way than blaming someone else.

I reckon it's Gravisham. Whiskers said he's still working with the pirates. And he knows about us, doesn't he?"

"But the Underground Gang! How did they know about the name? No-one knows we're called that."

There was silence for a few moments as they all stared at their feet, not able to piece it all together. It felt frustrating and hopeless, like being at the very beginning of a thousand piece jigsaw puzzle and not knowing which piece to start with. Jennifer wasn't here, Em sighed. She would know. But then she wasn't coming down in the passageways anymore.

Ellie looked slowly around the room. "One of us must be a spy! It's the only way they would know the name!"

Miranda still had a perplexed look on her face. She leant close to Fay. "Er, which name's that?"

Fay rolled her eyes. This girl was as thick as a plank. "The Underground Gang, of course!" Fay hissed back in a harsh tone.

"It's got to be Miss Robinson!" said Ellie finally.

There were whispers of "it can't be"… "never"… "but she's with us."

"No-one else knows about it except us and I can't see that one of us would have blabbed." Ellie looked around defiantly, challenging anyone to disagree or own up. "So it must be her." The mumbling ceased. Then it began to dawn on everyone what this really meant.

"She knows Gravisham," Em blurted. "It all makes sense! She tells Gravisham and he tells the pirates."

"So the pirates must know the way in and out… and everything," Joseph said slowly as it sunk in.

"That's how they are getting in to shore to steal things and then out again," Fay continued. "They must know all the routes through the passageways by now."

"Oh nuts," said Em

"That's rotten luck," added Izzie. In the silence that followed you could have heard a pin drop.

"So, that's bad, is it?" added Miranda. They ignored her.

"So what are we gonna do?" asked Scott in his ghostly voice.

"We're gonna have to catch them at it," said Fay, the twinkle back in her eye as she sensed an adventure looming.

"Er… catch who exactly?" asked Miranda.

As if the children were not worried enough already, when Emily, Izzie and Ellie returned to their class that afternoon, who was sitting at the front with Miss Robinson, but a policeman. Emily almost gave the whole game away when she turned round, white as a sheet, and just wanted to bolt from the room, but Ellie held her arm firmly and sat her down. The policeman introduced himself as PC Dweeble, which made the class laugh. Emily didn't laugh.

"Now," started Dweeble, "you may be aware that we have had a number of burglaries and incidents of beach huts being burnt down recently. It is believed…" Dweeble continued, pacing up and down the classroom as he went, and every now and then darting a suspicious look at some poor innocent child, who would then jump and sit up very straight, wanting to scream, "it wasn't me!"

"It is believed," Dweeble continued, "that this is down to young tearaways. These whippersnappers are nothing more than common vandals and we want to catch them. I want you to be extra vigilant. Watch everyone… it could even be someone you know… someone in this classroom…" his eyes slowly swept the classroom. As they fell on Emily, she had a sudden blockage in her throat and started coughing vigorously. His eyes moved on to Izzie whose hands were shaking so violently that she accidentally threw her pencil two rows in front. "So if you see anything… anything at all… I want you to report it to me. My name and telephone number are on the black board." Dweeble left, giving the classroom one more accusing stare, and Izzie fainted.

Mysterious things were happening that evening at the Ferry, the sleepy little village beyond Felixstowe golf course. Strange comings and goings at midnight, in and out of the Martello Tower and over the dark frosty ground. Small crafts rowing into the cliffs beyond the boat yard in the dead of night, like smugglers from olden days.   If anyone were to pay attention to the details they would notice, but then no-one ever did.   The only person who noticed was old Coleman Welch. Coleman limped out to the veranda at the edge of his wooden house, not much larger than a couple of beach huts put together and rocked in his rocker every night.   He would have reported it to the police, but then he didn't much trust the police, but he watched and took it all in.

The Ferry was a fishing village at heart.   Even in the dead of night you could still smell the fish, and along the gravel paths you would find small fish huts where fishermen sold their catch.   There was a small jetty, a boat yard and hundreds of tiny boats of all different descriptions moored in the harbour.

Yes, something was afoot, thought Coleman.   He noticed more figures darting past the café and settled down on his veranda to watch, gently swaying back and forth in his rocking chair.

It was pitch black in the middle of the night as they ran over the gravel path. "What are we doing? This is mad!" said Ellie.

"Shh! Come on," Em replied.   "You're just miffed 'cause we didn't get the beach hut watch. Don't worry. It'll be fun."

"I'm freezing," Ellie said crossly, rubbing her bear arms to keep the wind off. "And this is not fun! We spend half the night trekking down here to sit at the Ferry and watch for what exactly?... Nothing!" They had hiked the long tunnel down to the Ferry.   It came up in the middle of the golf course, and from there they had a long, cold and alarmingly dark run down to the Ferry village.

"Can't we go to the beach party?" Izzie suggested.   "Pleeeeeeas! It may be the last one this term."

"Shh!" Em insisted. But it was true.   They had got the bad end of the deal.   Fay, Miranda and the others were watching the beach huts for any sign of the vandals, and that was easy since Whiskers had a fully equipped luxury beach hut, with a special passageway built to it. Inside was a fridge laden with fizzy drinks and chocolate, and there was a cupboard with swim suits, a rubber dingy and towels. And even wet suits for when the swimming got too cold! Often during summer and even autumn they would have beach parties, play footie and sprinting down to the waters edge for a midnight swim. But instead they had been lumbered with watching the Ferry... boring or what!

They reached the tiny fishing village and decided to settle in the cafe which overlooked the harbour. The whole village was deathly quiet and there was a ghostly mist drifting in from the sea. It swirled around their ankles and seemed to get thicker as they looked into the distance, across the green and towards the boat yard. The whole effect gave Em the creeps, especially having just run across the deserted golf course.

The cafe was a very old building and it didn't take them long to find a window through which they could break in. They settled into the large bay, from where they had a good view of the boat yard and the harbour. If anyone came ashore they would see.

"Hey, pips! Look what I've found!" Izzie was struggling across the dark wooden floor, weaving in and out of the tables, carrying a large four litre tub of strawberry ice cream. "They've got chocolate and vanilla too."

"Mmmm," said Em. "This trip is looking up already." And so they sat and watched... and ate. The minutes dragged by and turned to hours very very... very slowly. There was a large grandfather clock in one corner of the gloomy old cafe, and Ellie sat watching it tick and willing it to sound the next hour. Izzie wandered in circles around the cafe like a caged animal desperately wanting to be let out, the monotony occasionally broken by requests for more ice cream. Em had brought her project book and was writing up what she had learned about Celts and Romans, which was, surprisingly, quite a lot. She had got so annoyed with Trevor, who seemed to know everything imaginable and kept dropping hints that she was thick, that Em had eventually told Whiskers and, as she should have guessed, an adventure immediately unfolded. The three girls had ended up in the Magic room and visited a real Roman chariot race. It had been faster, dustier and more dangerous than Em had ever realised... but now she had a real surprise which would get her top marks in her project... and silence the infuriating Trevor for good. She smiled to herself.

Em was pulled back from her daydream by a piercing noise from outside, then silence. Her eyes scanned the horizon through the bay windows.

Ellie whipped around. "What was that?"

"No idea."

"Do you think we should go out and take a look?" asked Ellie.

"Not likely!" Izzie replied with a shiver. "This place gives me the creeps." She rubbed her stomach. "And I'm feeling sick as well."

"Have some ice cream," said Em without the slightest hint of sympathy. "That'll make you feel better. Nice stuff isn't it?" She scooped up a chunk of choc-chip the size of a football, balanced precariously on the spoon and tried to force it into her mouth with the result that large chunks splodged down her jumper.

Izzie looked on feeling even sicker at the sight.

"I don't think I want any more ice cream... ever." Her face had turned a decidedly green tinge.

"I'm going out for a nose around," announced Ellie. "Anyone coming?" There was a loud silence. Ellie sighed and stomped to the door.

The air outside was fresh and chilly. Ellie pulled her cardigan tightly around her and, not for the first time that night, wished she had brought a coat. An owl hooted in the distance and as Ellie looked up she could see a grey swirling cloud moving in front of the moon. It cast a shadow over the whole Ferry, which suddenly looked darkly menacing. Everything was silent and Ellie could feel the grass crunch under her feet in the early morning sea mist.

"So much for friends!" she muttered angrily to herself. "Huh! Just let me wander out here on my own, why don't you! Anything could happen."

She wandered into the boat yard. Large fishing boats were suspended up on trailers and scaffolds in various states of repair. They looked like menacing monsters ready to pounce. The boat yard building was nothing more than a run down shack. Ellie walked up to the launch ramp. It must have been about twenty feet wide and had three boats sitting on it, each held still by chunky metal ropes, wound round large rusty reels.

Ellie stood very still in the silence and stared out over the harbour, straining to see any unusual movement amongst the boats.

"Oh, this is stupid!" she muttered to herself. All she felt like doing at the moment was climbing back into a warm bed. She lent back sulkily on one of the rusty metal winders. "What now?"

The silence was broken by a colossal noise. The large metal wheel Ellie was leaning on whipped around quickly and something rapped Ellie very hard on the head. Ellie sunk to her knees, temporarily dazed. The noise was deafening. It was one of the boats. The metal rope was unwinding furiously and the boat hit the water with a loud splash before bobbing up and down contentedly. Ellie looked around in horror, glancing at all the upstairs windows in the houses, expecting to see a swish of curtains or a light switched on. That noise must have woken half the Ferry up.

In the cafe, Em dropped her spoon of ice cream in panic. She had heard the noise from the boat yard.

"Quick! It's happening. Do something... er, what?" Em babbled on to herself. "What should we do Izzie? Call the police?"

"Ohhhhh," moaned Izzie. "I feel so sick. I can't move."

Em bit her lip and glanced out of the window again. They should have thought this out a bit more. If only Jen were here. She would know what to do.

Ellie climbed into the boat. How was she gonna get it back up the ramp? It was a small motor boat. Maybe it had a reverse gear like a car? There was a wheel with a key hanging next to it. She turned the key and a deep throaty sound coughed from the motor. The boat bobbed to one side and Ellie slipped forward grabbing the controls to steady herself. She felt the lever click loudly as her hand grabbed it and she immediately had that sinking feeling that this was not a good sign. There was a moment's silence. Then she was thrown back as the boat launched forward like a racing car, a deafening roar now coming from the motor. She tried to stand up but was immediately buffeted back down by the force of the spray in her face. Yuck, she was wet through! The little boat was weaving from side to side as if trying to throw Ellie overboard.

"What's she doing?" asked Em. She was sure that was Ellie. Why was she driving a boat? Em put the binoculars back up to her eyes. "She's not very good at steering it," she muttered. "Do you think we should go and help her, Izzie?"

Izzie lurched to one side, feeling very ill.

"When you've finished your ice cream that is," Em went on.

"Ice cream," whispered Izzie. "I never want to see another spoonful of ice cream ever again."

"You alright Izzie?" Em reached out and patted her on the back.

"Blgggggghhhhh!"

"IZZIE! That's disgusting! It's all over the floor. Yuck."

It was then that Em noticed the two men walking towards the harbour. She quickly put the binoculars to her eyes. They both wore balaclavas... just like bank robbers. They held what looked like guns, and large sacks, just like pirates or smugglers. They had found a large fishing boat. They were untying it. Alarm bells were going off in Em's head. This was it. They could catch them red handed.

"Izzie, Izzie, call the police now!"

"Blgggggghhhhh!"

Em crinkled up her nose in disgust. "That's gross!" Panic was rising in her. She had to do something quickly.

Suddenly there was the sound of a car engine. The car pulled around the dusty path and came to a halt at the entrance to the harbour. It was a police car. Two large policemen stepped out and made their way into the harbour.

"YES!" shouted Em as she danced around the cafe excitedly. "YES, we got 'em!"

But as Em settled back down to watch, everything suddenly

changed. A frown came over her face. What were they doing? They were talking to the smugglers. It was all friendly chit chat. Now they were pointing in her direction. They were looking her way... walking towards the cafe.

"Oh nuts! Izzie, come on, we gotta hide."

"Blggggghhhhh!" Izzie was sick again on the cafe floor.

The cafe door opened and the two policemen were silhouetted in the doorway. Two torch beams switched on and footsteps, which seemed so loud in the silence of night, pounded the floorboards as they walked in. Em immediately recognised PC Dweeble. Oh great, she thought. A pang of guilt swept through her. What if he caught her here? He would think she was responsible for all the break-ins. She bit her lip. What would her dad say?

"Blgggh—" Em stuffed her hand firmly over Izzie's mouth to stifle the groan and was rewarded with sick all over her hand. She quickly wiped it clean on her coat without thinking. Then regretted it... It stunk!

She looked up. The two girls were hiding behind a table and chairs in the corner of the cafe. Dweeble was working his way towards them. The torch beam was sweeping dangerously close.

"So who made the call?" asked the second policeman.

"Old Coleman called us out," Dweeble replied. "Good man, Coleman Welch. Kids broken in here, he reckoned."

"Kids! Always kids! You wait till I get me 'ands on 'em!"

Em was confused. What about the men stealing the boat, she wanted to scream?

"Charlie and Dez didn't see anything," Dweeble said. "Goin' for a late night fishing trip they were."

Em could have kicked herself. She had really screwed up. So they weren't stealing anything at all, they were just night fishermen.

Dweeble was now dangerously close. The torch beam was creeping around the table. She pulled back her foot but it was too late. It had been caught in the torchlight.

"Gotcha!" said Dweeble with a note of satisfaction in his voice.

He slowly bent down with the torch. "Come out now." Em pulled herself and Izzie back into the shadow. Dweeble was getting down on his hands and knees. Em swiped her foot and kicked the torch out of his hand. It spun noisily across the wooden floor.

"Come on now," Dweeble was saying. "There's nowhere for you to go."

All of a sudden there was the most colossal crash from outside. The whole floor began to shake. Dweeble pulled back and cracked his head on the table as he got up. Em sensed the opportunity. Her hand closed around something hard. She pushed Izzie forward.

"Run!" she shouted.

Izzie slouched forward and suddenly came nose to nose with Dweeble. A rush of shock ran through her. "AHHH!" she screamed. Then a sudden sick feeling overtook the shock. "Blggghhhhh!" She sicked down Dweeble's smart blue uniform. Em shot out from under the table, kicked as hard as she could at his shin and then swung whatever it was in her hand at his left ear. Then she tossed it and ran, pulling Izzie behind her. They met Ellie at the door and the three of them ran for the golf course entrance.

"What did you do with the boat?" Em shouted breathlessly as they dived down the passageway entrance.

"Don't ask," replied Ellie.

They heard footsteps behind them followed by a muffled cry of, "stop!"... CRACK, "Ouch!", THUMP... groan. And then silence.

When Dweeble finally gave up the chase and arrived back at the Ferry, his head hurt, he was limping, and he thought his foot must be broken. Stars were floating in front of his eyes, and... he shook his head, it couldn't be. There seemed to be a motor boat in the roof of his patrol car. The other policeman stared at the boat which was sticking up at rather a strange angle, and scratched his head. "Er... Sorry boss."

Chapter 13

Sewage…

"Emily, Trevor?" called Miss Robinson. They were all tasked with showing one special thing from their Celts and Romans project, and this was the moment Emily had been looking forward to. All the other children had bored the pants off everyone with rather mundane facts like how to count in Roman numerals. I mean, who cares about that, thought Emily? Jessica had brought a brass rubbing which had been half way interesting, she supposed. Emily, Izzie and Ellie had spent the morning discussing Emily's forthcoming sleepover. Everyone seemed to know about it and people kept asking Emily if they could come. The latest count was thirteen. Emily hoped her mum wouldn't mind.

"Emily, Trevor?" Miss Robinson called again.

"Hang on Miss," called Emily. "Just need to fetch something." She darted out of the classroom and returned a few seconds later pushing what, to everyone's astonishment, looked like a full size Roman chariot. It was only about three feet long with two wheels, which squeaked as she pushed it, and it had two long poles, one on either side, which would have attached to the train of horses. Long sharp spikes came out of the wheels, which Emily had seen used first hand when she had travelled back in time to watch the race. The spikes could be just as deadly as a razor blade.

"Er... Well, Emily," said Miss Robinson, lost for words. But Emily hadn't finished. It had been very hard work pushing this all the way back from the magic room. Now she wanted to make the most of it.

"Stand there Trevor," Emily ordered. She would get her own

back on this annoying little 'know it all' squirt. She placed Trevor between the two poles, fiddled around with the straps and within two minutes she had him pulling the chariot around the room like a horse. Tables and chairs went flying, Ellie yelped as the wheel spikes caught her ankle and calls of, "That's enough!" from Miss R seemed to have little effect as the classroom dissolved into chaos and fits of laughter.

The next lesson, however, was a different story. Emily almost fell off her seat when PC Dweeble walked into the classroom again.

"We 'ave," he stated firmly, after explaining that they were now a lot closer to catching the elusive Underground Gang criminals, "a good description of the three suspects we are searching for." Dweeble was sporting a black eye, what looked like a broken nose and was limping. Emily bit her lip. She didn't realise she had hit him that hard.

"The three criminals are female..." Emily glanced at Ellie who had gone quite pale. She then glanced at Izzie who was desperately chewing her fingernails. "They were all very young. Probably no older than twelve." Muttering erupted around the room as everyone whispered their suspicions to their neighbour. "The first was of slight build with long fair hair," Dweeble went on. His evil eye scanned the room. Emily felt like she was being photographed by an X-ray machine as his eye swept over her. But alarm bells were going off like little explosions in her head. "THAT'S ME!" her brain was screaming. Dweeble was describing her!

"The second one was shorter with very curly dark hair." Izzie's hands shot up to her hair. Then she tried to duck under the desk but cracked her head on the desk lid as she went down. She bounced around in pain, clutching her head. Everyone in the class turned to stare at her, including Dweeble. PC Dweeble stared very intently at Izzie for a few seconds. He glanced slowly down at the description he had just read, and then back up at Izzie who was now under her desk. Dweeble was just opening his mouth as if to say something when his thoughts were interrupted by Miss R.

"Do go on officer. I don't know what's got into her. Isobelle! Sit back up at your desk this instance!"

"Oh yes, yes," Dweeble looked back at his notes, now slightly flustered. "Er... We don't have a description of the third girl..." Ellie relaxed visibly in her seat... "but we do suspect that she is an expert in piloting small boats."

"Any questions?" asked Miss Robinson.

Trevor raised his hand. "Excuse me, mister... Is it true they drove a boat 'ta your police car? And how ya get that black eye?"

At lunch time they piled into the castle playhouse, but today it seemed packed solid with children.

"Yuck... What is that smell?" said Em. The stench was very strong. They all peered down through the trap door and into the depths of the passageway tunnel. All they could see was brown gunge slopping along a few feet below them.

"Gross!"

"It's sewage... Oh, it stinks!" said Izzie holding her nose.

"Cool!" said Jack with a look of wonder on his face. "What's sewage, E?"

"Ahgg, look!" shouted Ollie, who was already leaning over the tunnel opening, examining it closely. "There's bits of pooh floating in it."

"That's foul," groaned Em.

'I'm gonna be sick," said Izzie.

More people piled in behind them, and then Izzie leaned forward a little too far. She wasn't helped by the children cramming in behind her to see what was going on, and she may even have received a shove but no-one was going to own up to that. She tottered on the edge, hands flaying out to try to steady herself. Em reached out to grab her but her hands just slid over clothing unable to get a grip. Izzie's eyes went wide as she finally lost her balance totally, and fell. She hit the sewage with a scream, which was stifled as she disappeared totally under the surface. Everyone gasped. The flow took her out of sight down the passageways.

They just heard a distant cry of, "That's not sewage, it's chocolate! Mmmm, it's rather nice."

They all stared at each other in bewilderment. Ollie had a closer inspection and then jumped in.

Slurp, slurp...”Wow!... that's wicked!”

“How are we gonna get Izzie back?” asked Em. “We've got more lessons in...” she glanced at her watch, “ten minutes.”

Ellie shrugged, still staring in panic at the patch of sludge where they had last seen Izzie. As it happened, Izzie never reappeared that afternoon. Emily and Ellie spent the afternoon hoping she was alright and praying no-one would notice. Ollie spent the rest of the day looking as if he had been wrestling in a rather large mud patch, but then that was no different than normal so no-one really batted an eyelid.

“It's the factory,” said Whiskers later that evening, once everyone had fought and floated their way through the flooded passageways to the party room All the doorways were barricaded and trickles of chocolate were desperately trying to break through. The rich smell of cocoa wafted throughout the room. “Overflowed again. It happened back in... when was it?... nineteen forty seven. That was when—”

“Factory? What factory?” demanded Joseph. There was a large crowd, eager to hear Whiskers' story. Joseph and Ollie, Fay and Amy, Em, Izzie and Ellie were all there. Em had rowed herself and Ellie down to the party room in a rowing boat. They found they could fish for chocolate as they went, and their hands would reappear out of the gunge with huge chunks the size of boulders. They had also had to rescue stranded mice and children, who were sheltering helplessly in ducts and gullies. Mice were now running around, in the background of the party room, under the direction of Dufus, channelling the rivers of chocolate into vast vats so they could store it up for later consumption.

"Oh, er..." said Whiskers coming back from his reminiscing with a start. "Oh yes. Felixstowe has the largest chocolate factory this side of Manchester, you know." There were blank looks all round.

"That's rubbish!" Joseph retorted. "I know every square inch of this town and there are no factories. Cricky! Don't you think I'd have found out if it was something as good as a chocolate factory?!" The others looked on a little less certainly. After all Whiskers was always full of surprises. There were some whispered murmurs around the onlookers.

"But that's the point isn't it? If you knew, you'd want the chocolate. That's why they keep the location top secret."

"Top secret? A chocolate factory?" Izzie said, startled.

"This is a joke, right?" Joseph finished the thought.

"Oh, tell them, tell them," bounced Theo, who was perched on the table just behind Whiskers.

"A joke? Oh no, not at all," Whiskers said solemnly. "Government secrets, military installations and then come chocolate factories on the Government list of protected areas. Just think about it for a minute... Think how much chocolate gets eaten, thousands of tonnes, and yet, how many factory do you know of? When was the last time you visited one?" Whiskers paused to let it sink in. They were all standing with the same stunned expression on their faces. Of course Whiskers was right. None of them had ever seen or visited a chocolate factory.

"So, Whiskers... you knew all this time that we had a huge chocolate factory next door and you never told us?" asked Fay, a note of frustration in her voice.

"Top secret you see. And anyway, heavily guarded. You would never get in."

"Where is it anyway? You can't just hide a bloomin' great factory!"

"Oh, that's easy. The art of hiding things is to disguise them. It doesn't matter how big it is, if everyone thinks it's something else."

"So, where is it?" everyone called.

"The old telephone exchange."

Of course! thought Em.   No-one ever went in and out, the windows were shuttered up, and everyone assumed it was just full of telephone equipment.

As the chocolate level fell over the next few days, Ollie could be regularly seen in an apparently muddy state, lots of the children around town were complaining they felt sick, and Izzie, after the ice-cream at the Ferry and falling in the chocolate, had gone right off her food.   She didn't even help cook with the lemonade and ice cream counter anymore.   But Joseph, Fay and Emily were hatching a plan. They walked to school the next day, and stopped to cross the crossing by the round-a-bout.   On one side was the hotel, cafe.   On the other side was the boring brick building, pretending to be the telephone exchange.

"It looks so... sort of innocent, doesn't it?" said Emily.

"More to the point, how do we get in?" asked Joseph eagerly.

"But we can't," replied Emily.   "You heard Whiskers.   It's heavily guarded."   Fay and Joseph just gave her that, 'don't be so stupid' look.

"We'll find a way," said Fay.   "I have an idea.   I'm in charge of the wooden doors, which hide all the adventures, remember?"   And with that they crossed the road.

When Emily got home from school, she clambered over the yellow sports car and the 'Blue Pirate Eater' to feed Norman the sheep.   It was later that evening once she had gone to bed and carefully checked everyone was asleep, she climbed into her lift and buzzed down to the passageway level.   She was tense with excitement at the prospect of a new adventure.

Fay, Joseph, Izzie and Ellie were there too.   Fay had taken charge. They had traced the chocolate back to a large hole at one side of the Lake.   It was caked in thick gungy chocolate.   It opened out into a large tunnel.

"What do you think?" asked Fay, a bit doubtfully.

"This has to be it!" said Ellie. "It slants upwards." Ellie looked from side to side and paused for a moment, as if trying to calculate something. "I think that would be about the right place for it too." She pointed upwards. "The telephone exchange would be about there."

"Come on then," shouted Fay as she and Joseph ran ahead.

"Oh pips! This is great," squealed Izzie. "Wait for me!"

The walk was a very long up hill struggle.

"This isn't getting us anywhere!" complained Joseph.

"Come on," Fay persisted.

"It's boring," Joseph went on.

"Come on!" said Izzie and Ellie together.

"JINX!" shouted Izzie. "You can't say anything now."

"But—"

"No! Not till I say your name three times."

Ellie frowned, annoyed.

Eventually, after clambering over rocks and having to climb up steep walls onto shelves and ledges carved high up in the stone, they began to hear the metal clanking of machinery and smell the distinct rich chocolate aroma. Five minutes later they emerged in the chocolate factory, through a tiny trap door below a coffee machine. The noise of machinery was deafening. The big factory floor room was immense. Monster size machines were chugging and beeping. A large conveyor belt carried chocolate in various states, from machine to machine. First cocoa beans, then melted into vast vats, then moulded to shape and finally packaged up. The factory floor operated all by

itself and there were no people there, apart from one man sitting in an office, which was suspended up above the machinery on a platform accessible by some metal stairs. Em looked up. He was busy and hadn't noticed them.

"Right!" whispered Joseph, rubbing his hands together in glee, a broad grin permanently attached to his face. He ran off in the direction of one of the monster chocolate machines.

It reminded Em of the sweet shop, the first time they had ventured there at night and tiptoed around. "Harrychoc would like this!" she whispered to Izzie. Harriet, Em's friend from London, the girl who couldn't walk, and loved chocolate so much that she earned her nickname. Until they had visited the sweet shop at midnight one dark night and had found the strange mysterious sweet counter. Harrychoc had eaten the special sweet which had given her her legs back. Em had never seen that sweet counter again. So many strange and unexplained things happened in the passageways didn't they? She thought of Princess Annabel and the castle adventure. That was when Joseph had been knighted and become Sir Joseph of Orford... Em was daydreaming. The memory of the sweet shop had suddenly brought her memories bursting into life. A sudden thought hit Em. She reached across and tagged Ellie on the arm.

"You're IT."

"Hey!" Ellie protested. "We agreed. Passageways are base!"

"We're not in the passageways!" Em called, running off. "No returns!"

Ellie was fuming. Of course, they were on the surface now. It was so annoying!

"And you're not allowed to talk yet," Izzie added, edging out of arms reach. Ellie stared daggers at her.

Em reached down and pressed the two buttons on her pink passicom watch. Then she whispered a name and up came the bright lights which formed into a face on the screen. The face was surrounded by long bright red hair. "Harrychoc!" whispered Em.

"Emily!" the face beamed a smile back at her. "What are you up to?"

"Harrychoc, you wouldn't believe where I am!"

The others had run off to explore. Joseph had found the point where the hot liquid chocolate cascaded down a ten foot drop, like a huge chocolate fountain into the next machine. He whipped of his jumper and was using it like a bowl to catch the chocolate.

Another little face was hovering behind the coffee machine, hiding out of site. Little Jack's eyes were nearly popping out of his head. He had heard them all whispering about a chocolate factory and there was no way he was gonna miss out on that, so he had followed them in. But this was beyond his wildest dreams. His heart was racing fast and his eyes were darting backwards and forwards. There was just so much chocolate, he just didn't know what to do first. He was too little to climb up all the machinery and the others might see him anyway, so he would have to... what? Where would he find the most chocolate? He edged along the wall to a corridor at the end of the factory floor. He followed it down till it opened out into what looked like a storage room. There was a distinctly pleasant sweet aroma in the room and there were hundreds of shelves all piled high to busting with chocolate. There were a million different types... small bars, large bars, stocks of Easter eggs and chocolate bunnies, there were chocolate lollypops, packets of drinking chocolate, fancy boxes of chocolate... it was endless.

"Wicked!" whispered Jack, with a note of awe in his voice. He rushed over and reached up. It was then that he realised, to his frustration, that all of the shelves were out of his reach. He glanced around the floor for something to stand on... anything... there was nothing. He stamped his foot in frustration. The whole universe's supply of chocolate and all out of reach. Then he noticed the large metal door. It looked old fashioned with ornate designs on it. He walked over and put his hand on the lever style handle. It pulled down with a heavy 'thunk'. As he pulled it open there was a waft of cold air, a bright light and a low murmur of buzzing. It was very cool as he walked in. It must be a fridge, but big enough to walk in. There were more boxes, shelves and heaps of chocolate... and this time all within reach.

"Wow!" Behind him Jack heard a creak... thunk... clunk. His

head shot round. The fridge door had shut behind him, and he had the horrible feeling the metal clunk had been a latch or lock closing tight. He ran over and pushed. It didn't budge an inch.

"You stupid pooh door!" he fumed and kicked it hard.

"Ouch!" Then the light flicked off and Jack was left in the pitch black darkness.

Ellie and Izzie had climbed to the high conveyor belt leading up the foil wrapping machine. Ellie was picking up every fourth chocolate bar from the conveyor in a very organised fashion.

"What you doing that for?" asked Izzie.

"If we keep it regular, picking up every forth chocolate bar, no-one will notice. It's obvious, isn't it?" replied Ellie, counting out the next fourth bar.

"Ssh! You're not allowed to talk."

"You asked me!" Ellie retorted in an exasperated tone. Izzie just reached down, her arms as wide as possible, trying to encompass as many hundreds of chocolate bars as she could.

"IZZIE! You're messing it all up!"

"If I can just reach..." but Izzie had reached too far. For the second time that week she tottered on the brink of a chocolate disaster, desperately trying to keep her balance. Ellie reached out and grabbed, but couldn't get a good enough hold. She watched helplessly as Izzie's foot finally slipped and she fell onto the conveyor. Izzie climbed to her knees but it was too late. The conveyor turned straight downwards and Izzie fell with a hundred chocolate bars, into the foil machine.

There was a distant scream of, "Ellie! Ellie!" and then a crunching sound as the foil machine struggled with something rather larger than a chocolate bar. Ellie ran along the walk way by the conveyor. Her feet clanked on the steel surface. She got to the other side and looked down. There was a long neat line of silver foiled chocolate bars appearing on the conveyor belt ten foot below. There was a sudden thump and a large Izzie shaped foil wrapped thing was dumped on the conveyor. It wriggled, knocking chocolate bars everywhere and a face broke through. Izzie's face was covered in chocolate and hundreds of tiny bits of silver foil which were stuck on like glue. She also had a rather nasty bruise above her left eyebrow. Ellie giggled.

"Ellie, you're not allowed to speak!" shouted a very annoyed Izzie.

"You said my name three times," Ellie replied with a sparkle in her eyes. "Oh, and I tagged you as you fell. You're IT. No returns."

Ellie and the foil covered Izzie both suddenly looked up. There was a red light flashing on top of the foil machine. Ellie glanced up at the man in the office. He was staring at the red light too, a frown on his face. Then he glanced across at Ellie. A wave of panic hit her. The man blinked as if he wasn't sure whether to believe what he was seeing. Then the moment was broken as an alarm started shrieking.

"We need to get out of here," Ellie screamed. Joseph's head popped up from behind the conveyor belt. From all parts of the factory children scrambled out. Izzie's hair sparkled like a mirror ball at a disco as she ran, her fingers fumbling to pull off strips of rather sticky silver foil. They followed Em down a corridor and past the sign to the storage room. But the room at the end of it was a dead end. In the distance they could hear the clunk... clunk... clunk of the man in the office running down the metal steps of the staircase.

"Oh great," said Fay. "Where now?"

"In here. Quick. We can hide." Em pulled the metal handle down with a 'thunk'.

A rather blue shivering Jack ran out.

"What are you doing here?" Em started. "Oh never mind. No time. Go!" They all piled into the fridge, sweeping Jack back in, despite his kicking and shouting protests.

"E! E! The door," Jack shouted. "Stop the—"

Creak... thunk... clunk.

Everyone's head turned. Joseph launched himself at the door but it didn't budge. Then the light flickered off.

Em could hear the shuffling of feet. She was squashed back uncomfortably against the shelves. Something was sticking in her side, and her hands, feet and face were starting to burn with the cold.

"Ouch. Get off!"

"Who's foot's that?"

"Mine. Leave it alone!"

Thump.

"Hey! Who was that? That hurt!"

"I don't like the dark."

"Ssh."

"What we doin' E?" Jack whispered excitedly. "We playin' hide an' seek, E?"

"Oh for goodness sake, Jack!"

"Can I say boo when they find us, E?"

"I feel sick."

Joseph slammed into the door again with all the force he could muster.

"Ssh," hissed Em. "The man will be coming." The darkness went quiet for a minute.

"You're IT," whispered Izzie.

"Who?" someone muttered.

"I dunno. Whoever I tagged."

"Wasn't me!"

"Er... might have been."

"Shut up, Izzie!" a couple of voices shouted.

"Jinx!"

"Ssh!"

"You're not allowed—"

"SHUT UP!!"

There was more shuffling of feet and pushing and shoving. Someone was flapping their arms to keep them warm.

"Stop that... get off!"

"It's freezing in here. I'd give my right arm to get out of here."

"I'd give my left foot."

"I'd give the scab on my left elbow."

"What?"

"Scab on my—"

"Ssh. I heard you."

Em's hands were so cold she couldn't feel the end of her fingers; all she could feel was a dull ache. She stretched her sleeves over her hands. "Get me out of here and I'll invite the whole universe to my sleepover."

"Can I come?"

"Who?"

"Me."

"Who's me?"

"I'm me, stupid."

"Oh seriously, you lot," hissed Ellie angily, "how are we gonna get out of here?"

"Anyone got a passicom?"

"Brilliant!" Ellie enthused suddenly. "Anyone?"

"No."

"Er, no."

"Left it at home."

"No."

Ellie sighed.

"I have," whispered Em.

"Good. Call someone."

Em fiddled with it for a moment. "I can't use it in the dark. Which buttons?..."

There was the sound of frustrated muttering and deep sighs.

"Give it here."

More pushing, shoving and general moving about.

Clunk. "Oh, I dropped it."

There was the crash of heads and groping of hands as everyone bent down to find it at the same time, followed by angry muttering and a bit of less accidental pushing and shoving.

CRUNCH! Silence.

"What was that?" Em asked in a very accusing acid tone. Silence.

"E... Sorry E. I stepped on it."

"IDIOT! Our one hope and you... you trod on it. You stupid boy!!"

The conversation was then silenced by a loud clunk... thunk, and the fridge door swung open.

"Oh nuts!" Em shielded her eyes as bright light flooded into the fridge. The black silhouette of a very large man was framed in the doorway. For a brief moment Em was reminded of Gravisham but it wasn't. They were all still as statues, not quite knowing the next move.

"BOO!" shouted Jack, then looking round wondering why no-one was laughing.

"Gotcha, you little 'ooligans!" The black silhouetted figure walked purposefully into the fridge. Then he slipped on a pile of silver foil, slid up the centre of the stone floor, as bodies dived to get out the way, and he finally hit the back wall, cracking his head on a shelf. Em winced with pain just watching. The man fell back on the floor with a thump. No-one moved. Then a pile of chocolate bars collapsed on him. He lay still.

"Leg it!" shouted Fay.

"Cool E. Can I get some chocolate?"

"Come on Jack!" Em grabbed his hand and pulled him after her. Joseph and Ellie dragged the man out before they left. They didn't want to leave him in the fridge.

Back in the party room Joseph was peeling the dried chocolate off his jumper whilst Izzie picked small flecks of silver foil out of her hair.

"I still can't believe there's been a chocolate factory here all this time," Joseph broke the silence, "and we never knew about it. It's criminal."

At the circular counter in the centre, the tubby shape of Cook was dishing out drinks of all colours and descriptions. The food tables were full to bursting and the smell of chocolate wafted across the room.

"Izzie, are you not helping Cook tonight?"

"No... Not hungry. I've sort of gone off chocolate the last few days."

A very enthusiastic Whiskers suddenly scampered across towards them, neatly zigzagging through the feet and chair legs. He bounced up onto their table.

"Well done Emily, very generous..." Em was taken by surprise. She was expecting a lecture about breaking into the chocolate factory. "I'll make the announcement then?" Whiskers continued. "How exciting! All the mice are coming. Very excited, they are!"

"Er, what... OK," Em replied uncertainly. She had that vague feeling you sometimes get when you think everyone else knows something you don't.

There was a clink, clink, clink, as Whiskers chimed a rather large schooner of smoking yellow liquid, with a spoon. The room grew quiet as all eyes turned to Whiskers, now standing atop the circular centre piece of the party room. Em was as eager as anyone to find out what he was so excited about.

"What d'you think it is?" asked Ellie.

"Probably a new ice cream challenge or a competition on the Lake, or something," replied Joseph.

Theo, together with Rufus, Dufus and Bart, the three mining mice, and Em's partners in crime when it came to practical jokes, popped up onto the table and started patting Em on the back and shaking her hand vigorously.

"Very good show," Bart enthused.

"Brilliant idea! Absolutely brilliant! We are quite touched." Dufus wiped a mock tear from his eyes. Em was totally confused. Suddenly Izzie's eyes went wide. Her gaze shot from Em to Whiskers, back to Em again.

"Oh no! Sorry Em. Ohhh. I feel sick." And with that she bolted from the party room.

Whiskers was now in mid announcement. Em turned to listen.

"...and it is with great pleasure that our generous Guardian, Emily, has asked me to announce that she is having a sleepover at her house, two weeks on Friday, and everyone is invited." Whiskers led a round of applause. Em's mouth hung open whilst her brain worked in slow motion, trying to fathom what Whiskers had meant... surely he couldn't... could he?

"I've never, ever been invited to a sleepover before," Theo muttered dreamily. "What do you do exactly?... What should I wear? I have a bow tie for special occasions."

"I never said..." Em protested.

"Oh yeah, you did," Joseph replied. "In the fridge, remember? You said you'd invite the whole universe to your sleepover if you got out of there. And it looks like you just have!"

"But Mum said I could only have three friends," Em replied, stony faced, as the full extent of her dilemma set in.

"But how did he know?" Ellie began. Then it dawned on them.

"IZZIE!" they all said at the same time.

Chapter 14
The Balloon…

Emily jumped with fright as the doorbell rang, and a wave of panic ran through her. She ran to the front door. It was Izzie. Relief again.

"Did you tell her?" Izzie asked in a low whisper. Emily just shook her head. The summer holidays had now set in and today was the day of her sleepover… the sleepover where Mum was allowing her a maximum of three friends to stay. Emily had already had one argument because she had mentioned it to a couple of other girls. So how on earth was she supposed to explain that she had accidentally invited half the town, not to mention the mice! Her mind had been wrestling all week with whether to try and explain, or just to hope and pray it would all go away. She had opted for the 'hope and pray' tactic but now it was here she was very worried.

"Hello Isobelle," said Mum walking into the hall. "Got your pyjamas?" Izzie nodded. "What have you done to your hair," Mum continued, "it's all sparkling. Very nice."

Izzie frowned and Emily pulled her towards the stairs. "Come on." Izzie's hair was still full of tin foil and seemed to shine like a lighthouse, trying to warn the ships at night. She had spent hours picking the tiny bits of foil out of her hair.

The two girls raced up to the play room. They passed a puzzled looking Dad on the landing. He was holding something rather sticky looking in his hand.

"Em," he called absently, "why's your ceiling dripping chewing gum?"

Emily and Izzie exchanged worried looks. They had both forgotten that hideous night when Theo had upscaled the Blue Pirate Eater in Emily's bedroom and they had repaired the hole in the ceiling with pink chewing gum. Both girls shrugged innocently and raced on up the stairs.

The play room was a large room taking up the whole third floor of the Victorian house. It must have been the size of three bedrooms and Mum had said they could all sleep up there.

"Why didn't you tell her?" hissed Izzie. They had all been pleading with Emily for the last week and a half to sort it out.

"Maybe they won't all come," said Emily weakly, but neither of them really believed it.

"Mum said we can sleep up here tonight," said Emily, changing the subject.

"But how do we get into the passageways?" replied Izzie. "You don't have a doorway up here."

Emily hadn't thought of that, but there was no time now. The doorbell went again. It was Ellie. Within a minute it went off again and it was Fay. But her little sister Amy was also in tow. Emily hovered out of sight at the top of the stairs and listened to the debate at the front door.

"The problem is," explained Fay's mum, "she seems to think your Emily invited her too."

"It doesn't surprise me!" frowned Emily's mum. "I'm very sorry Amy, but we've only got room for a few girls up there."

"Oh, that's OK missus Em," replied Amy, undeterred. "I'm very small. I don't take up much room." And with that she marched in. Fay and Amy's mum just shrugged.

"Now Amy dear—" began Mum a bit more sternly.

"Emily said I could, you know, missus Em," Amy cut her off quickly, giving her a rather hard stare as if trying to explain something very simple to a two year old. "She invited all of us."

"All of you?" asked Emily's mum suspiciously.

"Oh yes... and the mice too." She held out her duffle bag. "There you go missus Em," and with that she marched upstairs. The two mums just stared at each other.

Emily bit her lip, listening at the top of the stairs. But there was worse to come. Thirty seconds later the bell rang again and seven boys trooped in, led by Joseph and Ollie.

"Oh no," said mum. "There must be some mistake. We only invited girls to the sleepover."

"Well Emily invited me too!" insisted Ollie, a distinct look of defiance on his face.

"NO! I draw the line at—"

"I'm coming! So there!" He stamped his foot hard on the hall carpet and gave Emily's mum his best hard stare; chin forward, eyebrows drawn together, bottom lip out. It normally did the trick.

"Emily!" Mum called up the stairs, as the boys lugged their bags into the hall.

Next Charlie arrived, then Jemima, then the Adams twins, followed by Jennifer together with the four blonde girls from down the Terrace... then Lydia and Jess... and the doorbell kept on ringing.

"EMILY!!" Mum bellowed up the stairs. For some reason Emily seemed to be keeping out of her way. Mmmm, I wonder why, thought Mum acidly.

When the coach party arrived Mum just gave in.

"Come on then," she muttered and ushered them all inside. Dad stood in the hall with a bewildered look on his face.

"That's forty seven," he said in wonder.

"Well you'd better go up and sort them out then, hadn't you dear," Mum snapped at him.

"ME?!" said Dad in shock. He glanced up the stairs, and could hear the noise coming from the play room. "I'm not going up there. Do you think I'm barmy or something. I'll not get out alive."

"Well I'm watching TV. They're all yours," Mum replied in that, 'just you dare say no' sort of tone. Dad shot out to the shed. He suddenly remembered something very important he had to find in there which might take him a few hours.

Many miles away, Emily's cousin Alice was fed up. She had lived in Felixstowe up until a few months back, then her family had packed everything into large wooden crates and moved up north to Durham. She liked her new house just outside Durham, and her bedroom was nice and large, although desperately in need of decoration to get rid of the horrible orange floral wallpaper. But it had to be said that the Durham passageways were dead boring. There was no party room and there was a distinct absence of weird lemonade cocktails and wonderful food to eat. Very few wooden doors would open for her, probably since the hinges were so rusty, and the whole of the passageways were uncared for and had a rather dark and sinister feel to them. And more than anything there was a distinct lack of children, since no-one bothered going down there. Added to which, the chief mouse was a real grouchy old codger called Romonic Chupot. He was so mean, Alice suspected he might be related to Spondic. There was just one chink of light. That was the presence of the passistation. Durham had a passistation, even if it was a rather dreary one, where not many passitrains stopped. She was nearer to Edinburgh here so she had been up to visit McG and all his brothers and she had received a special invitation to the annual Edinburgh Castle festival. But she hadn't managed to get down to see her cousin Emily, and she missed Emily and all her friends and the mice... and the adventures. Only one passitrain an evening ran to Crinkle Point, the East coast stop in Felixstowe and that left at midnight, not arriving at Crinkle Point till two in the morning, which left her hardly any time with her friends before having to get the three-o-clock train back home! But despite all this, she was going to have a try tonight, because tonight was a very special night, cousin Em's sleepover night, and Alice desperately wanted to be there.

And so Alice jumped out of bed, pulled on some clothes that she had hidden under her pillow for speed, and pressed in the second petal on the forth orange flower from the end of the wall (she really did have to get rid of this wall paper... it was truly hideous!) There was a slight squeak and a slim gap appeared between her wardrobe and her chest of drawers. You wouldn't even notice it on a casual glance. Alice squeezed between the two pieces of furniture and before she knew it she was clanging down the spiral staircase (avoiding the forth, fifth and seventh steps which were broken). She sighed. She had reported these numerous times to old Chupot, but he wasn't doing anything about them. Alice had another reason to do the trip to Crinkle Point as well. She wanted to have a word with Whiskers and see if he could get anything done about her disastrous passageways.

Alice didn't see anyone else on her way to the passtation and she eventually scampered onto the passitrain just in time and relaxed into her seat for the long journey, taking out the supply of food and sweets she had raided from the kitchen the day before, in her preparation for the trip. She also took out her passicom and spoke Emily's name into it. A moment later Emily's face appeared and the two of them giggled in excitement.

Every family has legends. You know, those strange distant relatives that everyone talks about at family events like weddings and birthday parties. It's normally some distant aunt or uncle who did something very silly as a child, or who went mad or escaped from prison. Well Emily's family had its legends too. One was a distant Great Uncle, who blew up his car. Another was a distant cousin, who won a medal at the Olympic Games. And another was Great Uncle Bogthwart, the stories of whom were too numerous to mention but included teaching the dog to chew up the cane which his mother kept hidden under the doormat. And of course Emily's dad was fast becoming a family legend too. Well, you don't just find sports cars and boats in your back garden and keep it quiet do you.

Anyway, the point is that every family had its legends and today was one of those special days when another one... or perhaps two... legends were soon to be born. And they would be the biggest family legends of all. The type which would be talked about for years to come, far and wide in the vast family network. And all because of little Alice.

Alice was very excited when she reached Crinkle Point, to be met by Em, Ellie and Fay, (who had only managed to escape from the play room into the passageways when Amy had suggested they use Rover, her pet hole). Alice was even more excited when Em explained that Whiskers had managed to get a two hour delay to the passitrain which would be taking her home. And, since Alice was arriving late and would miss most of the party, Whiskers had announced some weeks back that he would be laying on a waterski championship specially for the occasion. Then you can imagine Alice's joy when she won the competition. She was quite an adventurous little girl after all, and had been practicing balancing on her brother's surfboard in the bath for the last three weeks, much to her mum's dismay, who thought she had gone utterly bonkers.

It was a little later in the evening when the problems really started.

"What!" said Alice in horror, whilst struggling over a choco challange.

"I only asked how long you were staying at Emily's?" Whiskers repeated his question.

The two girls looked at each other. "But I'm not staying at Em's. She said you'd arranged for a late train back for me."

"A late train back?" said Whiskers scratching his head. "Oh no my dear, I had only commented that I hate grey rats."

"What's that got to do with it?" Em shot back, now getting quite flustered.

"I haven't got a clue, my dear," Whiskers beamed happily. "I never mentioned a train. You asked about rats and I said I didn't like the grey ones."

"No, no!" said Em. "I said 'Rats, it's a shame Alice can't come down', and you said..." her voice trailed off as she realised her mistake. "You said you hate grey rats, not that you'd get her a late train back?"

"Never mind," said an obviously cheerful Whiskers. "No harm done." And with that he hoped onto the food table and dived head first into a very large chocolate blancmange, and disappeared altogether.

Em and Alice stared at one another. "So there's no late train back?"

Em shook her head, and her face flushed red. "Doesn't look like it." There was now a large group of children hanging around the table, giggling at this rather absurd conversation. Alice glanced at her watch. It was now a quarter past three in the morning. She had missed the last train.

"Hey, I got an idea!" perked up a high pitched little voice. It belonged to a very little boy with mousy hair who looked as if he was far too young to be coming down in the passageways this late at night. "My dad hires out bouncy castles!" he announced.

"So what!" Em replied tersely. "What we gonna do? Bounce to Durham? Push off kid."

"No, no!" continued the boy, unphased by the harsh reply he had received. "You don't understand. He also owns a hot air balloon. You could fly back home." Em and Alice looked at each other.

"It's an idea," said Fay.

Charlie, as the kid was called, led them through a tunnel which led to his spiral staircase, which came up, not in his bedroom but in the shed at the bottom of his garden.

"Corr, that must be a bit cold in winter," said Ellie, "having to come all the way down here to get into the passageways."

"Yeah, it is," said Charlie. "I'm told this tunnel got built whilst Theo was off sick last year, and they got all the measurements wrong. First one they built came up in my dad's manure heap. It got real messy!" The girls cringed at one another.

"Well, this is better than the manure heap," conceded Ellie.

"So where's the balloon?" asked Em.

Charlie pulled a large wicker basket out from behind the lawn mower, and they heaved it out into the garden. The wind was chilly and none of them, apart from Charlie with his nightly run across the garden, had dressed for the outdoors.

The wicker basket appeared big enough for someone to stand in, and it was full to overflowing with cloth... what looked like the world's biggest duvet cover. Charlie directed them expertly as they unpacked it and connected the burners.

"I don't think this is a good idea," said Ellie. They all ignored her.

"How long is this gonna take?" asked Alice glancing at her watch.

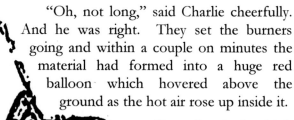

"Oh, not long," said Charlie cheerfully. And he was right. They set the burners going and within a couple on minutes the material had formed into a huge red balloon which hovered above the ground as the hot air rose up inside it.

"I really don't think this is a good idea," Ellie repeated, a little more loudly.

"Any better ideas?"

"Quick, quick, get in!" shouted Charlie. "We forgot to tie it down!" He was right. The balloon had reached its full height and the wicker basket was beginning to hover a few inches off the ground. Alice clambered into the basket.

"How are we gonna get it back here?" asked Em.

"Err," said Charlie.

"Someone will have to go with her, to fly it back again," said Em.

"No time," Fay replied. "She'll just have to fly it back next time she comes."

"Don't worry," said Charlie. "Dad hardly ever uses it these days."

Fay was pulling hard on the anchor rope to hold it down. With a final heave of the material the balloon lurched upright and without warning it rose into the sky. Fay was taken completely by surprise and, not quite knowing if she should try to hold it down for just a tincy-wincy bit longer, she didn't let go of the rope. She dangled, screaming as she rose up into the air... ten feet... twenty feet...

"Let go, Fay!" they all shouted. "Let go, quick."

Fay looked round and could see the ground growing distant. "I can't," she bellowed. Then without warning the balloon got pulled off left by the wind and her hand slipped. She fell backwards landing right in the middle of the rhododendron bush.

"Ouch!" Em thought to herself.

"Oh no, my mum's prize rhododendrons!" moaned Charlie.

Alice looked over the side of the basket and could see everyone getting more distant below her. A sudden thought hit her. "Hey, how do I steer this thing?" she shouted.

"You don't," Charlie replied. "You just go where the wind takes you."

"Well how's she gonna get home then?" asked Ellie.

The smile immediately fell from little Charlie's face. He hadn't thought about that.

"You great pillock. Get her down!" Em shouted.

"I can't. She's up there now."

"But…" Em's voice trailed off.

Ellie stood, hands on hips. "I told you this wasn't a good idea!!"

They watched as the bright red balloon rose as high as the clouds and floated away.

Em cupped her hands round her mouth and shouted. "Durham's that way!" She pointed to her right. "She's going the wrong direction. That's the coast."

"Great," said Ellie sarcastically. "She'll end up in France."

They watched until the last spot of red disappeared in the distance.

"I hope she gets back OK."

Alice hadn't heard any of the discussion which had gone on below her. She tried in vain to find the steering wheel, but there definitely wasn't one, she was sure. She watched as she headed out over the water. Was there water between Felixstowe and Durham, she wondered? Yeah, she was sure there was. After all, they had gone

over a few bridges in the removal van, hadn't they. That was rather a
large bit of water down there, though. It probably looked bigger from
up here, she thought. The land reappeared. That was good. The sun
was beginning to rise now. She hoped she would be home soon. She
could see fields below her and there were the first early risers of the
day. A few people waved at her and she returned the wave. She could
see someone below her on a bicycle. He was wearing a blue and white
stripy jumper, had a string of onions around his neck and wore a beret
on his head.

"Bonjour!" he called.

He didn't look like he came from Durham.

She was flying over a big city now. Straight ahead of her was a
large black tower. It was a metal tower which started wide at the
bottom and grew gracefully thin as it rose up. Hey, she had seen
pictures of that before, somewhere. She couldn't remember where,
but she was sure it wasn't in Durham. The wind changed direction
and she was drifting away from the tower again. She passed back over
the water and eventually, what seemed like hours later the sights below
her began to look familiar. She recognised Durham. The balloon was
getting lower now and she could even make out what she thought
looked like her house. Now, she thought, all I have to do is learn how
to land this thing.

Alice's mum was still in bed. The sun shone through the window
and woke her up. School day, she immediately thought. She climbed
wearily out of bed, grabbed her dressing gown and wandered down
the hallway. On each of the doors she knocked, put her head round
the door and shouted, "morning! Time to get up!"

Then she reached the final door... Alice's door. She turned the
handle and pushed open the door slowly. Now, where was that girl?
Alice's mum wandered into the room. Was she hiding again? The
little tyke! There was a sudden loud crack above her head. Plaster and
wood splintered and fell from the ceiling. Alice's mum jumped back
in surprise. The whole ceiling seemed to vaporise before her eyes and
a large wicker basket descended through the ceiling, amidst a cloud of
dust. It was followed by the ripped remains of a large red hot air

balloon. It all came down with such force that the left wall of the bedroom gave way and fell outwards onto the new shed in the garden which their dad had built the last weekend. Alice wiped the dirt and dust from her face and smiled sweetly at her mum. Her four brothers had now piled into the room behind her mum as well. They all stared at the wicker basket, now dangling in the middle of the room, the strings caught on the last remaining wooden beam running across the ceiling. Alice looked up at the damage.

"Sorry mum," she said weakly.

"Wow!" said her little brother George. "Wait till I tell my friends at school about this one!" And so the legend was born.

Chapter 15
The Red Snappers…

Jack was just lying on his bed fiddling with his passicom. It was night time but Jack never slept much. He didn't seem to need much sleep, which suited him. His torch was propped up on a book pointing the light over his hands so he could see what he was doing. "Stupid!" he moaned. He had arranged to call Ollie on his passicom, but the stupid thing wasn't working. He picked it up and thumped it hard on the wall. No, that didn't work either. His face turned red. He was getting annoyed now. He thumped it harder against the wall. Nope. He threw it as hard as he could out the window. It was a useless thing anyway! He grabbed the torch and headed for his chest of drawers. But as he pulled out the bottom drawer, a head popped up. It was Theo. He climbed out awkwardly, juggling a clipboard in one hand and a big yellow box in the other.

Jack frowned, still in an annoyed mood. "What you doin' here?"

Theo quickly looked left to right as if someone might jump out and catch him. "No time to explain." He seemed in a right panic about something, thought Jack. "Er…" he looked undecided for a moment and then made a decision. "Look after this for me." He handed Jack the small yellow box, which had an elastic band around it. In fact he almost threw it at Jack. He seemed eager to get rid of it. "Whatever you do, don't open the box." And with that he scampered off again.

"What is it?" asked Jack.

"No time… got to go…" was all he got in return. "Just don't open it," said the fading voice. "Phew… glad to get shot of that!"

Jack laid the yellow box carefully on the end of his bed and stared at it. It was a perfectly square cardboard box, with a thick elastic band holding the lid on tightly. He shone the torch all around it, to see if he could gain any clues as to what might be inside. Nothing. The house was deathly quiet, and the room was very black, apart from the thin beam from his torch. What should he do? It really wasn't fair was it, leaving him a box, but saying he couldn't open it. If he went down into the passageways it would be bugging him all evening, but if he just sat here and stared at it, what use was that. There was really only one thing he could do. Jack wasn't as cautious as Emily. I mean, what could be so bad that he shouldn't have a look at it. It really can't be that bad. He very slowly picked up the box. It was quite light. He rattled it from side to side. Yep, there was something small in there, which rattled around. Suddenly the box seemed to jump in his hand. He dropped it immediately. It landed back on his bed. He watched it closely, his nose about two inches away. It was still again. He prodded it with his finger. Suddenly it jumped again. He could hear whatever it was scampering around inside. It was alive! "Well, who are you?" he muttered. There must have been some kind of animal in there. He suddenly perked up with interest and his head rested to one side on his shoulder, as it often did when he was thinking. The box was now rattling and moving from side to side on his bed, a bit like a jumping bean, if you've ever seen one. "OK little guy, let's take a look at you." Jack picked up the box and curled his fingers underneath the elastic band. He slowly pulled it off the box and opened the lid.

Inside were three small... things. What were they? They were about three inches long with a shiny scaly back, and they were a pale red colour. Jack loved bugs. He loved nothing better than pulling the legs off spiders or chopping worms in half, but these were different to bugs. They had big soppy eyes. In a strange sort of way they looked quite sweet and cuddly, not like bugs at all. He picked one up and placed it in the palm of his hand. It ran in circles for a few moments and then stared up at him, making a faint noise, a sort of 'bzzzzzz'.

"Wow!" murmured Jack. "Wicked. You're a cool little bug guy, aren't you." He poured the rest out on his bed and they seemed to settle snuggled in the duvet.

It was early morning when Emily was woken up by a faint bzzzzzz noise. She hadn't gone down in the passageways the previous night. She had just been too tired. It was early, cold and frosty and she didn't want to stick even a toe out of bed, but that noise was bugging her... bzzzzzzzz. She slipped out of bed and grabbed her dressing gown. The first thing which alarmed her when she walked out of her bedroom was that the banister rail around the top of the stairs had totally gone... just vanished. Tiger the dog followed her out of the room and started barking. "Shh," she put her finger to her lips. She found Jack in the kitchen. She immediately spotted the red creature on the draining board.

"What is that?" she asked in surprise.

"He's a cute little thing, E." Tiger obviously didn't think so, he was snarling.

"What happened to the banisters?"

"I think they were hungry, E."

"They! You mean there's more than one!" As if on cue there was a bzzzzzzzzzzzz, and the nicely varnished antique pine kitchen work surface vanished in a shower of splinters and dust. Emily jumped back in surprise. A second, rather fat, creature appeared on the draining board, long splinters of wood still sticking out of its jaws.

"You little vandal!" Emily chided. And with that she grabbed a tea towel and swept both the little bugs into the sink. She quickly turned the taps on.

"Careful E, you'll hurt them," Jack complained.

"Hurt them? They're destroying the house you stupid boy. I'll do more than hurt them. Drown the little..." But as they both watched something very strange happened. The pale red creatures had now turned a very bright red, and they were now racing incredibly fast round the sink. But they didn't seem to be struggling.

"Don't think they like that, E."

"No," Emily replied. She was getting worried now. "Do they look angry to you, Jack?" Jack nodded.

Bzzzzzzzzzzz. Chingggg. There was the strange sound of breaking china as the sink vanished. The red things were even bigger, brighter and their jaws were munching. Emily was convinced she saw one licking its lips. They paused for a few seconds and then scampered off on lots of tiny little legs.

"Oh nuts!" said Em. "What are we gonna do?!" They both gazed round the room to see if they could spot the little insects. They couldn't, but there was now a noise coming from the hallway. They both rushed out.

Bzzzzzzzzzzz. The front door disappeared in a cloud of dust and splinters. Bzzzzzzzzzzz. There was a red streak across the ceiling swiftly followed by a cracking sound. Em grabbed Jack's hand and just dived out of the hall in time, before the ceiling caved in. There was a huge cloud of dust. Emily stared up at the ceiling. It was gone. All that remained were rough wooden beams. "Oh nuts," she groaned. "Jack, this is terrible!"

Jack was straining his neck to look at the damage. His eyes were wide in wonder. "Wow. Cool little guys, aren't they. They move really fast, E."

"Yeah, I know," she replied, a note of worry in her voice. The house was now silent. Emily had an idea. She switched on Dad's computer, and clicked on the encyclopaedia. She selected search... animals... Type? Insect. Red, three inches, scales. Legs or slithers?... She selected legs. The computer whirred for a few seconds and then up came the picture. That was the little blighter. *The Costa Rican Red Snapper'* it announced. *'Found deep in the South American rain forest'*. She read snippets of information. A pest, which eats up the forest. "Yep, I believe that!" she muttered. Sleeps when dark and dry. Aggregated by water. "Nuts!... that explains it. Right!" she said in a newly determined voice. She handed Jack a pair of scissors. "Go get a shoe box from Mum and Dad's wardrobe, cut a hole in the side. We're gonna make a trap for them." Bzzzzzzzzzzz. Red streaks shot up mum's favourite curtains. Emily stared. All that was left were thin strips of frayed looking material. Emily bit her lip. This was getting totally out of control.

Dad didn't want to get up. It was a Tuesday. He hated Tuesdays. Tuesdays were depressing. The previous weekend was gone and forgotten by Tuesday, and the next weekend just felt like it was years away. And he was desperate for a good Saturday to take the boat out again... The Blue Pirate Eater... it was a very posh boat. He snuggled under the covers. His thoughts wandered dreamily, as they do when you're half asleep. Why couldn't it just be a Friday? Maybe if he wished hard enough... he screwed up his eyes and wished... Nope, it was still Tuesday. He hated the office as well. Having to trudge in every day and work for Mr Bodington. Bod, as everyone called him, was large and round. He always seemed to be angry, always wanted everything done yesterday and he shouted a lot. Let's face it, thought Dad, I'm not even any good at my job really. Maybe I should skive off and go sailing instead. The thought made him smile. Then he remembered, today was the big meeting. He was suddenly nervous. The big meeting... it could mean promotion, a better job, a holiday. It was just then that he heard a faint but distinct bzzzzzzzzzzz, and then the ceiling collapsed on his head. It was to be the beginning of a very bad day.

When Dad sat up the thing which struck him first (apart from the ceiling that is) was why half the dressing table seemed to have vanished. Then he spotted the wardrobe. He was suddenly stunned. All his clothes were in shreds. In front of the wardrobe stood Jack holding a shoebox and a pair of scissors. "Er, Jack. What..." but Jack wasn't going to hang around and explain. He tossed the scissors and ran. Dad removed a rather large piece of ceiling from the bed, shook the brick dust out of his hair, and then wandered onto the landing, stunned at the absence of the banisters. He banged his head on the wall just to check he was definitely awake... it hurt... yes, this was really happening.

It was only a few moments later when the doorbell rang. Dad

would have opened it if there had been a door there. Emily hovered in the hall behind him. Jack was still trying to catch the last of the red snappers. He had the other two caught in the shoebox. Emily immediately recognised the uniform at the door. It was PC Dweeble, standing there, examining what was left of the half eaten doorframe. Her heart stopped, and panic began to fill her stomach. She remembered when Dweeble had visited her class at school. But now he was here. She must have been discovered! They had traced the Underground Gang back to her. She was going to be arrested and put in prison. This was it… the moment she had most dreaded… all her adventures were coming to a horrible, terrible end. She bit her lip and waited. Dweeble seemed to stand there for an age, keeping her in suspense before he slowly opened his mouth.

"Woodworm," Dad cut him off in an irritated sort of voice, before he could ask any stupid questions about the door.

Dweeble raised his eyebrows. "Good evening sir. I wanted to talk to you about your sheep."

That took Dad by surprise. He blinked. "Sorry, my sheep?" he asked, confused.

"Yes sir, that is your sheep in the garden there, I take it."

"Yes," said Dad. Then he reconsidered. "Er, well, actually… not mine exactly."

"No indeed sir, it isn't. We've had reports of a stolen sheep from Evergreen farm."

"Stolen!" Dad raged, now getting rather angry. "I haven't stolen it! I haven't been able to get rid of the stupid thing, however hard I try!"

"And how did you come by it in the first place sir, if you don't mind me asking?" continued Dweeble. Mum was now hovering nervously in the hall as well.

"I found it."

"Found it, sir?" repeated a disbelieving Dweeble. "You just happened to find a sheep… where exactly?"

"Well, in my garden of course," replied Dad, getting more and more agitated. He was waving his arms around now, which was a bad sign. "I wouldn't exactly have dragged it here, would I? Now if you don't mind, I have a few... er... domestic problems to see to!"

"I see sir," Dweeble continued undeterred. "This sheep was stolen from Evergreen farm in Levington. You claim it just happened to walk the five or six miles and settle in your garden here. Is that right sir?"

"YES! YES!" repeated Dad confidently. "Didn't you hear me the first time? Are you deaf as well as STUPID?!" Mum and Em froze as they heard Dad shouting the word "stupid". Calling policemen stupid was not a wise thing to do.

"Erm... Dad," whispered Emily.

But Dad didn't care. After all, what did he have to fear? That was exactly what had happened. The sheep had just appeared in his garden.

Dweeble bristled slightly, and continued. "And that nice yellow sports car. Is that yours, sir?"

"Well, not exactly," said Dad, his confidence beginning to wane slightly.

"That just fell out of the sky too, did it, sir?"

"Are you calling me a liar, constable?" Dad shouted, now waving his finger menacingly at Dweeble.

"Not at all, sir," Dweeble smiled. "If you can just show me the registration documents for the car that will be fine."

"Er... well..." Dad paused.

"You do have registration documents? You know sir the little green form that says you own the car." Dweeble smiled, a gleam in his eye. Dad was silent now.

"And dare I ask about the boat... yours?"

"Well..."

"Let me guess," Dweeble cut him off. He raised one eyebrow questioningly. "Not exactly?" Dad smiled weakly. "And you don't have a licence for the boat either, I assume? It just appeared in your garden as well?" Dweeble raised both eyebrows almost tempting Dad to say yes. There was a long pause. Dad nodded.

"Well, pretty amazing garden that," said Dweeble as he pulled the radio from his shirt pocket and held it close to his mouth. "Dave, yep that's right. Can you send a car round. We've got a right nutter here. Thanks Dave."

Dad was about to protest when the telephone rang. Mum picked it up. "It's Bod," she hissed. Oh no, thought Dad, his boss. That's all he needed.

He took the receiver. Emily listened... she could only hear her dad's side of the conversation. "Hello Bod... I mean Mr Bodington, sir... no sir... meeting? Yes sir, YES! I know it's important... of course, yes..." There was a long pause. "No I can't... er, why?... well, it's a rather long story... house falling down... police... arrested sir... what! Fired?... but you can't." He slowly replaced the receiver to its place on the wall. The wall tottered dangerously, paused and then collapsed with a large puff of white brick dust. Dad hardly noticed.

"They fired me," he said quietly to Mum, in total bewilderment. "I've lost my job." Emily smiled weakly. There was a long awkward silence. Emily thought her dad looked very small and sad and serious, as if he was going to cry... suddenly she felt really sad for him. She ran over and gave him a hug.

Dad wandered out to the police car with PC Dweeble. He knelt down to pick up a small piece of front door on the path. It struck him as silly as he did it. His whole house was collapsing, what did one piece of wood matter. For some reason he wanted his front path to be clear. He didn't know why... but then he didn't understand anything anymore. As he knelt on one knee a glint caught his eye. It was the glass of a watch. He picked the watch up, turned it over in his hand and put it in his pocket. Emily was pleased to note that Tiger bit Dweeble's ankle as he left. Mum gave Dad a reassuring smile and they all waved as Dweeble drove him off in the police car.

"Right!" said Mum, "I'm not even going to ask what you two have been up to." She looked at Emily and Jack sternly. "We've got a lot of work to do. You two are going to help me. I think we may need a new front door, to start with!"

Chapter 16
The Battle...

Emily sat in the cell with her dad. It was later that day and she had come to visit him. It was an awkward moment's silence. They were both feeling miserable, but trying not to show it. The prison cell was quite dark, lit by one small light bulb hanging from a wire. It didn't even have a light shade. The walls were bare white brick. There were no windows, just a bench, which also doubled up as the bed... a rather uncomfortable one by the look of it.

"Don't worry, Em," Dad said with a false smile. "They're just keeping me here over night and then they'll release me in the morning." He was sitting, fiddling with the light cord. It came off in his hand. He frowned and tossed it on the floor.

There were so many things Emily desperately wanted to ask him and tell him... she remembered seeing him as a school kid... she wanted to know if he had ever visited the passageways... she wanted desperately to tell him everything... all the mess she had got herself into. And she wanted him to be the dad she had seen in the cap and shorts on Twickenham green, the slightly silly, not good at much dad who would understand how much she had done wrong and forgive her, not the tough dad who would tell her off. But she was a child and he was an adult. Somehow there was a gulf between them. There was a huge chasm she couldn't cross. She wasn't allowed to tell any adult about the passageways. It was the golden rule. But Miss Robinson knew. Somehow her dad was different. She didn't know how to broach the subject. There was an uncomfortable silence.

"Dad, what sort of things did you do as a kid?"

Dad looked up at the ceiling as if pondering. There was even the glint of a smile on his face, as if momentarily distracted from his current problems. "Normal kids stuff I suppose."

"Did you ever... er... collect..." She paused, not able to bring herself to say the words... "toilet roll holders?"

"Toilet roll holders?" Dad looked at her in surprise. "Criky, that was a long time ago. How did you ever know about that?"

"Toilet roll holders?" Emily said in a scathing voice, raising her eyebrows and crinkling her forehead as if to say... Why?

"Yes," Dad mused, "don't really know why. I think I just liked doing things which surprised people once in a while. I do have a confession to make though, Em." Emily looked up expectantly. Maybe he did remember... maybe he would tell her about all his adventures in the passageways.

"Yes... my school report. I never did show you it, did I? It wasn't quite as good as I let on. It was pretty bad actually." Emily smiled. "Your report was very good, Em," he continued. "Not that bad at all. I'm proud of you... really, I am, Em."

She had to tell him. This was all so unfair on him. He was the one who had suffered from all her adventures. He'd been arrested because of the sheep and the boat and car, all of which were because of her passageway adventures. She had to tell him everything. That would be the right thing to do, wouldn't it? She bit her lip nervously. She would have to tell him about the fireplace, and the sheep, and the boat, and all about the Red Snappers.

"I'm sorry, it's all my fault," she blurted. "You see it was so much fun when it started... we played, explored all the passageways, went all over the place, you know, from the fireplace... but then there was the ship in my bedroom, and look at the state of the house and now you've lost your job and just everything..." Her voice trailed off as she looked up at her dad.

He smiled. "Never liked my job anyway. It was a stupid job. Not as if I was any good at it." He had a dreamy far away look in his eyes. Had he heard a word she had been saying? "I'll get out of here, don't you worry. Then we can spend our time sailing together on the boat, and enjoy ourselves a bit. I can teach you how to sail her if you like?"

"I'd like that," Emily smiled. "But what are you gonna do about your job?"

"Oh I don't know. You know, Em, the more I think about it, the more excited I get about doing something totally different. You know I think I am actually pleased this happened."

Emily smiled. Maybe he'd be OK after all.

Emily sat quietly in Mum's car for the trip home, lost in her thoughts. She had never got to explain it all to her dad. It weighed down heavily on her heart. She felt guilty. And the closer they got to home the angrier she felt about it.

They drove down Ocean View Terrace, past all the nice houses, the trees and shrubs, the people out peacefully in their gardens... then their house came into view, with the boarded up front door, and collapsed bay window. If you had walked down the street now you would have thought this house was vacant and uncared for, and about to be ripped down. As Emily wandered up to the boarded up front door, there was a large sheet of paper pinned to it. The corners were blowing in the breeze. She read it carefully.

BY ORDER OF THE COURT...

This property is declared unsafe and unfit for habitation.'

There was a gap. Then it said:

'Please contact Gravisham and Co Property Agents for
further information regarding rehousing and demolition
of this property.'

Gravisham! She thought. It made her so angry.

"Huh!" said mum in disgust and ripped it down, discarding it on the front lawn.

Emily ran in the house. "I'm going to bed!" she bellowed angrily and ran up to her room. She was about to go on a hunt for Whiskers, but she didn't have to. The mouse was sitting calmly on her bed, waiting for her. "YOU RAT!" she bellowed at him. She had gone quite red in the face. "This is all your fault. Have you seen the state of my dad? He's stuck in a prison cell!"

"Unfortunate, yes my dear, but all part of the plan—"

"UNFORTUNATE!" Emily cut him off. "It's always part of your plan isn't it," she yelled at him. "I hate your plan. I don't want to know anything about it. You're a stupid mouse. I hate you!" With that she grabbed Whiskers by the tail threw him into her sideboard cupboard, reached in and pressed the red button. Whiskers landed with a hard splat on the side of the lift. The mouse turned round and spoke quickly with a note of urgency in his voice.

"Look at the picture, Emily. You must look at the picture! It's happening, now!"

"I DON'T CARE!" she screamed back as the lift disappeared from view with a low buzz, and Whiskers was gone.

Emily lay on her bed. Her face was still locked in an angry frown. She was still red with rage and frustration, and was muttering nasty things about the mouse under her breath. She turned over and lay still trying to fall asleep, but that was hopeless. There was something nagging in the back of her mind... the picture. She was determined she wasn't going to look at it. Absolutely not! That would be giving in to the stupid mouse. Nothing would persuade her to look at it... but I wonder what it would show now? NO! she scolded herself. She didn't care what it showed. The feeling still nagged in the back of her mind like someone tugging the back of her collar. She sighed, slipped back out of bed and wandered out onto the landing. She stared. There was nothing there. The hook was still in the wall and she could see an outline of dust and dirt where the picture had once hung, but now it was gone.

"Mum!" Emily called as she ran down stairs into the kitchen.

Mum looked round. "Where's Dad's picture?"

"He took it down. Said there was something wrong with it. Put it in the shed I think." Emily raced out the back door and down to the shed. She grabbed the torch sitting just inside the shed door, and flicked it on. She rummaged around the shed for a couple of minutes until she found the picture. She pulled it out from where it was standing, behind a rack of shelves, and shone the torch on it. She gasped. In the little bay now stood a whole host of pirate ships. There must have been twenty or thirty of them.

Fay was in trouble. She was wandering aimlessly and alone in the passageways. Her cheeks were red. She had been crying. It was all going wrong and it was her fault. She couldn't believe she could have been that stupid. She had let Miranda into the passageways, hadn't she? And Miranda had told Gravisham, and now there were pirates. They were in the passageways, and in the town. After all the planning and work everyone had done, she had let them in... she had let everyone down. It had been Miranda all along. Miranda had betrayed them. And Fay had just found out today. GG, the other new boy at school, Gravisham's youngest, had cornered Joseph after school. Joseph had had to run very fast to avoid a beating, and GG had let slip about Miranda. The two of them had been passing on information to the pirates for ages, and Fay felt really stupid.

But now Fay was in trouble, although she didn't care anymore. The guards had been doubled on all the safe parts of the passageways, but the pirates now controlled large sections of the underground world. There had been skirmishes and battles... and there had been casualties. Dufus had lost his tail and was still in the hospital cave. And it was all her fault. And so Fay had wandered beyond the guards, into the dangerous section of the passageways, the part controlled by the pirates. To be honest she didn't care if she got caught anymore. She was just wandering aimlessly. She heard a scurrying sound and looked up. She saw Whiskers haring round the corner. She didn't normally see him moving that fast.

"Fay, my dear, come on. We have to get you out of here, quickly."

"Why?" said Fay, smiling weakly. "What's the point?"

"Come on, pull yourself together. Let's go!" The mouse pulled urgently at her ankle.

"So, I find you here?" came a mocking voice, she recognised. She turned to see Miranda behind her. Miranda stood hands on hips and with a smirk on her face. If looks could kill, Fay's stare would have destroyed an army.

"Why did you do it?" Fay asked. She couldn't keep the hurt and disappointment out of her voice. "You were my friend."

"I was never your friend!" Miranda spat. "Poor old stupid Miranda. That's what you thought isn't it?" Fay didn't answer. "Isn't it?" Miranda pushed. "I thought so. But who's the stupid one now? Haven't you even worked it out yet?" Fay looked blank.

"You're Miranda Attenbury, aren't you?" said Whiskers. "Charles Attenbury's granddaughter." The light began to dawn in Fay's eyes. She had thought the name sounded familiar to her. "Charles Attenbury," Whiskers continued, "closest friend of the very first Gravisham, all those years ago."

Fay groaned. She had been even stupider than she had thought.

"Yes, that's right," grinned Miranda as she saw the look on Fay's face. "And we've done more than you could imagine. Who let the pirates in?... us. Who found the Red Snappers?... us. Who got Emily's dad arrested and in prison?... us. We have it all organised. The pirates are coming, and you can't stop them now." Two large figures appeared behind Fay and Whiskers. They were pirates. Miranda turned and stalked off. "Goodbye Fay. I'll leave you to my friends here."

Em held the binoculars up to her eyes and stared out over the mist of The Lake. "Eighteen so far," she said, counting the ships. She lowered the binoculars. Joseph sat in a rowing boat. He was dressed in his armour and had a glistening silver sword resting in the bow of the boat. It was the sword he had received a year ago when he had rescued the Princess Annabel and her castle in Orford... yet another of the many passageway adventures he had had. It was the sword used by the princess when she had knighted him 'Sir Joseph the Brave of Orford'. He pulled on the oars of the boat. He was going to rescue Fay and Whiskers.

"What now?" asked Em.

"You must find Jen," Joseph replied. "She has the plan." It seemed a long time ago when Joseph and Jennifer had been given responsibility for designing the plan to fight the pirates. It was a difficult task since the pirates were fighters and they were just children. But if anyone could do it Joseph and Jennifer could. But Jennifer wasn't here any more. She had gone, hadn't she? "We've sent the call out. There is nothing else we can do till Jen comes. She will know." With that Joseph started to row out. "The call," was something rather special. It was the emergency call, which could be put out on the passicoms. It was only to be used in dire emergency... but then it didn't get much more dire than this, did it? Would anyone come? She didn't know. They had never used it before. They didn't have a clue what sort of range the passicoms had. Would anyone have heard the call? Em hoped so. They watched Joseph row out into the mist. Em bit her lip thinking of the last words she had spoken to Whiskers. What a mess!

"Good luck!" shouted Izzie as Joseph grew misty. There were about twenty of them standing on the shore of The Lake. Em raised the binoculars again.

Emily's dad lay on his mat in the police cell. It was cold, there was a smell of damp and it was now very dark. He didn't like it in here. He wrapped the blanket around him. "Beep beep... beep beep... beep beep." The sound stirred him from his thoughts. He looked at his watch. Nope, it wasn't that. He reached into his pocket and pulled out the strange looking watch thing he had picked up outside the house. He had no idea what it was, but it was certainly beeping at him. He had never seen a passicom before… in fact Jack's passicom, which he had flung out of the window in frustration the night before. Dad turned it over in his fingers. "Beep beep… beep beep… beep beep" it continued. He pressed one of the buttons… nothing. He pressed the others… it continued. He tried pressing two buttons together. The digital face of the watch turned totally black and then swirled into a picture. Amazing, thought Dad, it's a watch phone thingy of some kind. Then he looked closer at the picture. "Emily!" he muttered to himself. Emily's voice began to chirp out of the little speaker as she gave out the call. The picture wasn't great and the voice wavered up and down as the signal was obviously weak, a bit like the TV when you can't get the aerial in the right place.

"Calling all passageways, calling all…" she began, but then it just turn to hissing. "…We're being attacked… We are in trouble… kidnapped… " More hissing. "…Pirates… Get here as quickly as you…" and then it was gone. Dad stared at the watch in horror. She had used words like "kidnapped… being attacked." She was in trouble.

Dad banged on the cell door as hard as he could. A few seconds later a little rectangular hole opened up and Dad could see Dweeble's eyes looking through.

"What?" asked the policeman in an annoyed tone.

"It's my daughter," Dad blurted, "She's in trouble. I have to go and help her."

"Yeah right. And you just want me to let you walk out of here do you?"

"But she is!" Dad protested.

"Pull the other one, it's got bells on," Dweeble replied. The rectangular hole shut again. "Hey, Dave, we got a right one 'ere," said Dweeble as he wandered back to the Custody Sergeant.

Right, thought Dad. I'll just have to get out of here on my own… I'll have to escape!

Back at The Lake things were beginning to happen. As Joseph

was disappearing into the mist there was a loud clanking noise behind them. Into view came Sir McDavish. He was a large broad Scotsman, dressed in the full armour of a knight, an enormous sword hanging by his side. Em recognised him immediately from the adventure they had had at Orford castle the year before. The knight ran straight out and splashed into the water of The Lake. "Sir Joseph!" he called in a broad Scottish accent. "Ya Dunna think you're goin' without me, now lad! We fought together once. And we'll do so again, me lad!" With that he climbed into the boat with Joseph, the two of them clasped hands tightly in greeting and they vanished in the mist. There was more disruption and noise from the tunnel behind them as a tall girl appeared in a flowing silver gown. She had a tiara on her head and behind her two knights and five or six hand maidens appeared. She held her chin up and her shoulders back as if she was balancing a pile of books on her head. She walked straight through the crowd of children as if she just expected them to get out of her way, which they did. "Emily, my dear!" They hugged. It was Princess Annabel. Emily was so pleased to see her. This was amazing, thought Em. All the friends she had made in the passageways through countless adventures were coming to help. "We came as soon as we received the call," the Princess continued. "Any news?"

Em didn't know what to say. "Wow! Am I glad to see you. News? Well, we're, er…"

"Right!" Annabel took over. "Are the tunnels behind us safe?"

"Er… I don't think so," Em replied uncertainly. Annabel was a princess, Em remembered. She had defended castles and won battles. Finally, someone who knew what to do.

"Lincoln, Galavan!" she called in a voice which would have frightened Emily's school teacher. The two remaining knights snapped to attention. "Search the passages and secure this section. We want no attacks from behind."

"Yes Ma'am!" and they hurried off.

Annabel turned back to Em. "Do we have a plan?"

"Well we could poison them with the food?" Izzie suggested.

"Wouldn't be difficult with your cooking!" came an anonymous voice from the crowd.

"Weee Monsieur!" came shouts from the French mice who were now pouring out of tunnels, back for the fight.

"Or we could fill in all the tunnels?" suggested Ellie. The mice frowned and shook their heads.

"No time for that," one of them squeaked.

"We could blast them with laser beams!" shouted a small lad with red hair. Everyone gave him dismissive looks.

"We need Jennifer," called a voice from the crowd. It was Theo. The little mouse ran forward. "We must have Jennifer. She's in charge of the plan. But she's not here, and anyway, she won't come. And her entrance is on the other side. In the dangerous part of the passageways." The poor little mouse looked frantic. He was rambling and pointing this way and that. Annabel bent down and picked him up on her hand.

"Thank you little mouse," she said in a voice which silenced him immediately. "We'll get her." She turned to her hand maiden. "One of you will accompany this mouse—"

"I'll go!" came a voice from the tunnel entrance. "I'm faster than anyone."

"Harrychoc!" Em shouted. It was Harriet. Things were improving by the minute. Harriet, who had found her legs in these passageways and now she couldn't just walk, she could run faster than anyone… in fact she ran in the Olympic Games! But the special thing about Harry was her determination. It was something Em thought she had learned from not being able to walk. Even when she couldn't walk she had been determined to enjoy life. She picked up Theo, flicked back her long red hair, spun round and sprinted back down the tunnel. As she left there was even more noise from the tunnel and out ran seven lads. You could tell they were brothers. They all had the same, unkempt blonde spiky hair, and they wore kilts. It was McG and his brothers from Edinburgh. Then, to Em's surprise, the divers in wetsuits rose up out of the water, a troop of soldiers marched in from the tunnel, closely followed by an astronaut in a space suit. Em's jaw dropped. Who were all these people?

"Charlie!" shouted a boy from the crowd to the astronaut. That had obviously been one of his adventures. The commander of the troop of soldiers looked around lost for a minute, desperately trying to identify someone in authority and then his eyes locked onto the princess and he marched up to her. "At your service, ma'am!" he saluted. Annabel didn't miss a beat.

"Thank you General. Please deploy your men here, here and here..."

Well, thought Em glancing down at her passicom... the call... it had worked a treat. Then the kangaroos arrived.

Harriet ran as fast as her legs would carry her, following Theo's directions. "Look out!" screamed Theo, as she sped round one corner and straight into two pirates. Harriet's feet didn't even slacken their pace. She dodges straight under their grip and was gone like the wind.

Jennifer was sitting at her desk struggling with her maths. She had another test tomorrow and was determined to get top marks. Of all the passageway children she was the most organised. But being organised had its problems. She had realised that she did not have the time to do well at school and to be part of the passageway world. And she knew what was most important. Most of her friends didn't see it. They would struggle on with both. But Jennifer knew she was right, and she had made her choice. But her heart ached! She had to admit that she missed it. She missed the adventures and her friends. She sighed, and looked again at her maths revision. It was then that her wardrobe door burst open and Harriet and Theo fell into the room.

"What on earth..."

Harriet was breathless. Theo went back into ranting mode. "The plan! The plan! Pirates... they're here... now... Lake!"

"What?" replied Jennifer, screwing up her face in confusion.

Harriet straightened up. "The pirates are here. Everyone's down there. They need you."

Jennifer was in two minds for a minute. "No," she said calmly. "I've made my decision. I'm not coming."

But Harriet didn't have time for this. She picked up Jennifer's maths book and flung it out the window. "Hey!" Jennifer shouted.

Then Harriet pushed her into the wardrobe. The bottom gave way and they were all sliding down the ramp into the passageways.

Emily's dad wasn't hungry. He used his spoon to scrape the paint off the brickwork at the bottom of his prison wall. He then poured his drink onto the plaster to loosen it up. Another half an hour of scraping and the first brick slid out of the wall. YES! thought Dad. This was quite exciting. He had never been an escaped convict before. Four more bricks and he was able to slide through the small hole he had created. Now what? There, sitting in front of him, was a car park full of police cars... well he had to travel back into town somehow, didn't he? He kept his head low as he walked up to the car, opened the door and climbed in. Keys were in the ignition. He fired it up and drove it out into the road. Now he could rescue Emily. And he had always fancied driving with the sirens on. He found the switch, flicked it and shot down the road as all the other cars moved out of the way. Oh, this was really cool!

This night was getting stranger by the minute. But it was going to get stranger still, and it would be a very long night indeed!

Chapter 17

Jennifer's Plan...

Ten minutes later it was all go at The Lake! Jennifer had taken charge. They had been divided into ten battalions, each including children, mice and troops.

"Theo... Upscaler!" she shouted. Everyone watched in utter amazement as Theo produced a small rusty metal device from his pocket. It was long and thin, tapering at one end. It was no bigger than a hand, but it looked very old. Theo pointed it at the first three inch toy boat as Jennifer placed it in the water. It made a clicking noise like a toy gun and the three inch boat began to grow. Jennifer had no time to wait.

"The next one. Come on Theo!" They were now growing to full size ocean going ships. The General shouted orders as his troops kitted out the ships with guns and cannons. Now they had their own fleet to fight the pirates. Harriet, Annabel, McG, Ellie, Izzie and Jemima all captained ships, as they sailed out from the beach. Em was on board Jemima's ship, from where she would coordinate the attack. As she looked back from the deck of her ship the beach was growing misty and she could see Harriet standing on the bow of the ship behind, eager to get going. The pirate ships would be in range in a few minutes and the battle would begin. Amy, Jack and Ollie were going to do most of the damage with their secret weapons. But they weren't expecting to win by fighting. They had other plans. The ships were just decoys.

Jennifer remained on the beach. She watched the ships go, and watched as Ollie and Jack climbed into the aeroplane, perched by the side of the pier. Ollie pulled on his goggles and started it up, and the plane began to trundle along the long strip of beach. Then she turned to set about her secret task, which would be the key to success or failure. She suddenly felt very alone and nervous.

Miss Robinson was having a relaxing evening with Uncle Oscar. She reclined in the smart leather armchair. Oscar Gravisham poured her a glass of wine. It was the Chablis 67, a very nice taste. She liked Uncle Oscar, but there was still a niggle in the back of her mind. Joseph and Emily had told her such wild stories, you just wouldn't believe. In fact, all of the children seemed to think that her Uncle Oscar knew more about the passageways than he was letting on. She pushed the thought aside. What nonsense! It just couldn't be.

"So how are the class this year, Lily?" Gravisham asked.

Miss Robinson took a deep breath. What could she say? This year had been extraordinary. She had changed, she realised for the first time. She hadn't even worried about her yellow sports car, which she had never got back. No there seemed more important things now, than cars and trinkets. She had thought for so many years that she knew and understood the children she taught, but now for the first time she was actually spending time with them in their world... the passageways, and seeing their successes and problems and dreams... she was enjoying them rather than just teaching them. It was refreshing she thought.

Gravisham saw the glassy, dreamy look in her eyes. "Lily?"

Miss Robinson came to. She didn't like being called Lily. She was Lil... just Lil, or Miss Robinson to the children in class... or Miss R, as she had become known in the passageways. She smiled. He was the only one able to get away with Lily. "They're fine," she smiled.

"You have some troublesome ones this year. That Emily girl for one. She is a bit of a trouble maker. And Ellie and that Isobelle."

Miss Robinson had a sudden sinking feeling. "Why's that? How do you know them?"

Gravisham put his finger in the air in a kind of, 'I know more than you think', gesture. "Uncle Oscar knows them, believe you me." It was then that the phone rang, and Gravisham left Miss Robinson to her thoughts. She was suddenly uncertain of her ground. This house, which had always been a friendly place through her teacher training days, suddenly seemed less friendly. It couldn't be... could it? He couldn't really be plotting against them?

"Gravisham!" he answered the phone. "Yep... uh-huh...OK. You captured them. Good. GG OK? Good. You captured the mouse too. Excellent! You know what to do." He dropped the phone into the cradle. He turned to Miss Robinson. "Another glass of wine?"

Miss R had heard enough. She now realised how wrong she had been. She put all the nice feelings she had had for Gravisham behind her. An icy coldness came over her. Her eyes narrowed. This was now war.

"So who was that, Uncle?"

"Oh, not important," he dismissed the question with a gesture.

Miss R changed her tone. "Oscar, can I trust you with something very important?"

Gravisham turned to her. "Of course, my dear. What is it?"

Miss R reached into her bag, fiddled for a moment and then extracted the passicom. She passed it to Gravisham, who tossed it over in his hand.

"It's a watch," he shrugged. "So what?"

"I don't know how much you know about young Emily in my class, but that is hers and it's more than a watch. I'm not sure what I should do about it." She watched carefully for his reaction. Gravisham seemed undecided. Maybe he was trying to decide whether to let her in on his secrets. "I just wondered if you could help," she pushed with the sweetest smile she could conjure up for Uncle Oscar.

"My dear, I do know what this is," he said tossing the passicom on the sofa. "Little Emily is mixed up in things far too big for her. I am afraid for her safety." There was a chilling note in his voice. He crossed to the window and stared out for a moment, sipping his drink. "Lily, I'm going to tell you a story you just wouldn't believe. It all started a very long time ago, with a strange but distinguished gentleman called Mr Bruthersharken. Believe it or not, he was a pirate…"

Fay and Whiskers sat in their cell. The metal bars in front of them were rusty from all the sea air. They were in a small dark room, separated from any thought of escape by the rusty metal bars. The floor swayed. They must be on board one of the ships. Fay rubbed her ankle. It was sore from the iron shackle around it. At least the pirates had left them alone for a few minutes.

"Sorry," Fay whispered. "What's going to happen to us?"

"Oh, don't blame yourself, Fay, my dear. If anyone is to blame it's me. I should have put a stop to this months ago, or closed the passageways down, like old Spondic said. Maybe he was right all along. But I just couldn't bring myself to do it, you see."

Fay smiled at the little mouse. He looked just as despondent as she felt. They went quiet for a while. She couldn't think of anything else to say.

"But always remember, Fay, that hardships sometimes make us stronger. And friendship is a very powerful thing."

Fay wrinkled up her nose. What was that supposed to mean? What could her friends do about it now?

Em screwed up her face as the first pirate ship appeared mysteriously through the mist. Panic and fear swept through her like a cold chill on a snowy winter's day. There was a CABOOM, a flash of fire as a canon shot from the enemy ship. Em felt sick with dread. The two seconds till the shot hit seemed to last a lifetime. Em had a sudden urge to jump overboard. Then she remembered. The Roman chariot race... the racers had been brave and courageous, and relied on their skill and instinct... all the things they had learnt, as they raced within inches of their life. Well she had learnt and trained through all her adventures in the passageways, and it all seemed like training for this moment. They had a plan, and her part was here. She had to be brave and see it through. Then the canon fire hit.

Jack sat riveted to the seat in the tiny one prop aeroplane. His eyes were wide and the wind blew hard against his face making them sting. This was just so wicked, he thought. Ollie, or Biggles as he liked to be called, sat in front wearing his lucky scarf. He banked to the left and Jack could see the battle below him. Three pirate ships were positioned side on to Ellie's ship, and they were battering it with cannons. It wouldn't last long at that rate. The little plane shot over the scene, banked right and his view changed. He could make out Princess Anna... whatever her name was standing at the helm of her ship below. The ship was going full pelt towards the side of another pirate ship. It was going to ram it. There was a loud crack as the boats met. He saw the Princess fall back as the ship sawed through the other ship as if it was butter. The pirate ship broke up and faded below the surface as it sank, shedding pirates into the water. Jack was pulled back round by Ollie's shout.

"OK! Here we go. Be ready and don't miss."

Jack scrambled with the yellow box under his arm. He pulled the lid off and felt the plane dive sharply, as Biggles overflew the ship. Jack picked up one of the Red Snappers and lent out. They were very low, just feet above the deck. Jack flung the thing down. It hit the deck... "bullseye!" The plane pulled up and round to the right. Jack twisted and strained to see. There was a distinct bzzzzzzzzzzz, from the ship below as they flew back over, followed by a loud GULP,

GULP as water seeped into the holes made by the Red Snappers.

"YIPPIE!" shouted Jack. "Next one, Biggles!" Ollie gave a thumbs up and the plane pulled sharp left. Biggles lined up his next target. They overflew low, rolled neatly to avoid a cannon shot, and dropped the next Red Snapper. Bzzzzzzzzzz... GULP, GULP. Jack smiled.

Ollie pulled up and Jack's hands fumbled with the last Red Snapper. "NO! Come back!" he shouted.

Ollie looked around. "What's up?"

"Dropped it!"

"What! Find it quick!" Jack crawled down under the seat. Where was the little blighter? But it was too late. Bzzzzzzzzzzzz. Oh no! Bzzzzzzzzzzzz.

Jack looked up out to the cockpit. The tail fin was gone and there was now a rather large hole in the left side of the plane. Bzzzzzzzzzzz.

"Oh pig snot!" shouted Ollie in frustration, now struggling with the controls. For some reason the plane didn't want to go where he was steering it. "So much for my lucky scarf. Hold on tight!" Jack glanced down at the left wing. It wasn't there. It took his brain a few moments to register the fact. This definitely wasn't good. The plane started spiralling downwards.

There it was! Jack spotted the horrible little thing. He stamped hard, and again. "Gotcha!"... well maybe. It was hard to tell. Jack was getting dizzy as the plane span round and round. In fact he felt sick. But he didn't have long to think about that. Bzzzzzzzzzzz. Suddenly something gave way below his seat. He grabbed for the arm rest... it came off in his hand. He gulped. This definitely wasn't a good sign.

Ollie was in trouble. Even the great Biggles himself couldn't have flown a plane in this state. His eyes narrowed and he pulled back as hard as he could on the stick. It was no good. The whole world seemed to be spinning before his eyes. He couldn't tell which direction he was pulling the plane. He heard a large clunk and a yell from behind. He swivelled round to look. Jack was gone. There was just a rather large hole there now. He turned back round to see the deck of the ship just before he hit it. Oh no! This was gonna hurt!

Joseph and MacDavish rowed quietly up to the left side of the pirate ship, where a loose rope hung down from the ship's anchor. They had approached unnoticed due to the mist, which still covered the Lake. They could hear the gentle sound of water lapping up against the hull, and in the distance the sound of fighting, yells, and splintering wood, the explosions of cannons. It seemed distant from where they sat. They had picked up a rather wet and bedraggled Amy on the way. Her ship had collided with another one in the mist. The three of them looked at each other. They had been creating a plan on the way across but now they sat quietly, none of them really wanting to board the ship and face the dangers.

"Right!" whispered McDavish. "Let's go." McDavish raised himself silently up the rope, which was some feat given the noisy and heavy armour he was wearing. As he reached the top he jumped over the rail and Joseph could hear the yell of the broad Scottish accent and the clink of metal swords meeting. Joseph and Amy waited for a couple of moments to let the diversion get underway. Then Joseph nodded.

Splat! went the hole on the wooden side of the hull. A black hole appeared and grew wide. Joseph climbed through and Amy followed, peeling the hole off the inside of the boat behind her. "Good boy, Rover," she whispered giving him a pat.

They were in the cargo hold. It was dark, and they were surrounded by crates and barrels, large chunks of salted meat hanging on hooks and chests overflowing with bright yellow gold. They could see a chink of light from the hatch above them, and they could hear the pirates shouting up on the deck.

"McDavish said the brig… that's where they keep the prisoners… will be at the back of the ship," Joseph whispered. "Come on." They were just making their way to the back of the cargo hold when there was a loud thunk! as a pirate dropped the ten feet down from the hatch, and landed right in front of them.

"Eye-eye! So what have we here then?" he said with a grin, drawing a dagger from his belt. He was at least four times as wide as Joseph and three times the height. He was huge. He had a bushy black beard in which Joseph could see bits of food. And he smelt. He obviously hadn't washed for a week, but that didn't worry them too much just at that moment. Joseph gulped and drew his sword with a loud ching. The grin faded from the pirates face to be replaced by a growl.

"This is stupid!" shouted Amy. "Look how big he is!"

"You got any better ideas?"

Amy pulled the black squidgy ball of stuff out of her pocket, pulled back her arm and threw it at the pirate. The hole hit him right in the midriff. The pirate was totally astounded. He glanced down and couldn't believe his eyes. There was a hole, right where his stomach used to be. His legs now looked as if they went right up to his shoulders.

"Run!" shouted Amy and with that she ran straight through the middle of the pirate, who gave a shiver. Joseph didn't wait to be told twice. Amy gave a loud whistle and Rover the hole obediently jumped off the pirate and raced after them.

"Ahhg!" moaned the pirate dropping his dagger and feeling his stomach and legs carefully to make sure he was all there.

Splat! They were through the end of the cargo hold and into the brig. Suddenly they stopped dead. Joseph glanced over his shoulder to see if they could go back… more pirates were coming. Amy quickly peeled Rover off the wall. But now they were trapped. They were in a small room, not much larger than your bedroom probably. The walls were all dark wood. There was an old wooden desk on their right, strewn with maps and charts, and ahead of them was a prison cell with thick rusty metal bars. Inside the cell, separated from them by the rusty metal bars were Fay and Whiskers. What caught Joseph's eye immediately was a tall man standing over a fire of red hot coals. He was holding a long curved blade, which was glowing orange as he held it close over the flames. The sight stopped Joseph cold. He knew exactly what the man was doing. He recalled what Whiskers had told them… "yes they do cut off hands and feet and tails of those they capture." What Joseph hadn't noticed were the other two people there, until they stepped out of the shadow. It was Miranda and GG, obviously there to watch the spectacle.

"Splendid," said Miranda with a sly grin on her face. "More

hands and feet to chop." George Gravisham laughed.

The pirate moved very fast. He waited for Joseph and Amy's eyes to glance away to the prisoners, then he covered the distance in three strides. Amy dived for the floor. The blade struck Joseph on the left arm and he screamed and fell. His armour saved his arm. But the metal armour had buckled under the strength of the attack, and his arm hurt like he had just been hit by a truck.

The pirate towered over Joseph, raising the curved orange blade above his head. They heard a muffled cry from Fay, wide eyed in the cell. Joseph curled into a ball, waiting for the blade to strike.

But the pirate had made his first mistake. He had taken his eyes off little Amy. Splat! The hole landed right between his feet. Joseph was convinced he could hear a giggle coming from the hole as it very slowly widened and grew bigger. The look of surprise on the pirates face turned into a look of pain as his feet moved further and further apart, until, with a loud scream, he fell. Rover gave a loud burp, shot back over to Amy and circled her feet like a restless puppy. Joseph climbed to his feet, stunned and shaken. He raised his eyes towards Miranda and GG, who were now standing gawking in the corner. GG suddenly lunged. Joseph was relishing this moment. He had been waiting for this sort of opportunity for so long. The well oiled sword left its sheath with a sharp ching. He swiped the blade round in an arc, and the flat of the blade connected with GG's left ear with a crack. GG hit the ground with a thud.

"Yes!" screamed Joseph in triumph.

Suddenly there was a distant CABOOM, followed by the high pitch whizzing sound which followed it. They all stood motionless and waited. The whizzing got ominously louder and then the room rocked like the world was about to end. There was the sound of splintering wood and screams from on deck above them, as the cannon hit and crunched through the wood. The side of the room caved in behind Miranda and small jets of water started to shoot through the splintering wood, like a garden sprinkler. "She's gonna blow!" shouted Fay. "Get us out of here!" She rattled the rusty bars of the cell.

Whiskers jumped onto his little feet.

"Key's," he called, "find the keys."

Joseph started searching around the desk for keys. None. "They must have been with the pirate."

"Use the hole!" shouted Fay, urgently. Amy wrapped it around the bars of the cell, and stepped inside. "We need to get these off too!" Fay barked, shaking the shackles on her leg. Amy pulled a little piece of black squidgy stuff from the lump and spread it over the shackle. It dropped off. She did the same for Whiskers. They were free.

The floor rocked again. Miranda was frozen to her spot in the corner, her eyes glazed over in terror. Water was now gushing through the wall and the room was filling up. Above them they heard an ear piercing crash and something heavy fell across the hatch, cutting out the light and cutting off their escape. The room went black, Amy screamed and the room seemed to descend into chaos.

Fay could feel the water rising up to her waist. Whiskers was standing on her shoulder. Joseph dropped his sword with a clank. That was no use to him now. His eyes squinted around the room, desperately searching for some light or way out… something, there must be something.

SPLAT!

"Through here!" squeaked Amy. Joseph could hardly hear her above the noise of creaking floorboards, splintering wood and crunching bones. He was going to ask where the hole led, but what was the point. They just had to get out of here.

"Pick up the boy!" Whiskers called. "Quick now. We have few seconds left." Joseph dragged GG, still unconscious, over to Amy, barely discernable in the dark, and he climbed through the hole, dragging GG behind him.

"Miranda!" called Fay. There was no response. "Miranda! Come on."

"No, I can't move," came a soft scared voice. Fay was now swimming. She reached out her hand. "Miranda, where are you?"

"Come on, Fay my dear! We must go," called a worried Whiskers, through a mouthful of water. He leapt from Fay's shoulder, grabbed Amy's sleeve and the two of them fell into the hole. Fay was still reaching out when, with one final creak, the upper deck gave way above her.

Miss R rushed from the house. Gravisham had told her the long tale. Unbelievable, the depths people would stoop to! But she smiled to herself. She was wickedly clever, even if she said so herself. She reached into her bag and took out the small tape recorder she always carried around. She used it to record ideas for lessons at school. But this time it had recorded Gravisham's whole sorry tale. And that would be finding its way to the police. There was enough there to put him in prison for good. She also took out the little rectangular piece of paper. It was a bank cheque paying a very large amount of money to Gravisham. The pirates were paying a lot to Gravisham for his help. But he had made the mistake of showing it off to her. And she had stolen it. With great satisfaction she tore it slowly in half. The sound of ripping paper echoed up the street. She smiled.

Her high heels made a clipping noise on the pavement as she walked in the quiet darkness of late evening. But she knew that far below her, the children... her friends she realised... were fighting for their lives. She had a very long night ahead of her. What was it Gravisham had said... "the pirates couldn't lose. There were too many of them."

Well, they would see about that, wouldn't they.

Meanwhile Jennifer was on her special mission. So far it was going well. They had put out the call and upscaled the ships. The attack had been launched. She and Joseph had planned it all out months before. Her organised, logical brain had seen it all happening in her minds eye... and now it was! But this bit was the key to her plan. No-one would ever have guessed it. She was panting and breathless when she reached her destination. It had been a good ten minute run. She opened the secret entrance and climbed through onto the dark cold factory floor. Apart from a small shadow of moonlight which shone through the windows high up in the ceiling, the room was black. It was the chocolate factory. The huge machines lay quiet on the vast floor like sleeping monsters on the plain of Africa. She found the panel of light switches and flicked them on. The tube lights blinked on one by one and a quiet buzzing sound filled the factory. In the middle of the panel lay a large red push button. Above it the notice read:

'Production line START/STOP - Only to be operated by supervised personnel.'

That was the button she needed.

The passicom beeped on her wrist. The beeping echoed around the room. Theo's face sparkled on the tiny passicom screen. He gave a thumbs up. "All done!" The picture flicked off again and she was alone. Theo and Benji had been rerouting the chocolate factory pipes. They had linked the output pipes through to the sewers and from there down into The Lake tunnel. Theo also had the upscaler. If they could just get this right… it was all down to her now. She had to get the machinery working. The big red button was covered with a see through plastic cover to stop anyone accidentally hitting it. But the cover was shut fast. She curled her fingernails under the edges and pulled and pulled, but it wasn't going to budge. She kicked it and then punched it with her fist.

"Ouch!" That hurt. It didn't budge and the plastic was too thick to break. She realised now that she would not be able to get to the red button. This just wasn't fair. She couldn't get this far and stop now. The room was still silent around her, apart from the buzzing from the lights, and she was all alone with no-one to ask. Suddenly the enormity of the whole situation hit her. Up to now she had just been working mechanically through her plan… but what were they doing? They were fighting pirates with weapons. Commanding boats and rescuing hostages. It overwhelmed her like a huge wave crashing onto the beach. She sank down to the floor and sat still. She couldn't do this. She was just a little girl, after all. She really wished she could just be back in her bedroom doing her homework and revision again. She sat on the floor, buried her head in her arms and cried.

Oscar Gravisham sat thoughtfully in his study. The lights were low, and classical music played softly in the background. He smiled to himself. There was nothing more he needed to do. All the pieces were in place. It was like a gigantic game of chess. And he was the master chess player. He couldn't lose now could he? He rose and walked over to the book case. He extracted the book in which his bankers cheque sat. All that beautiful money which would be his once he had finally got rid of those disgusting children and handed the passageways over to the pirates. He flicked through. It wasn't there. Strange, he thought. He glanced at the floor to see if it had fallen out. No, it was gone…

LILY! Red hot anger boiled up in him. He threw the book with all the force he could muster. It slammed into the wall. How could he have been that stupid! "Blast it!" he shouted. Suddenly it dawned on him that maybe there was another master chess player in the game. "Right, Lily. We'll see just what you're made of." He picked up the phone and dialled a number he knew well.

The Pirate leader, Nathanial Mitra Bruthersharken III was rubbing his hands with glee. The battle was going well. Prince Bletcher was tied up and securely imprisoned below, and he, Shark, as he liked to be called, was now in full command of the platform, known as Sealand. He was keeping in contact with his ship commanders by radio, and even though Gravisham was getting cold feet, everything was going according to schedule. He looked over to some of his men making a poor job of tying off the ships and bellowed a reprimand at them. When he looked back a strange sight met his eyes.

The mice attacked from the South. Mice were only little creatures but they had the element of surprise. Blotch had led the attack. After all, he was the fastest they had. They had already cut all the ship's loose (sharp teeth you see), and McSmallenby with his band of Scottish mice, who had arrived to help, were now flooding the sea tunnel so that no more pirates would be able to reach The Lake. With no ships and no tunnels the pirates would be stranded. All they had to do now was rescue the prince, and get out. And high above their heads a red hot air balloon hovered. Cousin Alice had the rope ladder ready for them to make their escape.

"Pull yourself together girl!" Jennifer muttered to herself. She raised her head and spotted the fire extinguisher. She jumped to her feet, rushed across the room and picked it up. It was very heavy. She hefted it onto her shoulder and then, with all her might, ran over to the panel and launched the extinguisher at the button. There was a loud crack as it smashed through the plastic cover and hit the button. Then it fell to the floor with a loud metal clang, which reverberated around the room. Jennifer watched... nothing. She rechecked the panel. Yes, the big red button had been pushed in. What had she done wrong? Her eyes darted around the room in panic, but what could she do? She didn't know how any of this stuff worked. "Come on!" she pleaded.

Behind her she heard a very faint trickling sound. She darted back and climbed onto a chair to see into the machine. There was a slow trickle of chocolate. To her left she could hear a faint but distinct grinding noise and then a pumping as another machine moved into operation, large pistons moving up and down with enough force to crush a car. All around the room machinery was working up speed. The silence of a minute ago now sounded loud enough to rival a football stadium. Jennifer pressed the emergency button on her passicom.

"Everyone retreat!" she shouted. "Everyone get out of The Lake." She had given the order, and with a sense of satisfaction she would now wait and watch.

Deep below the ground the dark brown sludge dripped slowly. Then it began to drip faster and then it began to run down the tubes.

It slithered slowly through the pipes which Theo had rerouted and into the sewer. It took three minutes for the chocolate to fill the sewer pipe before it overflowed into the down pipe. This emptied down past Theo's upscaler and into the passageway tunnel. As it passed the upscaler it was magically transformed into an avalanche of thousands of gallons... a vast waterfall of chocolate. That created so much force that it exploded out of the passageway tunnels into The Lake... thousands of gallons of it, like a water canon. One unfortunate pirate ship was sitting quietly by the tunnel entrance when the chocolate fountain hit it so hard that it shot right up to the roof of The Lake where it hit the stone ceiling with the force of an elephant and shattered into a million pieces. The children's ships were already retreating as the tidal wave of chocolate spread over the Lake shattering everything in its wake.

Emily's dad was quite enjoying himself, driving his very own police car. He had already pulled up a group of teenagers and given them a telling off, for no particular reason. It was quite fun, everyone thinking you're a policeman. The police radio crackled again. It had already given out a description of him, the escaped convict. "Armed and dangerous" it had called him. "Do not approach this man." But suddenly it caught his attention again. What was that they had mentioned. He squinted trying to make out the crackling radio, which sounded like a TV not tuned in very well.

"Car forty seven. Can you do a drive past on 127 Rosary. We have to pick up a mister Oscar Gravisham and bring him in for questioning."

Gravisham… the name rang a bell. He was the idiot from that property company who kept trying to pull down his Terrace. 127 Rosary Avenue. That wasn't too far. He could have some fun here, he grinned to himself. He took a left and then a right. There was a figure walking quickly down the lonely street. He could just see the outline silhouetted in the street light. It was someone very large… Gravisham. Dad flicked on the blue lights and siren, and pulled the car up. Gravisham had stopped dead in his tracks, a look of horror on his face. Dad quickly grabbed the police cap lying on the dashboard. He didn't want Gravisham to recognise him. He climbed out of the car, and flashed his wallet at Gravisham. He did it quickly so Gravisham wouldn't see that it was really his library membership card rather than a police ID.

Gravisham was beginning to get flustered. "Officer, officer, I can explain everything." He reached into his inside jacket pocket, and Dad took the opportunity to spin him around and push him up against the side of the car.

"Right, spread 'em! Firearm in inside pocket," said Dad, putting on the most serious deep voice he could muster.

"No, no!" said Gravisham, very alarmed now. Dad pulled out the handcuffs and slapped them on Gravisham's wrists, his arms now secured behind his back. YES! It was a great feeling. He'd always wanted to be policeman when he was a kid.

"So give me one good reason why I shouldn't take you in?"

Gravisham quickly saw a possible chink of light. "I have money... I could pay you! How much? A thousand? Ten thousand?"

"So, bribing a police officer now, too?"

"Oh no, no!"

"Right Mister Gravisham. I think we're gonna throw the book at you."

"No, please officer. I'm a very well thought of businessman here. Please!"

Gravisham was now down on his knees begging. Dad grinned. This was just too good to be true. "You're a menace to the public, aren't you?"

"Yes, yes," Gravisham agreed.

"Well say it then!"

"Er... I'm a ... yes, I'm a menace to the public."

This was just amazing, thought Dad. "You're a crook!"

"Yes, yes... a terrible crook," repeated Gravisham, who would now have done anything to get himself out of trouble.

"And you're a total bafoon! Thick as a plank!"

"Definitely. I'm a bafoon. Thick as two planks." Gravisham was obviously getting into the spirit of this now.

"Right," said Dad. "I'm gonna let you off this time. But you are closing down your property business in this town and moving on. You understand me?"

"Yes sir. I will."

"Well?" asked Dad. Gravisham looked at him, not quite sure what he was supposed to say next. "Aren't you going to thank me?"

"Oh yes, yes of course. Thank you officer. You have been most kind."

Dad climbed back into the police car feeling quite satisfied, and drove off.

"Erm... what... what about the hand cuffs," called Gravisham from the pavement as the police car disappeared into the night.

At first Em thought she was asleep in bed. It felt like that Saturday morning lazy feeling. She stretched her arms and yawned. Her eyes were still tightly shut and dreamy. Her nose gave a twitch. There was a very strange smell this morning. It wasn't like the normal bakers smell from Mum's bread maker. It was a strong bitter smell... cocoa! And come to think of it, her feet felt wet. She opened her eyes.

She was lying on the beach by The Lake. Everything was very still around her. As she moved to get up a sharp pain ran through her chest. She felt winded, as if someone had just hit her very hard. She sat up slowly. The bitter smell was from the chocolate. And everything was chocolate! She couldn't believe it. A small chocolate wave lapped at her feet. She gazed out over the now chocolate Lake. It was setting solid over the centre of The Lake, and looked like squelchy mud, dried by the sun. She could see the remains of ships sticking up out of the mud. It looked like a ship's graveyard out there. She noticed a wing sticking out... that was from Ollie's plane. There was not another soul in sight. Where had they all gone? There was a soft clank at her feet. She glanced down. It was Joseph's sword. She recognised it. It had an inscription from the princess on the blade. She picked it up and placed it carefully on the beach.

Her hair and back felt uncomfortable. She was caked in dried chocolate. As she moved it cracked and crumbled. She ran down the tunnel to the party room, but that too was silent and empty. It felt as if time had come to a stand still and she was the only person left in the world. What did it all mean? Who had won the battle? Why weren't her friends here celebrating?

She wandered aimlessly back through the tunnel. There was now a solitary figure kneeling on the beach. It was Ollie. He was kneeling by the edge, drinking. He looked up, his face covered in brown gunk. His lucky scarf looked like it might need a wash. He didn't seem to care.

"Mmmm... Could you ever have imagined it, Em? A whole sea of chocolate!"

Just for a moment Em smiled. Yes, that was every kid's dream wasn't it. But she didn't feel like a kid anymore. She had grown up. Where were her friends?... Had they survived?

There was a shout behind her. She turned and Harriet almost knocked her off her feet with her hug. There was a whole crowd there... mice, children, some nursing wounds, some holding mugs of chocolate. Em had never in all her life been so pleased to see them. She pulled slowly away from Harry.

"No chocolate for you Harrychoc?" Em teased.

"No... I think I've seen enough chocolate for a lifetime," she replied.

And with that Em ran to wrap her arms around Izzie and Ellie, and from there to Theo and Bart. She even gave the Scottish boy, McG, a hug, to his embarrassment. They looked as bedraggled and tired as she did. Scott and Jemima had collapsed in a heap on the beach. Jack, she could see, had picked up a great lump of muddy looking chocolate and was using it like hair gel to see if he could spike his hair with it.

"We did it, Em," said Izzie. "We beat them."

But as Em looked around something wasn't right. "Where's Fay and Whiskers and Joseph?" There was an uncomfortable look around the crowd, shuffling of feet... no-one wanted to count the casualties. The sinking feeling hit her chest like a bullet. She closed her eyes as she remembered her harsh words to Whiskers.

But all of a sudden a black hole appeared on the beach. A hand reached up and pulled itself out of the hole. It was Joseph. He dragged the soggy limp body of George Gravisham behind him. Then he collapsed on the beach, still clutching his arm, where the blade had cut into him. Amy followed him out, Whiskers perched on her shoulder. And behind her came Fay. Em dived on them, so excited she must have almost suffocated poor Whiskers as he lay there exhausted. In fact she was so excited she totally missed the look of horror on Fay's face. The beach party started, and the celebration would go on till morning. No-one cared about school... it seemed so far away.

And as they partied Fay continued to look down into the black hole. Her eyes were blurred with tears and her mind was going over and over the scene on the ship. It would continue forever in her nightmares... She had never managed to reach Miranda's hand.

Chapter 18
The Rainbow Palace...

ONE YEAR LATER...

Emily woke up in the comfort of her own bed. Well, it was her new bed, in her new bedroom. The fireplace was gone, and the sideboard too. The room was long and thin and a little tatty. Dad still needed to do some work on it.

Her mind drifted back to the battle, as it so often did. Miranda hadn't been the only loss. When the party had ended and they had sat quietly around the fire that Bart had lit on the beach, Theo had ticked everyone off on his clipboard and then they had all tried to remember. McDavish had last been seen sinking into the chocolate in his heavy armour. No-one had seen him surface. And Princess Annabel's ship had taken a direct cannon hit and exploded in flames. The princess was feared lost. And of all the mice, Rufus... her good friend Rufus had been killed by a pirate's blade. She remembered fondly all the tricks he had played on her, and eventually she had played on him. He had been her friend.

But everything had changed since then, hadn't it. That was over a year ago now. She didn't play tricks on people anymore. It wasn't the same without Rufus. Emily pulled back the bed clothes and looked at her pink pig clock. Both ears on it were broken now, ever since she had dropped it again. It stood on the bookshelf next to the mirror and in amongst the many abandoned makeup tubes and bottles. She smiled, looking at the mirror. The message Ellie had written in red lipstick was still there. The girls had makeup parties now and discussed boys and things. Yes, they had definitely changed. Fay never went down in the passageways anymore. It had all been a bit much for her. They talked about it a lot though and laughed as they remembered... but no-one ever mentioned Miranda. It seemed like a different world they had once lived in... a distant dream. The rest of them still went down sometimes, but they had had their time. They were growing up, Emily realised, and they had other interests. Emily had even given up being the Guardian. Amy was the Guardian now. Joseph had joined air cadets and had even had a flight trial in a real aeroplane. They had said he was good. He wanted to be a pilot one day. And as for Jennifer... well, what could you say? Being organised had finally got to her. It was as if something had snapped inside her brain. Now she wasn't organised anymore... how would you describe her? Now she was wild with her orange spiky punk haircut, and she did the wildest things you could imagine. Yes, thought Emily, they had all been affected by the passageways, hadn't they. Even her dad. Above the bookshelf was the framed newspaper article. It had a grainy black and white photo of her dad with the heading '*Escaped Prisoner! Armed and Dangerous*'. It was one of those events which had now become a family legend. Every now and then when they had relatives to stay, someone would crack a joke about it and Dad would look embarrassed, but Emily thought, underneath it all, he quite enjoyed the attention and the look of awe he received from people because of it. Of course, at the time he had been in a lot of trouble, but somehow it all got sorted out.

The police cars had tuned up at old Gravisham's house and hauled him away. It was very pleasant having a Gravisham free little town. Weeds and ivy could now be seen growing over the once smart gatepost of Gravisham and co Property Agents. The council were thinking of making it into a museum.

And rumour had it that Whiskers had been to visit the Prime Minister about reforming the mice's relationship once again with the government, but he refused to answer any questioned about that.

Emily had made the mistake of lying back down, once she had switched her alarm off, and now she was almost dreaming again, but she just caught herself in time. Half past seven, she suddenly realised. It was her turn to get them all up today. She pulled on her dressing gown, and checked her hair in the mirror, before running down the very long hallway corridor. It was a strange hallway in her new home. It had stain glass windows on the right hand side. The sun shone through them in the mornings and it cast a rainbow of colours down the hall. Emily had been allowed to name the house 'The Rainbow Palace'. She knocked on each of the doors as she ran past them, pushing her head round the doorframes and making sure the boys were awake, before she ran downstairs to start on breakfast. There were ten of them in all. There was a sort of low groaning and mumbling sound, which stretched through the huge house at breakfast time. They all moped around angrily, not wanting to get up. Emily sat at her end of the long rough oak breakfast table and listened to the creaking as everyone gradually made there way down the stairs.

She sat and daydreamed. It was old Whiskers who had said it. "All part of the plan," he had said, just before Emily had shouted at him, called him a rat and thrown him into the lift. She smiled as she remembered. But he had been right, hadn't he? Dad had moped around at home for a couple of months before the letter had arrived. And what a strange letter it had been. That's what had first put the idea into his head. And who had the letter been signed by? *'The honourable HR Whiskers'*. Emily had been suspicious as soon as she had seen that name on the letter. Whiskers seemed to be able to do anything. But the letter had definitely planted an idea in Dad's head. Then one day Mum and Dad had called her and Jack into the room to explain that they were moving house. It was no surprise, since the old house was still a wreck from the Red Snappers and Dad had no job and no way to pay for it to be repaired.

"So where are we gonna live?" Emily had immediately blurted out, with a worried look on her face. So many thoughts had gone through her head in that moment... being homeless, losing her entrance to the passageways, leaving her friends, but most of all leaving her Terrace and the seaside behind. That was when Dad had shown her the letter.

It said it was from the *'Department for Children'*, and had been enquiring about the establishment of a foster care home in the area for children who had no parents, or who had difficulties of one type or another and needed to be away from their home.

"And that's what we're going to do!" Dad had announced.

"But where are we gonna go?" Emily asked. "I don't want to leave here! I'm not going!" But Dad had a wicked look in his eye.

"I'll show you," he had replied calmly. "We've found just the place. You'll love it."

Ocean View Terrace led into another road which had a very steep hill which led right down to the beach. Emily always remembered one fantastic winters day when the snow had fallen thick and they had sledged right down the hill and onto the prom. The beach had been covered with thick white snow, right up to where the sea lapped up the sand. As you walked down the steep hill, on the left was a huge house. It wasn't actually a house anymore. It was divided into six apartments, each one as big as a house. It was so big that it looked like a palace, or it would have done if it was posh enough. In fact it was more like a number of different houses stuck together in a row. At one end was a turret, like you would see on a castle and at the other end was a wooden panelled front. In front of the house was a long garden which, since it was the last house in the street, ran down a long way to a fence, which was spitting distance from the beach. The whole front of the house overlooked the sea. It was quite extraordinary. Dad walked them all down Ocean View Terrace and round the corner till they were standing in front of the huge old house. Two men were there pulling down the 'For Sale' sign.

"So we're just moving round the corner?" Emily asked.

"That's right," Dad replied. "She'll need a lot of work, of course. But you can have that room there Emily." Dad pointed up to the window. "You will be able to see the sea from there."

Emily was pulled back to reality as ten boys thundered through the kitchen door. She was on breakfast duty. Giles was the first into the kitchen, still rubbing the sleep out of his eyes. Breakfast duty for Emily didn't actually mean doing much, since the boys were all used to fending for themselves. Giles was the oldest of the ten. He went silently to the toaster. The twins ran in, rattling the doorframe as they came, followed by a sleepy Colin. They always had to keep an eye on Colin... he always got lost, just had no sense of where he was, as if he lived in another world. They all filed in, in various stages of dress, and they chattered away filling the kitchen which noise and activity. The twins were throwing cornflakes in between thumping each other. Nigel was taunting Malcolm with last night's football results, it was the usual routine.

"Mornin'," Malcolm glanced at Emily as he passed, and then resumed his conversation with Nigel. "... Face it, they're rubbish! They can't even kick a ball," he said despondently. The smell of toasting bread filled the spacious kitchen.

Emily's eyes came to rest on Bernard, sitting on his own, away from the table on a stool in the corner. Giles passed him a plate of toast without comment. All the ten boys came from different, but equally unpleasant, backgrounds, but they knew little about Bernard. He didn't speak, you see. He was little, with scared eyes and wherever he was you often didn't notice him since he was so timid he sort of blended into the background. Emily's dad said that all the children who came to stay had, as he described it, scars on the inside. She thought Bernard's must be the worst. Dad said that The Rainbow Palace was about helping them. Her thoughts were then broken by a bit of toast, thick with jam, which hit the side of her face and slid down her neck.

"Disgusting!!"

Chapter 19

Dragon Snot...

Emily woke on the stroke of midnight. Usually she would wake ready to slip out of her room and through the secret door, a large arched stain glass window at the top of the stairs. But today she was woken by the sound of someone sobbing outside her door. She slipped out of bed, grabbed her dressing gown and opened her door.

A beam of street light shone through the stain glass window, lighting up the solitary figure of Bernard with a spectrum of different colours. He sat on the top step of the stairs. It was as if God was watching him, as he cried. Did God care? It suddenly seemed an important question. The moment lingered. Emily didn't know what to say. There seemed a world between the two of them, which words couldn't bridge, especially since Bernard never spoke.

There was perhaps only one language which she had learnt could reach any child. She hadn't shown any of the foster children the passageways, but there and then she made her decision.

"Come with me," she beckoned. Bernard looked up. Emily beckoned him to follow with her hand. No other words were said. She clicked open the stain glass window and they both climbed inside.

In fact there were many passageways running through The Rainbow Palace. The kitchen connected to the study and from there a secret staircase ran up to this stain glass window on the landing. Em was convinced there was more to find too. One day she would get around to searching them out. Bernard had never spoken, but as Em showed him around the passageways and introduced him to the mice, something in him seemed to warm to this different world. Maybe this was how they were supposed to help the children, Em wondered.

Music was playing from the juke box on one side of the party room, there was now the permanent smell of chocolate which lingered, and the newbies would run in and out of the passage to The Lake just to see the legendary lake of chocolate. Stories would often be told, as the younger children sat around in awe, of how the Chocolate Lake had come to be, and the downfall of the pirates.

Tonight was a purple evening so decoration, tables, chairs and even the food was purple, and Em had to admit that purple ice cream did not look at all appetising. She found Jack in one corner with a purple choco challenge. He still held the record for eating the most choco challenge in the shortest time.

The evening progressed and Em was pleased that Bernard seemed to be enjoying himself. He was still silent, still almost hiding in a small corner, but now his big eyes didn't radiate the fear they had before. After a while Em looked across but she noticed he had left the party room.

"Come on Jack. We better find him. You never quite know how safe he'll be down here in the passageways. He's a newbie after all."

They searched the Lake, the games room and all the obvious places with no luck.

As Em rounded a final corner, in her search for Bernard, the most extraordinary sight she had ever seen in her life met her eyes. She stopped dead in her tracks. Jack ran straight into the back of her and the two of them starred, agog. They were standing at the beginning of a rather long passage, which led right across town, towards the cinema. Bernard was standing ahead of them, about fifty yards down, his back to them, watching the same sight. They couldn't see his face, but Em could imagine he was paralysed with fear. In the distance, down as far as they could see, where the shadows grew and darkness overtook the passage, something large and green was rattling towards them very fast. There was a rapid thud, thud, thud of huge feet. Into view came a huge...

"That's a..." started Jack. "It can't be..."

"It's a dragon," Em finished the thought. "That's not possible!"

The dragon moved faster than anything Em had ever seen of that size. It was a dirty dishwater greeny brown colour. It was so large that it took up most of the width of the tunnel and its neck and head were stooped low, in front of its body. It almost flew down the passage towards them. Its body crashed off the walls and roof like a pinball as it shot chaotically towards them. Every time it crashed into the walls green sparks flew, lighting up the passage, and it carved large crevices out of the rock with scales which Em thought must have been made of solid steel. Piercing red eyes shone like laser beams and seemed to bore right into her soul, casting a chill like ice in the pit of her stomach.

It was all too much to take in. Before Em's brain could process another thought the dragon suddenly looked awfully close.

"Bernard," Em murmured. Then the urgency hit her. "BERNARD!... RUN!!"

But Bernard could have been a statue. He was rooted to the spot, hypnotised by the piercing red eyes of the dragon.

"BERNARD!" Em screamed.

Jack's eyes were wide. He tugged at Em's sleeve.

"E... We gotta go, E!"

Em began to run up the tunnel towards the boy, but she already knew it was too late. The bottom jaw of the dragon dropped, a wind blew, knocking Em to the stone floor and a bright cloud of fire erupted from the dragon's mouth and engulfed the tunnel. It roared up the passage like an explosion, filling every corner and crevice. Em watched in horror as the orange yellow flames swept around Bernard like the thin yellow fingers of a gigantic hand... and he was gone.

"NO!!!"

The flames continued to race up the tunnel. Em had no time to think. She scrambled to her feet, turned back and ran, sweeping Jack up as she went. They skidded around the corner as the roar of the flames deafened their ears and the heat singed the back of their necks and clothes.

Em grabbed Jack and pulled him into a passage on their right. She was running so fast she couldn't breathe. The heat and noise was subsiding. Em stopped and looked around. It was gone. She collapsed on the floor wheezing.

"Poor Bernard," she moaned. She couldn't believe what she had just seen. She glanced at Jack. He was just standing mesmerised, his eyes were glazed over. In Em's mind's eye she could still see the flames as they closed around the sad little boy and he disappeared from sight. And it was she who had brought him down here... brought him to his death.

"The others," Em said, "we must warn the others. Come on Jack."

Em burst into the party room.

"Help! Help! A dragon... It got Bernard!"

But no-one was listening. There was far too much noise. The twins and Malcolm were on one side of the room and they seemed to be waging war with the mice on the other side of the room. Food was hurtling across the room at a startling pace, and since it was all a deep purple it almost looked like real blood stained war wounds where the food missiles hit.

"The foster kids?" Em glanced down at Jack, confused. "Oh no! I must have left the door open."

Just then the evening got even stranger (Were that possible!) Into the party room staggered a knight. He was very short and broad, wore a dirty but thick looking leather tunic, a dark black singed metal breastplate and helmet and he held a rectangular wooden shield. The shield looked like it had once had an emblem on it but it was burnt black. And the helmet may have had a colourful feather plume in the top once but now it was just a short black stick. He looked nothing like the smart knights of Princess Annabel... and it looked like he had lost his sword somewhere along the way. He staggered into the centre of the room, was hit side on by a purple slice of pizza and collapsed on the floor.

"STOP!!" bellowed Whiskers, in the most commanding voice she had ever heard from the little mouse. The room fell silent.

"Sir Cuthbert!" Whiskers exclaimed jumping down from the table and tossing away the piece of purple chocolate cake he was about to launch at the enemy. "Are you alright?"

"Oh yes, old fellow," Cuthbert replied, climbing very slowly to his feet and brushing himself down. He removed his helmet to expose a thick tangle of jet black hair covering an equally black fire singed face.

"Is it Broncs again?" asked Whiskers. The knight nodded. "Theo, Blotch!" the mouse called across the hall. "Broncs has wandered back into the tunnels. You know what to do." Theo and Blotch rushed off whilst a large group of mice led Sir Cuthbert off to a chair and some purple lemonade.

"Poor Cuthbert," Whiskers commented as he passed Em. "Been chasing the dragon for years, he has. He's on a king's errand you see, to wipe all dragons from the land, back in the year 1172 that is."

"Dragon..." muttered Em, then she remembered. "DRAGON... Bernard!!"

"No, not Bernard," Whiskers corrected, "the dragon's called Broncs. He gets awful bronchitis you see. And then when he sneezes it's—"

"No, no," Em insisted. "I don't mean the dragon. I mean the boy, Bernard... The dragon got him! It burnt him up to a..." She whimpered slightly for a second. "Burnt him to a crisp! He's... gone!" she almost sobbed. She waited for Whiskers to react. It felt like a weight off her chest now she had told him. What happened down here was his responsibility after all.

"How curious," Whiskers replied, running his tail thoughtfully through his paws. "Well I never did. There's always a reason for these things you know. Never a coincidence. I'm sure he'll be in a better place now."

Em crinkled up her nose in a frown. "Better place?" she snapped angrily. "The kid's dead! Didn't you hear what I said? Your nice dragon microwaved him... Frazzled him to a crisp. Anyway... there's no such thing as dragons!"

"Try telling Sir Cuthbert that," Whiskers nodded over to the flame grilled knight.

At that moment there was a kafuffle going on in the passage outside the party room and in wandered a strange... thing. It was green, slimy, short. It reminded Em of an alien from out of space on a bad low budget movie.

"What is that?" exclaimed Em.

"Aha!" Whiskers suddenly looked delighted. "Our lost boy returns! Bernard."

"What!... But—"

"Dragon snot," Whiskers cut her off.

"I beg your pardon," Em now felt this conversation was getting totally out of hand and to be frank (which she wasn't since she was Emily) she didn't have a clue what Whiskers was talking about.

"Dragon snot. I told you... Broncs gets Bronchitis, and he sneezes the most terrible bogies. Great insulating properties though. Would have saved him from the flames."

Em watched as the green lump stretched and pulled trying to break free of what looked rather like a thick layer of extra sticky green treacle. None of the mice seemed to want to touch him for fear of getting caught up in the stickiness. An arm emerged and peeled back enough green gundge to reveal a face... Bernard's face. Em was so pleased, she could have kissed him... but then on second thoughts she would wait till all the snot was removed.

"Does amazing things to people, dragon snot, you know," Whiskers babbled on. "Healing properties you see. And it dulls the memories. We use it with the children when they leave the passageways, you know."

Healing properties? Em suddenly wondered, looking across at Bernard. He had a broad grin on his face and a glazed peaceful look in his eyes. She had never seen that before. The terrified puppy eyes had gone.

"Any chance of some lemonade?" called Bernard.

Chapter 20

Memories...

Bernard had changed. The lost little boy had turned into a talkative, confident... even rather cheeky... boy.

"Of course, it's all down to how we run the home here, Em," Dad had explained to her proudly, with that air of confidence and superiority of someone who is truly misguided. "You know, I think I have quite a talent for this looking after children stuff, Em." Emily just smiled at him. In actual fact, it was she who now had quite a job organising the passageway trips for all of the foster children. And she knew that in the passageways each one would find just the right the adventure they needed, hidden behind a short wooden door, which would creak open all by itself as they passed it by.

Anyway, tonight was sleepover night. This was her treat. Emily remembered her last sleepover which, lets face it, was a bit of a disaster. The good thing about this house was that it was big enough to sleep all the friends she wanted. In fact tonight they were having a girl's dorm and a boy's dorm.

When evening came they all gathered in the larger of the two dormitories as Dad drew up a chair to read them a story... a scary story. The lights were out, the room dark, and everyone sat in rapt attention as Dad told them the story of the ghostly house on the hill. There were "ahhs" and "ooohs" and shudders in all the right places as they heard about the deserted house on the hill. Emily looked around at all her friends. Fay and Amy were there, Fay in wide eyed rapt attention and Amy yabbering away in her ear. Jennifer was laying back in her bed listening, her orange hair almost glowing in the dark, it was so bright. Joseph and Ollie were so loud tonight and kept interrupting the story, Ollie wearing his very dirty lucky scarf. And Izzie and Ellie

were there too, Izzie chewing on a long curl falling forward from her head.

"Now," Dad continued, "The boy crept up the dark staircase towards the haunted room upstairs."

"You said it was downstairs!" Ollie interrupted, pointing accusingly at Dad.

"Ollieeee!" everyone shouted, "shut up!"

"Creek, creek, creek went the stairs..."

Emily glanced across at Amy who was still yabbering away to herself... hang on... no, no, she looked very cross and was pointing her finger, like she was trying to tell someone off. That could mean only one thing. Emily's eyes swept the floorboards and stopped on a small circle which looked blacker than the shadow... it was Rover, the hole. Why had Amy brought that?... the silly girl! It was dodging around, sweeping teasingly up the floor towards Amy and then dodging back again, always keeping just out of reach. Amy was staring daggers at it. She had never been able to keep the thing under control. Emily glanced up and immediately noticed that everyone's eyes were now fixed on the hole, except Dad, that is, since he had his back to it.

"And this is my best bit," Dad went on, unaware of Rover behind him.

Fay had a distinctly worried look on her face, and Emily could see why. Rover was now wandering temptingly near the back legs of Dad's chair.

"He put his hand on the door handle and twisted slowly..." Dad read on, even though no-one was listening to him anymore.

There was a collective gasp around the room as Rover shot within inches of the chair leg.

"... Wait for it," said Dad, quite enjoying himself, and rather pleased that everyone seemed to be gasping in all the right places in his scary story. "I know... It's the way I tell them," he said with a chuckle.

Rover changed into the distinctive shape of a smile. He gave out a little chuckle and swept underneath the chair legs.

"Woooooaaaaaaahhhhh........"

There was a sudden and rather swift look of utter surprise on Dad's face and then he was gone. The scream faded very slowly like the sound of someone falling hundreds of meters off the edge of a cliff.

"Oh nuts!"

"Rover!" scolded Amy, "you naughty boy. Give him back at once." The hole shot out of reach into the corner of the room and gave a loud burp.

"Oh that's disgusting," someone moaned.

"Give him back!" Amy ordered, "or no bed time story for you tonight," she scolded as if it was a puppy dog.

"Er, Amy, it's a hole," Ellie reminded.

Emily's jaw dropped. "You give it bed time stories?"

"Seriously Fay," Jennifer whispered, "you need to sort your sister out."

"You give my Dad back right now!" Emily shouted. Rover growled softly but menacingly, his shape changing to a jagged set of teeth.

"Please Rover... there's a good boy," Amy goaded.

"Oh, for goodness sake!" Emily rolled her eyes. "It's a hole, not a pet dog!" Amy straightened her back and shot her a superior look.

"Come on Rover, don't listen to her. You're a lovely hole. Now, give Em's dad back for us, there's a good boy." The hole shot up the wall and onto the ceiling. Then there was the sound of a distant scream getting gradually closer, a bit like an express train coming towards you. Then, out fell Dad tangled around his chair and the two hit the floor with a thump, splintering the legs of the chair in the process.

Dad slowly climbed to his feet. He looked stunned and slightly bewildered. He shook his head to clear it. Everyone held their breath, wondering what he would do next.

"Well," he concluded, "I don't know what happened there." He glanced down at the broken chair. "Goodness me! That's seen better days." He rubbed the back of his head. "Must have bashed my head when I fell... everything just seemed to go very black for a moment."

Everyone nodded vigorously.

But the highlight of the sleepover evening was to be the passageways. The long line of children tiptoed out of their dorms and through the secret entrance behind the stained glass window on the landing. When they reached the party room Whiskers was in full flow. It was his welcome speech.

"... When old Winston Guthry..." It was the same speech he had done last year and the year before. Em had forgotten it was that time of year again. She glanced at the newbies. They looked so young... so unknowing and naive. They had a lot to learn.

"... And my two bits of advice?" Whiskers continued, "don't eat two much and get a good night's sleep..." Em was more interested in getting to the food table today.

"... And of course sadly today we say goodbye to some of our..."

Em glanced at her watch. Another hour till she could see if her cousin Alice had managed to make it on the passitrain.

"... Emily..." Whiskers continued.

Em wished that Alice—. Hang on... What was that? Em looked up. Whiskers was looking at her. So were many of the others. Theo wore a frown. Some of the younger children looked embarrassed. Em could see Joseph's face, the look of horror on it. Had Whiskers really said what she thought he'd said?

"Of course we will all remember when Emily and Joseph got caught by old Arthur in the sweet shop..." Em's eyes began to mist over. "… and the legend of the Chocolate Lake..." She felt light-headed, as if she was just floating above it all. Whiskers was saying his farewell speech. This was to be her last evening in the passageways.

Whiskers came to see her after concluding his speech. She remembered the look in his eyes and the hug he gave her, but she didn't take in a word he said. For the first time it had dawned on her... it was the summer, she had had her birthday... she was now ten years old.

Emily climbed into bed that night with a very strange feeling she had never felt before. Her tiredness was intermingled with unfamiliar feelings of regret and a stabbing emptiness in the pit of her stomach. Could this really have been her last night in the passageways?

It was two weeks later when she woke up in the dead of night. She wasn't sure why. Ever since she had started going down to the passageways her senses had grown sharper at nights. She knew she never awoke at night without a reason, or unless something around her was strange or unusual. She immediately glanced around the room... nothing. She climbed out of bed and checked her secret door but there was nothing there. It had been removed the evening after her farewell. Then she noticed the letter. The familiar writing on the plain white envelope was a give away... Whiskers. She ripped it open and read...

> *Dear Emily,*
>
> *Time seems to have flown by so quickly since that first day when I met you and Fay and gave you your first tour of the passageways. Do you know what I enjoy most down here? It is seeing the way the children change, the skills they gain and challenges they face as they grow up. You know, not even I know quite how things are going to turn out. You will always have a special place in my heart, Emily, for you have shown the greatest of all attributes, your courage and your love has overcome your fears.*
>
> *Now you are probably feeling very sorry for yourself at the moment, and wondering why it is that you have to leave the passageways. You may even think this is the end of something, but you would be wrong. Your part in our adventure here may be finished (and a very important part it was) but you have so many more adventures to come. Life is one big adventure. You have to find your place in it... find the purpose for which you were put there. Everyone has a purpose. There is something out there*

which only you can do.

And you never know, maybe as time passes we will meet again. Occasionally there is the odd one or two who remember. Maybe you will remember, Emily.

Oh, and one tip for you... look out for Methuselah. He'll help you.

Goodbye and good luck

HM Whiskers'

Emily stared at the letter. She didn't know quite how to feel. She lay down and shut her eyes to think. Whiskers was a wise old mouse and she was sure he would be proved right. And yet she had a great big empty feeling inside, as if she had lost something really important, a treasured possession. And who was Methushla? Maybe she would...

She came to with a start. She had fallen asleep. Her hands felt around in the dark for the letter but it was gone. It had been a real letter hadn't it? Maybe she had dreamt it. She had a sudden rush of panic, jumped out of bed and switched on the light. No letter. She pulled open the bottom drawer of her chest, pushed aside the makeup bottles, brushes and mirrors, and reached for the tin box. Her hand clamped around it and pulled it out. The padlock rattled. It was her memory box and sometimes late at night she just needed some reassurance that it had all been real, not just a dream. She placed her key in the lock, turned it and pushed the lid open. The panic rose to her throat. It was empty. The piece of wallpaper, the letters from Whiskers, all her passageway memories. They were all gone. Maybe it had all been a long dream after all. She smiled to herself... a good dream anyway. She had a sudden thought. She grabbed her dressing gown and ran silently down the hall to Jack's room. She peered in expecting to see the empty bed... But no, there he was, still and fast asleep, tufts of hair sticking out from below the duvet. She sighed and carefully shut his door. So that was it then, none of it had been real, just her wild imagination.

"Hang on." Something struck a cord in her memory. Something wasn't right. She slowly opened Jack's door again and walked in. She tiptoed up to the bed and reached down. Very lightly she lifted the covers. Then she saw it. The pillows were arranged specially with the wig sticking out to look like hair... just like she had used to do.

"Yes, you were real. Be careful little bro. It's a dangerous world down there."

A month later Emily stopped dreaming so much, the memories of the passageways faded and became distant. Two months after that she found herself laying in bed, wracking her brains, desperately trying to remember something vitally important... something she used to do... what was it? She just couldn't remember. It had been something secret... she vaguely remembered something about carvings on walls and a large lake. Strange, she thought. Her thought was interrupted by her dad's head peering around the door.

"You coming out in the boat with me today?"

Emily smiled. "You bet!" She jumped out of bed and pulled on her clothes. As she helped Dad push the trailer down the steep road to the beach, strange thoughts ran through her mind, like 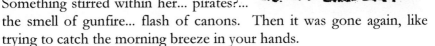 distant memories long forgotten. There was Ellie running a boat down a launch ramp in the dead of night. Dad pushed the boat round into the right position on the beach. The name plate flashed in front of Emily's eyes... '*The Blue Pirate Eater*'. Something stirred within her... pirates?... the smell of gunfire... flash of canons. Then it was gone again, like trying to catch the morning breeze in your hands.

THE END

Printed in the United Kingdom
by Lightning Source UK Ltd.
130494UK00001B/220-249/P